Dragon Fire Academy 2:

SECOND TERM

a series written by Rachel Jonas

Dragon Fire Academy: Second Term

Copyright © 2019, Rachel Jonas

Dragon Fire Academy 2
Synopsis

The good news: my four guardians are more than just a brood of cocky dragons. I was drawn to this island to find them … my mates.

The sucky news: an ancient evil has marked me as its vessel, but I suppose one girl can't have all the luck, right?

I was warned that second term would be a challenge, but nothing could have prepared me for this. As if things aren't already hard enough, one innocent slipup threatens to cost me big time.

Every day, it gets harder to tell friend from foe. Especially with more than one enemy who wants to make sure I lose everything.

Thing is, no one has any idea how fiercely I'm willing to fight. I guess they'll learn the hard way that I'm no pushover.

Giving up simply isn't in my blood.

***

Note: DRAGON FIRE ACADEMY is an upper YA/NA reverse harem romance. This series will take you on a brand-new journey with a descendant of the beloved Seaton Falls shifters, featured in THE LOST ROYALS SAGA. So, keep an eye out for cameos from some of your favorite characters! New readers, rest assured; it's completely unnecessary to read the first five books before embarking on this fresh chapter set in a world filled with fierce wolves, hotheaded dragons, and powerful witches you don't want to cross.

Thank you for your purchase!

Come hang out in "THE SHIFTER LOUNGE" on Facebook! We chat, recommend YA Paranormal Romances, and engage in other random acts of nerdiness. We also have tons of giveaways, exclusive ARC offers from me, and guest appearances by some of your favorite YA authors!

For all feedback or inquiries: author.racheljonas@gmail.com

CHAPTER ONE

NOELLE

My surroundings slowly came into focus.

First, there were fragments of light, then glimmers of strange shapes and colors. There wasn't a single inch of me that didn't ache, like I'd been tossed into a blender, ripped apart, and then pieced back together.

It took a few seconds, but my cloudy vision eventually settled on four formidable figures, four sets of eyes staring back at me. Each one was just as concerned as the others.

Peering up, the stone ceiling of a cave darkened the space, but it was definitely morning. The orange glow of sunlight and chirping birds made it obvious. Seeing as how there were no plumes of smoke, warning sirens, or at least restraints on my arms, I guessed this meant I hadn't freaked out and tried to destroy everything when I shifted.

Then again, I could have very well died, and this was heaven. The hard, bronze-toned bodies hovering around me made that a total possibility.

"You're okay?"

The question left Ori's mouth barely louder than a whisper. The words were filled with so much concern, and his gentle tone took me by surprise.

Until now, he'd only addressed me with frustration and intolerance. Neither was present when he'd just spoken, which only added to the feeling of disorientation as my head swam.

When I peered up, his gaze took hold of mine. A spark of unexpected emotion passed between us, making my heart thunder. Ori must have felt it too, because the next second, his eyes suddenly lowered to the ground.

A memory flickered inside my thoughts and I blinked, feeling confused as it rushed in from the fringes of what felt like a dream. Only, this vision of Ori hovering above me, leaning in to press his lips against mine … I hadn't imagined it. Nor had I imagined gripping the back of his neck, inviting him to get even closer.

Apparently, the Omega I once deemed heartless and intolerable now made my heart skip a beat. The same potent sense of clarity that overtook me after I'd given in to the others, now existed within me for Ori.

"I'm fine, I think." When the delayed answer left my mouth, he nodded to acknowledge my response, but still avoided eye contact.

A warm hand gripped my shoulder and I glanced over, seeing that Rayen had been the one to touch me. Beautiful curls rested over his shoulders, partially hiding the red lips tattooed on his collarbone. My eyes wandered down to his chest, the one side covered in ink, connecting to more of the elaborate art that colored his arm in a full sleeve.

"You scared us pretty bad last night." The depth of his voice made me draw in a breath, one I didn't release until he offered a faint smile a moment later.

I imagined how wild things must have gotten and had to agree with him. "Yeah, I was kind of terrified, too."

Suddenly aware of how they'd stuck by me, the urge to reach for Rayen's hand was hard to fight. However, I held back, still feeling a bit overwhelmed by these changes in our little group's dynamics. I'd gone from being the pest whose very presence annoyed the heck out of them, to somehow being stared at like I was the center of their universe.

Well, for the three who were *able* to look at me, that is.

"We think you should stay with us." I turned toward Paulo when the suggestion flew from his mouth. "At least until classes start again," he added.

"I … what?"

His expression didn't change even when I protested a bit. He exuded so much confidence it was clear he thought this was the right thing to do.

The *only* thing to do.

I, on the other hand, stared at him like he was insane.

"There's no room for me there," I retorted.

"We'll *make* room." He hadn't even taken a second to think about that, just barked out the response as if he'd been ready for me to object to the idea.

My heart pounded. I mean, I was definitely aware of our connection, was drawn to them with a degree of intensity that was off the charts, but the timing felt all wrong. It had been one thing when I hunkered down with them after the Pinning Ceremony. Then, my life had been in danger and we hadn't acknowledged our bond. However, now that we had, I was keenly aware of the need to take things slowly.

Well … slow-ish.

The change of heart came when Paulo leveled another of his stormy gazes on me. It was all heat and tension with him. Heck, with *all* of them.

I scrambled for another excuse.

"I can't just bail on Toni," I countered. "With how I left last night, I'm sure she thinks I'm out here hurt, scared, or worse."

Paulo shook his head. "People saw Ori take you from the courtyard. Trust me, she knows you're not alone," he asserted.

I hated that he was probably right, blowing a hole right through my excuse. I also hated that I knew what Toni would say if I told her I was invited to stay at the guys' bungalow. Her advice would likely be something along the lines of, *'keep painkillers and an icepack close by, and load up on protection. Lots and lots of protection.'*

Squeezing my eyes shut, I pushed aside the flood of kinky images of myself entangled with the four, lifting my lids again when my heartrate spiked.

"It's just that … I think … what about—"

"I'm starting to think you don't trust us," Rayen interrupted with a smirk, cutting me off as I stammered. Unknowingly, he taunted me by wetting his lips.

"It's not that. I—"

"Or maybe she doesn't trust *herself*," Paulo suggested boldly.

My neck and face warmed too quickly for me not to have turned red.

Ori stood and the movement stole my attention for a moment. He seemed so far removed from the conversation as he locked both arms across his chest. His gaze finally met mine, and he stared at me like I'd break into a million little pieces if the wind blew my way.

The look reminded me of what Nayeli and the other hive queens had shared about his past, about the one he once loved, but couldn't save.

"It's not like that," I forced out, finally tearing my eyes from Ori as I looked to the others.

Okay, yeah, Paulo was at least *partially* right, but my weak will wasn't the only valid argument against staying at their place.

"What if my parents try to get in touch with me?" I asked. "I know it's tough getting calls to and from the mainland, but I'm positive they'll be trying since today's my birthday. What if they get through and then find out I'm staying with *you* instead of at the dorm? You four don't know my dad. He's … intense."

That was a good word for the man who once threatened to decapitate a guy for bringing me home fifteen minutes past curfew.

Yup … my dad was intense.

"There's a simple answer for that; you're twenty now," Paulo reasoned. "Old enough to make your own decisions. Even ones your father might not approve of," he added. "We're only trying to protect you, not knock you up."

Neither the laugh that left his mouth after speaking, nor the wicked way his eyes swept over my body, were innocent.

"Besides, you're worrying for nothing," Rayen chimed in again. "I'm almost positive your parents are gonna love us. Most do."

Aww ... how cute!

He was so chill and confident. Like most were before coming face-to-face with *The Reaper*. After? Totally different story. Explaining to my dad that I'd met and fallen for *one* guy on the island would have been one thing. Telling him I discovered I was the mate to four wouldn't be so easy.

To put it plainly, that wasn't a conversation I looked forward to having.

Suddenly overwhelmed, I attempted to sit upright, but the world tilted when I did.

"Whoa, take it easy." Kai's hands braced my shoulders, and he lowered from standing to kneeling behind me. When I glanced up over my head, seeing how he still carried so much worry from the night before, I realized just how bad things must have gotten. *All* of my memories from the last twelve hours were foggy, which left me with the sense of having lost time.

In my opinion, the guys should have been relaxed and happier now that I was awake and hadn't, you know, sunk their island. Only, their moods were so sullen I knew something was off.

"What aren't you telling me?" It was hard asking that question, because I didn't really want the answer.

Ori's large shoulders moved with a deep breath, and he locked eyes with the other guys before finally finding the courage to look into mine.

"It was touch-and-go for a while, but you were strong," he asserted. "We did our best to keep you comfortable, and then took turns watching over you while you slept."

He stopped, but I knew he hadn't told me everything.

"And?"

Dead silence meant *none* of them wanted to answer my question, but Ori looked especially distraught. I reached for his hand without thinking and the way his body stiffened made it clear the contact had caught him off guard. Not quite like he didn't want to be touched, but rather that he hadn't been this close to someone in a long time.

"I'm grateful for what you guys did," I started again, realizing I hadn't told them this yet. The words were so true, emotion strained my voice. "Whatever it is you're not saying, you can tell me," I added. "Did I … hurt someone?"

Ori's eyes quickly darted back toward mine, filling with sympathy. "No," he assured me.

"Thank God." I breathed a sigh of relief, but when the hand I held tightened around mine, I knew I'd celebrated too soon.

"You have the mark, Noelle." The information Ori had just given caused my brow to tense.

"The … mark? I don't understand."

Paulo turned to expose the back of his neck, pointing a finger to the nape where a symbol I'd seen there before glowed brightly — a flame within a flame. Still a bit confused, I reached beneath my hair.

"All queens receive them, but … *yours* – "

When Ori trailed off again, I became uneasy, breathing wildly as panic set in. At first, I didn't understand what he meant to imply, but then, as my fingers traced the warm outline of my mark, I was pretty sure I'd figured it out.

Like theirs, the symbol swirled slightly to the left, coming to a point. Only, mine didn't stop there. Above it, there was something more. Something I didn't understand and had the feeling the guys didn't either.

"Slow down, Noelle."

I ignored Rayen's plea when I scrambled to get to my feet again, stumbling like a toddler while getting my bearings. Three sets of hands were on me, and then the fourth looped an arm firmly around my waist.

With no idea where I was headed, or what I hoped to accomplish, I slumped against the wall of the cave, breathless.

"Why does mine feel different?" I asked, still panting.

The lack of an immediate answer only made me more anxious.

"Honestly? We're not sure," Paulo admitted, "but we're gonna figure it out." There was no doubt in my mind that he and the others had every intention to keep this promise, but that didn't mean they'd be successful. I was a wildcard. They knew that as well as I did, and this was just another glaring reminder.

I traced my symbol again. "What's it look like?"

"The bottom half is identical to ours," Kai answered, "but the top half is inverted—an upside-down flame, purple instead of orange."

My eyes slammed shut, knowing this was a sign. Of what, I didn't know, but it couldn't have been good.

"This is why you wanted to keep an eye on me," I said aloud as their intentions became clear. "You think something's wrong with me, think I might still be a problem."

"…Not exactly," Kai answered. "We just—"

"It's fine," I interjected. "You don't have to explain. I'll stay with you," I gave in, which came as a clear relief to all of them. "But if you don't mind, I need to stop by the dorm. Toni's probably worried sick and I need her to see I'm okay."

Rayen seemed to understand when he nodded. "Of course. We'll take you."

The rapid breaths that made me lightheaded were starting to subside. Not because my circumstances had improved, but rather because I was reminded that I wasn't in this alone. As I glanced around at all of them—so alert to my every move—I'd nearly forgotten I wasn't surrounded by actual family.

Then again, I knew family came in many different forms.

"Thanks for offering to take me in. I—"

"Don't."

The command had come from Ori, and it stopped me just as I was letting the hive know how much I appreciated them.

"We got off to a rocky start," he admitted. "I'll be the first to say I don't always know how to be soft when a situation calls for it, and my tone doesn't always match my intentions, but just … give me time. Please," he added gently. "In the meantime, while we're all figuring things out, anything we have is yours. As our mate, our *queen*, you're more than welcome in our home. Always."

His offer was so kind, I smiled. He stared thoughtfully and I didn't doubt the sincerity of this gesture for even a moment. He was a work in progress, but he knew it. So, if he needed time to adapt to our new dynamic, I'd give him that.

This declaration made me even more grateful that the four were so determined to stick with me. It wasn't so much that I *needed* them, but I *wanted* them, and the feeling was mutual.

It was during this thought that I was reminded we weren't yet out of the woods. For all we knew, this mark was a sign that my fight against the Darkness had been over before it even started. Yes, I'd had a successful face-off with it, but the odd symbol on my neck suggested things were far from over.

I'd won the battle, but who's to say I'd win the war?

CHAPTER TWO

NOELLE

My intention was to head straight to my dorm, barge in like I *hadn't* had some sort of episode the night before, and just … move on with my life. Instead, here I was, back at the guys' bungalow so I could "clean up a bit first".

That was the excuse I'd given anyway.

Sure, I *looked* like I'd crawled through mud and got caught in a monsoon, before spending the night on the floor of a cave, but I *still* would've gone back to school looking like hell to see about my friends. Yet, I made it seem like this detour was necessary.

Because I was terrified.

Facing the other students would be a nightmare. Without a doubt, word had gotten around, and I didn't have it in me to ignore the stares, the whispers. So, I did what *any* smart person would do.

I hid, of course.

Freshly showered, and still sporting only a towel, I'd fallen asleep curled up on Ori's bed—*my* bed during my stay. I was still exhausted from the shift, and the never-ending rainstorm that rolled through hadn't helped. The sound of it tapping the shuttered window while I rested had been to blame.

I breathed deep, deciding not to rush to sit up. When I did draw in air, Ori's scent was everywhere, lingering in the room, on his linen. Of all the guys, being connected to him was the strangest. I'd been fairly certain he hated me before this, but now, as I breathed him in, I smiled a little. It seemed the bond was more prevailing than I realized.

Not even the added power of my wolf and dragon being awakened rivaled my connection to the Omegas. Their energy was somehow a part of me, moving through me like a surge of electricity every time my heart beat. It was like all four were in my bloodstream now, and I was aware of them belonging to me, and me to them. I wasn't sure how to manage suddenly being so open, but I guessed they were equally as uncertain.

It would definitely take some getting used to.

The queens came to mind—Nayeli, Lehua and Kalea. Their lives were so full—full of love, happiness. One day, *my* life could mirror theirs, but I hadn't forgotten that my circumstances weren't exactly cut and dry. Although they were each able to fulfill their deeper purpose, none of their dreams required them to leave Sanluuk. Mine would *certainly* take me away from this place, away from the hive. At least for a while. So, for however long I was with the Guard, I'd have to live with the hole that would develop being away from the Omegas.

Since I was young, I'd known I wouldn't always have the luxury of living within my family's fortress. More than anything, I wanted to be useful, wanted to be a part of some greater good that was bigger than me. Bigger than my title. Bigger than my family's legacy.

I had an unquenchable need to do something that mattered.

Flipping over onto my back, I stared at the huge fan with palm leaf-shaped blades whirring above. The nap had done nothing to clear my head. For starters, I still had so many unanswered questions. Like, what was with my mark? I'd taken a mirror to it before my shower, and sure enough, it looked exactly as Kai described. The more I thought about that, the more anxious I became. Even with Paulo's promise that he and the others would do everything they could to help.

It had to be the Darkness.

My eyes flitted toward the window when I tried to push that thought out of my head. The storm had darkened the sky, making it impossible to tell how many hours had passed while I slept. I glanced down to my arm when the weak pulses of electricity in my veins surged a little faster now. It happened at the precise moment I found myself wondering where the guys had disappeared.

I pushed off from the bed and moved toward Ori's dresser. He'd given me permission to rummage for clothes after Rayen offered to wash mine. A laugh slipped out as I pushed a few t-shirts aside, praying I didn't find a porn stash like I'd run across during my stay in *Paulo's* room.

They were all so different—no two the same.

Pausing my hunt for clothing that would actually fit me, I observed the small, tribal statues Ori kept on a shelf above. They appeared to be hand-carved from wood. Beside them, a stack of old books supported a blue box with a gold lock that sealed it shut. The space was masculine but neat, whereas Paulo's had been the opposite. Still masculine, but his room definitely fit his laidback, unapologetic personality. Ori, on the other hand, was all clean lines and organization. The few belongings he *did* have seemed sentimental, items with purpose.

Surprisingly, being here didn't feel so strange now. Before, I wondered if my presence had been an inconvenience. *This* time, I knew beyond the shadow of a doubt I was wanted.

I moved down a drawer and found a stack of ribbed tank tops. They were usually pretty slim fitting, so I lifted one into the air, laughing a bit at how long it was. What would have fit Ori like a shirt, would practically be a dress on me. The one I held was white, and would've basically been see-through, seeing as how I didn't have anything to wear underneath, so I swapped it out for a dark blue one. For now, it was the best I could do, so I dropped my towel and slid the material over my head.

'*She's been out for a while. Think we should check on her?*'

The soft voice startled a gasp out of me, and I turned toward the door where I thought I'd just heard Kai ask the question.

'*I peeked in on her about an hour ago and she was fine,*' Paulo answered. Only, as I stepped near the door, I was beginning to think that hadn't been where this conversation was taking place.

It was too clear, too ... *close.*

'*You peeked in on her?*' Ori asked, repeating Paulo's statement, but as a question this time. '*You shouldn't have done that.*'

'*Relax,*' Paulo said with one of his chilled laughs. '*She was covered, but what's the big deal? It's not like she has anything I won't eventually be allowed to look at.*'

Covering my mouth when I nearly laughed out loud, I realized this was no ordinary conversation. I was in their heads. The feeling of static moving over my skin while I eavesdropped aligned with how my mother described the sensation. It accompanied the ability to telepathically communicate with someone you're tethered to, like she was linked with my father. The only difference was, Mom had *intentionally* connected herself to my dad, so the two could speak in thought, see through one another's eyes when the other allowed.

I, on the other hand, had done no such thing with the hive.

'*Don't start,*' Ori shot back, and I imagined the unamused look on his face.

There was still laughter in Paulo's voice when he spoke again. *'Just sayin'. She's basically ours now. It's just a matter of time before we get to see the goods, right?'*

'You think she's obligated to sleep with you?'

'You're putting words in my mouth,' Paulo answered in defense, sounding lighthearted despite Ori's brash tone. *'I'm only pointing out that, eventually, she's gonna want to.'*

He was so freakin' cocky. When my face tightened with a big, stupid grin, I had to admit I liked that a little. The next second, I exited the bedroom and stayed quiet as I continued to listen.

'I won't allow you to make her uncomfortable here,' Ori said gruffly. *'Our home should be her safe haven. Don't be the dick who ruins that because he can't keep his in his pants. Besides, we have to stick to protocol, so you're just gonna have to deal with it.'*

There was a lull in their conversation, and I had time to think about what I overheard. Mostly, I was acknowledging all the pent-up frustration that had accumulated between the five of us. All of it, locked inside us waiting to be released. My imagination ran away from me and I swallowed hard when the thought of painkillers and ice packs returned.

But my next thought centered around one word I heard mentioned — protocol — wondering what the heck it meant.

'Whatever, Boss,' Paulo eventually griped. Resentfully, of course.

There was no missing his sarcasm, nor the frustration aimed toward Ori after he'd put his foot down, establishing the standard he expected the others to uphold during my stay.

I moved toward the front door where the four were seated. Two of their large frames were visible as they sat on stools outside the windows. Finally stepping out onto the porch, I laid eyes on them all, including the pair I'd just heard arguing about charged hormones and bad timing inside my thoughts.

Rayen stood when I joined them, and the gentlemanly gesture caught me by surprise. A gesture that brought yet another smile out of me. Their gazes all slipped to what I wore — the thin, ribbed material that hugged my body down to where it stopped mid-thigh. I was breathing unevenly as they observed me, and when the self-consciousness that came with it got to be too much, I reached across my torso for my arm. It didn't hide me much, but it made me feel at least *somewhat* hidden from their stares.

" … Hey," Kai said awkwardly. Too much time had passed for it to feel natural that he'd just now decided to speak.

My face warmed when I smiled at him. "Hey."

"Here, take my seat," Rayen offered, stepping aside before I could even respond.

"Um, thanks," I answered breathily.

I moved closer to the beautiful specimen who towered over me as I peered up at him. He leaned against the tall, wooden beam behind him to give me room to pass. When I did, our bodies brushed against one another and I inhaled sharply. His hair — damp from either the rain, a swim, or a shower — clung to his skin. Whatever the case, there was something about him that was always so inviting. Like he wanted to be touched.

Or maybe it was simply that *I* wanted to touch *him.* Totally possible.

When I lowered to the stool and made sure I was covered appropriately, I realized I still had the Omegas' undivided attention. The conversation between Ori and Paulo came to mind again. Specifically, the part where Paulo mentioned the inevitability of our hive's physical connection.

At the thought of it, I was left to wonder what an appropriate wait time would be. I mean, I wasn't going to rush things, but ... I felt the pull already. Whether it was being mated to them, or just being *near* them, waiting seemed super unnecessary at the moment. Especially when I observed them right back—like how their clothing clung to them in the sweltering heat.

So much for taking things slowly.

I'd lived under some pretty tight restrictions back home, which taught me to bridle my feelings when it came to things like this—being chaste around guys, keeping in mind I was under near-constant surveillance. But maybe it wouldn't have been so bad if, just this once, I ... gave in? Went after what *I* wanted for a change? After all, the Omegas weren't just some random dudes.

Just as quickly as the thought came, I was reminded of my proper upbringing and knew I didn't have it in me to make the first move.

Stupid morals.

Stupid waiting.

"Sleep okay?"

I glanced toward Kai, grateful he'd spoken. "I did. The rain made it hard to keep my eyes open."

All around us, a continuous downpour beat against the roof and dock, rolling off the overhang that covered us. It was beautiful here at their place. Apparently, in rain or shine.

"Ori, your bed is perfect." I met his gaze with a smile he returned. "Thanks for offering it to me."

"My pleasure," he answered with a nod.

We were plunged into kind of an awkward silence after that, and the sensation of static crawling up my arms and legs returned.

'Soooo, we're just gonna pretend she's not practically naked?' Rayen asked. *'I'm tempted not to give back her clothes.'*

When I peered up to observe him, his gaze was focused on my boobs, where the tank top posing as a dress left them exposed. Clearing my throat, I discreetly tugged the material up a bit.

'Just don't let Ori hear you say that,' Paulo replied. *'Dude's in major cock-block mode, being a dick about protocol.'*

There was that word again.

Apparently, this conversation excluded their alpha. Which accounted for why he hadn't jumped in to rip Rayen a new one like he'd done when he felt Paulo had gotten out of line.

'Well, if we're waiting for him *to give the greenlight, guess that means Sanluuk is about to have its first ever lotion shortage.'*

Hearing Paulo laugh at Rayen's comment inside my head, I nearly laughed too.

'Maybe. Maybe not.'

Rayen shot Paulo a thoughtful look. *'Don't get any bright ideas,'* he warned. *'Just stick to Ori's plan. It's times like this we have to trust he knows best, respect rank.'*

Paulo didn't seem as content as Rayen, but he said nothing.

Hearing Rayen's rationale confused me, though. All this talk about protocol and rank seemed so cryptic. How did any of this relate to Ori being their alpha?

For a second, I thought I should probably tell them I could hear their inner-hive conversations, but then realized that might be embarrassing — for them *and* me. After a few seconds, I decided against it and instead asked a question to make things a little less weird.

"So, any idea where we should start our search? To figure out what's up with my mark, I mean."

Not a search for lotion. Definitely not lotion.

The others' gazes shifted toward Kai and mine followed.

"I believe my aunt can help," he spoke up. With how the others had all looked to him, I guessed this was something that had been discussed while I slept.

"She knows about things like this?"

"Yes and no," was the answer I was given. "Yes, she's sensitive to Spirit and the island itself, but I don't think *anyone* really has experience with what we're dealing with," he answered honestly, although his delivery was kind. "Talking to her is probably the best place to start. She's a seer," he added.

I'd heard of certain supernaturals having intuitive abilities — my aunt Hilda being one of them — so I didn't think it strange that one dwelled here on the island.

"Well, hopefully she can at least point us in the right direction," I said with a smile, doing my best to seem optimistic.

My gaze left theirs for just a moment when my thoughts drifted again, but my attention was called back a second later.

"There's something I think needs to be said." I glanced toward Kai when he spoke again. "Now that things have come to light, there's really no need to continue holding this information, but … the incident at the Pinning Ceremony and the orphanage weren't Noelle's only encounters with the Darkness. It communicated with her at Makoni Lagoon." He turned toward me next. "I'm sorry for having to break my promise to keep it secret, but they need to know everything. It all has to be out on the table for us to help you."

I nodded, feeling it was unnecessary for him to apologize, but I appreciated that he valued my confidence in him so greatly.

"What do you mean it communicated with her?" Ori practically growled. I mean a full-on, teeth gritted, snarling growl. "You took her to Makoni Lagoon?"

"No," Kai answered, "but I didn't stop her when she and some of her friends went."

"*We* didn't stop her," Paulo jumped in, deciding not to let Kai take the fall alone. It reminded me of how I sometimes stood with my siblings when they did dumb things that got them into trouble. Lord knows that was pretty often.

There was so much tension among them now, mostly coming from Ori who hadn't even blinked as he stared the two of them down.

"Do I even need to tell you how stupid it was that you're just now saying something? Makoni is only a few miles from the hemispheric border. Who's to say that, if you'd sent them all back to the dorm like you were supposed to, maybe the Darkness would have never found her?"

Kai's head lowered, taking Ori's accusation to heart.

"I was already having dreams," I cut in. "So, it's not their fault."

"What dreams?"

I peered up after Rayen asked. "Well, at first, I wasn't sure what to make of them, but after coming face to face with the Darkness at the Lagoon, I knew it was all related. It would speak to me, never really showing itself."

"What did it say?" Ori's expression was stern, unrelenting.

"In the dreams, I was never really sure. But at the lagoon … it told me I belonged here. And it said something similar that night at the orphanage."

Being forced to recall the details made my skin crawl.

All four of the guys were silent. Likely for different reasons. Kai and Paulo may have felt guilty, but Ori and Rayen were clearly stricken with concern. The deep creases in their foreheads as each stared at the wood slats beneath our feet said as much.

"She can't be out of our sight," Ori concluded. "When we retrieve her things from the dorm, we retrieve *everything* and bring it back here. She has to be kept under around-the-clock surveillance."

"No." When I objected, all their gazes shifted to me.

"No?" The way Ori asked, repeating my statement like he couldn't believe I spoke up, I guessed he wasn't used to being challenged.

"I'm sitting right here. Yet, you're discussing this like I have no say. You're *their* alpha," I reminded him, pointing at the other Omegas. "Not mine."

As Ori and I squared off, the three watched in silence.

"I intend to finish what I started here, which means I'm not moving out of the dorm. I get that you're only trying to protect me, but I deserve a vote on this, too. It's *my* life we're talking about here."

Ori's furious stare bore a hole through me, making my heart race. For a moment, those harsh edges of the relationship we'd carved out when I first arrived were glaringly visible. We seemed to have both forgotten about our bond.

"I don't disagree with you; this *is* your life. But … don't you get how that fact makes this our problem, too?"

My heart lurched when he aimed the harshly spoken question at me, pointing out how the two were no longer mutually exclusive anymore — my life and their interest. We were a unit now, no matter how strange that felt.

The other queens had shared Ori's past with me, and I should have been more sensitive to that, less defensive considering I knew he only meant to help. I wasn't wrong to let him know how I felt, but my approach could have been more thoughtful.

"I'm sorry," I forced out. "I'm a bit high-strung from all of this. It was wrong to snap at you."

"It's fine," he said with a nod.

Surprisingly, the flash-flood animosity that rose between us receded and I knew it had to be the bond. Under normal circumstances, the interaction would have been closely followed by visions of what it would feel like to rip his head from his shoulders.

"Something else we need to figure out is why Chief wouldn't let you leave." Rayen lowered to sit on the porch after speaking. "We heard you mention it when Ori carried you to the cave."

Naturally, my gaze slipped to Kai. After all, this was *his* father we were getting ready to discuss. I wasn't sure how much I could say without offending him.

"Well, I intended to speak with Ms. Long that night, about withdrawing, but your Chief was there instead. He wouldn't listen to anything I said, my reasons I thought it best that I return home. He just seemed adamant that … I had some greater purpose."

The four shared a look I wasn't sure how to read.

"Sounds like him," Kai mumbled under his breath, giving some insight into the relationship between he and his father. His gaze lifted to meet mine again. "He never elaborated on that?"

I shook my head. "No. That was all he said." A thought occurred to me, so I shared it. "Is it possible he knew I was your mate? Maybe he was aware that Spirit had brought me here and *that* was the greater purpose he mentioned?"

"You have no idea how badly I wish that were true," Kai scoffed. "My father's not the man he used to be. He's never been soft by any means, but he's somehow become even more callous over the years. If this had been a while ago, I'd believe his intentions were that pure. But lately, I barely recognize him by the decisions he makes."

"Besides," Rayen cut in, "Spirit hadn't even told *us* you were our mate, so Chief wouldn't have sensed it. That's not how it works."

Well, there went *that* theory. It seemed that the one positive spin I could put on why their Chief kept me here had just been shot out of the water.

"We know he's definitely up to something. That's not even a question," Kai sighed in frustration. "What we need to know now is what that *something* is."

CHAPTER THREE
NOELLE

Shortly after our talk on the porch ended, my clothes were returned to me—against Rayen's better judgment, apparently. Then, it was Ori who suggested we head back to the dorm to grab some of my things before it got too dark.

Besides, I didn't want to let anymore time pass without letting Toni know I was okay, without letting her see for herself that I was fine.

As Kai's Jeep rocked and swayed over uneven terrain, I was grateful for the nonstop conversation the guys kept up. They were full of questions, maybe intentionally because they sensed my nerves.

"So, which one is dominant?" Paulo asked with a grin. "Witch, dragon, or wolf."

With everything going on, I'd barely stopped to think about it. Still, it didn't take me long to know.

"My dragon," I revealed. "Which feels kind of strange, having only identified as a witch for so long."

He nodded as we hit a pothole and my body bounced back and forth between him and Ori.

"Guess this means we need to teach you how to fly," Rayen added, drawing my eyes toward him. The hint of a smile on his lips had me biting down on my own.

"Guess so."

"What are your classes for this term? Any combat?" Ori chimed in, stealing my attention.

"Um, yes. They wanted us to get more of our general studies out of the way first term, while we were getting used to things," I answered.

Understanding, he nodded. "Nervous?"

"About fighting?" I smiled and it was almost arrogant. "No. My dad's been sparring with me since I was six. He had this thing about always being prepared for the worst. Apparently, some stuff that happened before I was born made him super protective of me. Even though I'm not a kid anymore."

After sharing that snapshot into my life, I recalled what it had been like. I wasn't smothered, but my parents — mostly my father — kept a tight rein on me. Hence the reason the four dragons who now surrounded me had been called in on guard duty.

"What sort of stuff? I mean, if that's not too personal to ask," Kai corrected, keeping his eyes on the bumpy, dirt road ahead.

"Well, it's not personal, but it's definitely complicated," I began, trying to speak loud enough so he and Rayen could hear me where they sat in the front seat. "Do you know *anything* about my mother?"

I only asked so I'd know where to start, but when they each shook their heads, it became apparent just how separate their people were from ours.

"She was born hundreds of years ago … the *first* time, anyway."

Paulo turned to glance at me when the strange statement left my mouth. "The first time?"

"She was killed, but her soul was collected inside a stone on her necklace, a talisman my grandmother had made for that very purpose. That's how she was resurrected present day—no memory of her past life, no memory of who she was. They weren't sure why she'd been killed. Until about twenty years ago. When *I* came into the picture."

I felt Ori's eyes on me as he stared.

"It was because of me," I admitted.

My life was so much weirder than they realized. It was rare for me to tell others of my family's past. Some knew because they had studied our history. But they definitely never heard it from me. However, it was different with the Omegas. They weren't just anybody.

"How is that possible?" Rayen interjected. "You said she was killed centuries ago. What did that have to do with you?"

I nodded, letting him know he hadn't misheard. "She was pregnant at the time of her death. When her soul went into the stone that night, mine did too. My family later discovered that the Liberator hadn't been after *her*; it was after me. Mine was the life it sought to end."

The thought of it made me even more aware of the symbol on the back of my neck. Seemed I'd been outrunning evil my entire life.

"Why?" Ori's expression was no longer curious, like it had been a second ago. It was fierce.

I shrugged with a smile that didn't quite fit the heavy tone in Kai's Jeep at the moment. "Beats me. Because I'm a weirdo, I guess."

No one laughed, so the grin I wore to mask my real feelings faded.

Ori turned to gaze out the window, deep in thought.

"What's a Liberator?"

"A rare lycan," I answered when Paulo asked. "There have only ever been two. The first killed my mother, the second tried right after I was conceived — again, I guess — twenty years ago."

"Tried? Was someone able to kill it?" Rayen asked.

I shook my head, thinking about someone very special in my life — my godfather, Nick. "No, he's still alive. It's a long story, but he tried and failed. Then, fast forward to about five years later, where he's helping my dad teach me to ride a bike," I added with a smile as I thought of him. "Things started out bad, but like always, love won. He's basically one of my favorite people in the world."

My heart was a little heavy when I thought about not getting to tell him goodbye before leaving for the academy, but he wasn't absent just for the sake of being absent. His wife, my aunt Roz, was giving birth to their second kid. Otherwise, they would have been right by my parents' side. Like they always had been.

"Sounds like your life's just as complicated as ours," Paulo said with a grin when he glanced back over his shoulder.

Pushing aside the strong emotion that crept in, I nodded. "Agreed."

Ori had been really quiet, so I turned to him next, finding his attention still focused outside the Jeep. Just as I was beginning to wonder what he was thinking, his gaze shifted toward me.

"So, this … Liberator," he began, "it came after you twice. Did your family ever figure out why?"

I wished I had a better answer than the one my Aunt Hilda had given me. "All they've ever told me is that I'm special, that they believed the supernatural world was all about balance, and my potential gifts may have thrown things out of alignment for a while."

There was a brief moment that he stared into my eyes thoughtfully, but then I lost him again to whatever thoughts he was keeping from me.

Static moved over my skin and I breathed in at the feel of it.

'I don't like any of this,' came a stern voice inside my thoughts. It was Ori, sharing with his brothers what he wasn't yet comfortable sharing with me. Well, not on purpose anyway.

'What are you thinking?' Kai asked.

'That what happened in her past, and what's happening here might be connected somehow,' was Ori's answer. 'It all sounds a little too close for that not to be the case. We may need to get in touch with her family?'

"No!" The word flew from my mouth so quickly, I barely realized I'd said it aloud.

Four sets of eyes drifted toward me. Had it not been for needing to see where he was going, Kai would've stared longer. If I didn't say something to recover from what I'd just done, they'd know I heard everything they said — now, earlier.

Think fast, idiot.

"Uhhh …Shoot! I just remembered something," I said slowly, making things up as I spoke. "I—I don't have my ID. They'll never let me back on campus."

My heart was racing a mile a minute, and I was grateful dragons' sense of hearing wasn't as keen as wolves. The four settled down, thinking this was the true reason I'd freaked out.

"It's fine," Rayen assured me. "We know a few of the guards. They'll let you in."

Faking a smile, I breathed out with relief. "Oh! Well, everything's good then, I guess."

Hot, awkward mess. Yup, that was me.

I kept my mouth shut the rest of the ride—it was better that way—and sure enough, Rayen was right. We got in without a problem. Once the guard saw who escorted me, there were very few questions asked.

We passed through the iron gate and I glanced around. The added security posted around the perimeter, and the extra sigils etched and glowing in the stones of the border wall, led me to believe the academy had been on lockdown. My guess was that they hoped to ensure no one else got off campus.

Maybe even hoped to ensure *I* couldn't get back inside.

Yet, here I was, being gawked at like a failed science experiment.

We came to a stop in the small parking lot on the west end of campus and Kai shut off the engine. My heart still hadn't slowed, and I was grateful for the heat. It hid that I was *also* sweating because I had no idea what I'd experience once I came face to face with the other students.

I was certain that, even those who hadn't *seen* what happened, had at least heard. Add that to what took place at the Pinning Ceremony, and I'd be lucky if they didn't take off running when they laid eyes on me.

Scooting toward the far end of the seat, I planned to just hop out on my own. However, a hand stretched toward me. I caught Ori's gaze the second my palm touched his, and I let him help me down onto the pavement.

He was still strong-willed, and a pain in the neck with his I-am-man-hear-me-roar attitude, but I could admit to seeing something else in him, too. Something that made my stomach flutter when he touched the small of my back to let me walk ahead of him.

It dawned on me that I had Paulo's attention, and it made me a little fidgety.

"Are you really that scared to be back here?" he asked, calling me out.

"What? I didn't say that," I shot back, trying to play it cool as I walked very, *very* slowly toward the dorm.

"You didn't have to say it," he reasoned with a laugh. "You're pale as a ghost right now, and your hands are shaking."

I glanced down at them before shoving both inside my pockets.

"You don't have to do this, you know. If you just need clothes, we all have sisters," he revealed. "It would take two seconds for us to get enough stuff to last you a couple weeks."

While I appreciated the offer, getting some of my things wasn't the only reason I was here. That wasn't even the *main* reason I was here. It was about Toni, the twins, and Tristan.

When I breathed deep, the guys stopped walking, forcing me to do the same. They made it very apparent they weren't moving until I explained myself. Kai stood posted in front of me with his arms locked across his chest. Paulo braced his back against the brick of the building we'd halted beside. Ori and Rayen were moving in closer from their respective positions and, before I knew it, I was surrounded by walls of flesh and muscle.

One firm word touched my ears. "Talk."

I peered up at Paulo when he made the demand, not even blinking as he waited. Typically, I didn't like being forced to do *anything*, by *anyone*, but … these four made even being a dick kind of sexy.

Exhaling sharply, I realized I would be better off just telling them. It was the only way I'd ever get out of the… dragon huddle they formed around me.

"I just get weird about things like this, having to face people who know about me."

"Know *what* about you?" Ori asked, that hard look still present on his face.

My gaze lowered when I removed both hands from my pockets, wiping damp palms down my jean shorts. "People who know … I'm different."

The four were quiet. For ten straight seconds the only sound was that of the distant conversation and laughter as others did their own thing in the courtyard. During that time, it felt like the guys had moved in even closer. Or maybe that was my imagination, and the "walls" were just closing in on me because I didn't particularly like having this conversation.

"You're a princess. Supernatural royalty," Paulo stated, as if I needed reminding.

"I know who I am," I mumbled. "But things aren't like you think. I was never popular, or first on anyone's list for anything. I've always been … kind of on the outside."

I knew they probably didn't understand this, but I wasn't really in the mood to explain it. However, when I tried to push past Kai and Rayen, the two moved closer, until their shoulders nearly touched, boxing me in again. They were huge, to the point that they blocked out the setting sun and all I could see were their silhouettes. It was no use.

"I was bullied, okay," I finally forced out. "I had a hard time controlling my magic when I was young, and I was always a little weird, I guess. Then, there was a girl who just kind of made everything worse, and I suppose I never fully got over it. Which I know sounds *really* pathetic, but—"

"It's not pathetic," Kai interjected.

I peered up at him, exhaling sharply.

"Your parents didn't put a stop to it?" Paulo asked.

Frustrated, I rolled my eyes. "They would have, if they'd known."

"You didn't tell them? Why?" Now it was Ori who asked. I was gonna get dizzy if I kept whipping my head to see who'd spoken.

So many questions.

"Because," I huffed, "I didn't want them to look at me differently, didn't want them to think I was weak and needed them to step in. I had enough of that already."

There was more of that silent, broody staring, making me frustrated and hot for them all at the same time.

"Anything else you wanna know?" I asked sharply. "I mean, because who doesn't love being pressured into reliving those awkward, teenage years."

After speaking, I crossed both arms over my chest, realizing how exposed I felt. Only, I wasn't allowed to pout and wallow, because my arms were pulled back down to my sides by Paulo.

"You said you know who you are, right?" he asked. When I nodded, he tilted his head a bit, deepening his stare. "Then, tell me. Who are you?"

I didn't understand at first, but answered anyway. "I'm Noelle, daughter of the mainland's king and queen."

"And what else?" he pressed.

I blinked hard, trying to think of whatever answer he was after.

"I'm … a witch," I added, "a dragon, and a wolf."

"And what else," he pushed again.

"And … a student at—"

"Wrong." The depth and conviction in Paulo's voice when he interjected shook me to my core. My shoulders were taken and I was made to face him, looking right into his eyes.

"Whoever others had you convinced you were before," he continued, "whatever you believe they saw when they looked at you, from this day forward, none of that matters." His finger went to my chin and I wasn't allowed to look away. "All any of us see is you, our queen."

My stomach fluttered again when he finished making his declaration. I was at a loss for words, only able to nod in response.

I was turned loose, and now that I'd been set straight, the Omega huddle I'd stood in the middle of, suddenly broke apart and they fell into formation again—Paulo and Rayen walking at either side, Kai ahead of me, Ori at my back.

With them, I felt … untouchable.

CHAPTER FOUR

NOELLE

We approached my dorm and, too tall to fit through the doorway otherwise, the guys all ducked their heads. Being escorted certainly dulled my anxiety, but it hadn't left completely.

Although, with how Paulo had just put me in my place, I guessed that was something they'd see to it that I overcame.

There were so many strange looks and stares to dodge, and I pretended not to hear the whispers. It all made me grateful that being back here was only temporary for now. Maybe a couple weeks spent elsewhere, hanging with the guys, would give everyone a chance to forget what happened in the courtyard.

Despite my effort to avoid eye contact, there was a guy posted in the vestibule whose stare was impossible to ignore.

A snide grin was set on his lips, and as he held my gaze to lean in toward his friends, I felt sick. There was no doubt they were talking about me.

It seemed no matter how hard I tried to just be normal, tried to fit in, I sometimes thought I simply wasn't meant to.

The small seed of boldness Paulo had managed to plant, was gone in an instant.

Unfortunately, the ones who'd just been whispering about me were unavoidable, because they'd chosen to stand right along the path the guys and I had to follow to the stairs. Still pretending not to care I was the center of attention, I breathed deep as we passed.

Wolves—I caught their earthy scents right away, immediately noting how it differed from the smoky aroma of the Omegas. It hadn't been that way before shifting, but my sense of smell wasn't the only thing that was keener. My eyesight and hearing were almost annoyingly clear, too.

Which was why, when the guy *thought* he spoke quietly enough for only his friends to hear, I caught every word.

"She only got in because her family put in a word to the Advisors. Guess they didn't want her at home either."

Their laughter rose into the air, so smug and entitled. Like they truly believed they had more of a right to be at the academy than I did. My throat suddenly felt tight and raw with emotion, igniting a strange burning sensation in the center of my chest. Something I'd never felt before. However, it only took me a moment to identify it, thanks to something my father had warned me about.

It was rage.

All dragons were born with a supernatural chip on their shoulder, ready to fight first and ask questions later. We were, literally, hot-tempered. He said it was our cross to bear, our responsibility to contain it.

So, that's what I did. I stuffed the white-hot anger down into my gut where it wasn't threatening to burst from my lips in the form of curse words, or maybe even actual fire. Instead, I clenched my fists. Losing my cool would have only proven these idiots right.

"Control yourself." My steps slowed when Ori grumbled those words. "Lay a finger on *any* of these kids and Chief will be all over us."

At first, I thought the comment had been meant for *me*. However, noting how Ori's watchful glare narrowed toward a furious, scowling Paulo, I realized *he'd* been the one Ori meant to correct with his command.

As Paulo's eyes locked with the mouthy wolf, anger distorted his otherwise handsome features. When the smirk the guy wore began to slide off his face, one thing became clear.

He knew he had the attention of the mountainous man beside me.

I didn't even have to question whether the guys were all thinking about the conversation we just had, not even ten minutes ago. While *I* had decided to ignore the insult and take the high road, Paulo clearly had *not*.

Our steps halted and I read his body language — stiff shoulders, veins throbbing in his neck as hints of fire made them glow beneath his skin. There was an unwavering scowl set on his face that made me extremely grateful I wasn't that kid.

The sound of heavy footsteps echoed through the vestibule like my wildly beating heart. I held my breath, watching as Paulo crossed the tile. It seemed Ori's order had gone in one ear and out the other, which I wasn't even sure was allowed.

Coming nearly toe-to-toe with the guy, Paulo stared down his nose, harnessing what looked like the fury of ten dragons. The fire that glowed in his veins had spread to his arms now, too, flowing toward tight fists.

"Mind repeating what you just said?" The request left his mouth far too calmly, which accounted for the dead silence that suddenly filled the crowded space.

I peered around discreetly, noting how all eyes were on us now.

"I-I didn't say anything," the wolf stammered. Right after, he shot a sideways glance toward his friends. Sort of a plea for help. Only, they made it clear this wasn't their fight and wanted nothing to do with the Omegas. In fact, the group took one big, collective step back, leaving the lone wolf to face my guardians.

"Your name." Paulo's command ricocheted off the surfaces like thunder.

Needless to say, kid didn't hesitate to give up the info. "David, Sir. David Sinclair junior."

Paulo nodded, never letting his gaze falter. Beneath the thin material of his white tank, his large shoulder muscles stiffened when he reached out suddenly, taking David by his collar before lifting him into the air. The sound of his back slamming the wall next was accompanied by loud gasps exploding from the crowd.

'Don't be stupid,' Ori cautioned him in thought.

Peering up toward the terrified wolf dangling above him, Paulo ignored the warning.

"Well, it seems you picked the wrong day to be brave, David Sinclair Junior," he smirked. "It's been a crazy twenty-four-hours, I'm on edge, and I'm starving." He paused to eye the kid again. "Do you have any idea how long it's been since I had wolf for dinner?"

A menacing grin spread across Paulo's face and I wasn't sure he was kidding. "I might be unstable, but I'm fair," he stated a little too rationally. "I'm gonna give you a ten-second head start."

The only sound to be heard was David's breathing as he panted, staring into the eyes of the dragon who just threatened to eat him alive. I don't think any of us realized just how petrified he was, until a dark stain appeared on the front of his khakis. It grew larger by the second as he hung there, pinned to the wall. Paulo was the last to notice, once liquid trickled from David's pantleg, down to the tile in a puddle.

"Did he seriously just piss himself?" some brave soul to the left announced, seemingly unaware of the tension the moment still held.

The statement prompted a girl near the stairs to laugh so hard she snorted, which set off a chain reaction that moved through the room like a wave. David meant to shame and embarrass *me*, but that came back to bite him.

Hard.

Karma and whatnot.

"Put him down. Now," Ori seethed.

Redness had flared in David's face, and then a sheen of sweat. Disgusted, Paulo did as he was told, dropping the one who taunted me so quickly he couldn't quite get his footing. The result was a mortifying scene, ending with him falling into the puddle of his own waste.

"Consider this your warning. There won't be another," Paulo said sternly, holding David's gaze to make sure he understood. After slipping in the mess a few times, he finally got it together and took off through the front door, disappearing somewhere across the courtyard.

Thanks to Paulo jumping into action, the heat was suddenly off me. The name "Sir Piss-A-Lot" was floating around, and I had a feeling David wouldn't soon forget this lesson in what happens when you cross an Omega.

Ori, still frustrated by Paulo's insubordination, stormed toward the stairs with Kai and Rayen not too far behind. Taking slow strides as I walked beside Paulo, I couldn't quite put my finger on how seeing him stand up for me made me feel.

Years ago, my family had no idea the hell I'd been through, so I hadn't given them a *chance* to come to my rescue. Not that I needed it. I endured the merciless teasing and solitude on my own, but it might have been nice not to have felt so alone.

Now, I somehow had these four in my life, more than willing to defend my honor even without me asking. Suddenly, as I settled into the idea of this being my new normal, those feelings I searched for a moment ago were no longer so elusive. Paulo acting in my defense proved I didn't have to worry about being safe while with the Omegas. In their presence, I would always be protected, valued.

"Thank you," I said quietly. "You didn't have to do that."

The warm smile he lowered toward me made my heart melt. The backs of our hands brushed one another's just then, and my fingers twitched a bit when I kind of wished I'd had the courage to hold his.

"What do you *mean* I didn't have to?" He let out a confused laugh, as if I'd just spoken a foreign language.

I shrugged. "You went against Ori to put that kid in his place."

"Ori will get over it." Paulo chuckled a bit. "I'll never let anyone make you feel like you did back in the day. You're with us now, and that means when someone's against *you,* they're against us all."

The sense of pride and belonging that filled me when he said those words was indescribable. It was almost as intense as the rush that came next, when he took my waist and led me up the stairs.

We reached my door and I swear I only got my fist into the air to knock when it suddenly flung open. Staring at me from across the threshold was a very worried girl with red-rimmed eyes, and matching dark circles beneath them. If I had to guess, Toni hadn't slept much.

The guys hung back a few feet while Toni stared at me, eyeing me like she wasn't sure how to feel now that I stood before her. I could only guess the thoughts she had while I was missing, could only guess what she thought could have happened.

I didn't say a word while waiting for her to react. Mostly, because I wasn't sure *what* to say. There was guilt just sitting on my chest, like a weight. I wanted to go back in time and do things differently. Starting with trusting her enough to share my whole truth, my plan, my fears.

While I was still overthinking things and trying to read her thoughts, Toni practically leapt on me. Both her arms locked tight around my neck, like a vice.

"I should kill you for leaving without me," she threatened with broken syllables, spoken between sniffles.

"I'm sorry. I just wanted to keep you safe. *All* of you," I added, hoping she understood that.

I felt her head shake against my shoulder, protesting. "I get it, but … dude. That was a serious dick-move. I told you I'd be right back and you ghosted me! *Knowing* I'd be worried."

She was seriously hurt, and that was on me. I guess I really wasn't used to having friends who stuck by me like this. Still, there was no excuse.

"You have my word. I won't shut you out anymore," I promised.

Finally pulling away, she nodded, wiping huge tears from her cheeks that only made me feel worse.

She looked me over again, and then finally seemed to notice the guys standing behind me. The sight of them sobered her a bit, prompting her to swipe both hands to gather the fallen tears.

"Sorry," she said with a soft laugh. "Come in."

No longer blocking the door to our room, she gestured for us all to step inside.

"You probably want privacy," Ori spoke up, drawing my eyes toward him. "We don't mind waiting here."

While I appreciated the offer, I had nothing to hide from them. "It's fine," I reassured them.

He hesitated for a moment before nodding toward the others, prompting them to enter.

The room usually felt pretty spacious, but with the guys present—their foreboding height, the expanse of their broad shoulders—it felt like the walls were closing in on us.

Ori stood beside the window, peering down into the courtyard while the others didn't wait for permission to drop down onto my bed. I glanced around, taking note of the blankets and pillows sprawled out all over the floor.

"The others stayed over last night and I haven't bothered to clean up yet," Toni explained. "When you went missing, the twins and Tristan wanted to be here in case you came back. Seeing as how the guards wouldn't let us go look for you."

I glanced up when she said that. "You were going to come after me?"

She seemed confused that I asked. "Well, duh. Not just because we knew you were going through your first shift, but because of all this talk about it being dangerous out there after dark. We needed to know you were okay."

My chest felt tight when the idea of it overwhelmed me.

Toni chuckled and I was glad for it. It was hard not seeing her chipper, ready with a joke on the tip of her tongue.

"You should've seen Marcela. Apparently, chick's a psycho when it comes to her friends," Toni shared. "I, legit, thought she was gonna fight those guys when they told us the campus was on lockdown. It got so heated, one of them threatened to taser her, which got Manny fired up. You would've thought we had an army behind us when we stormed that gate—super bold, overly confident, totally prepared to get our butts handed to us by security," she added with a laugh.

"You all went through so much trouble for me. I—"

When my sentence trailed off, Toni stepped closer, looking me straight in my eyes.

"We love you, Noelle. None of us have our families out here, so we have to stick together. We were prepared to do whatever it took, because we knew you would do the same for us."

And I would have.

In a heartbeat.

She took my hand, squeezing it once before a knock at the door stole our attention.

Toni's eyes lit up. "That's probably the others. They went to the dining hall to scrounge up some dinner. They're gonna be so geeked you're here."

I hoped she was right. Hopefully, no one was too upset with how I left.

CHAPTER FIVE

NOELLE

"A full pizza, a carton of fries, and the finest freezer-to-dinner table hamburgers Dragon Fire Academy has to offer," Tristan announced, staring only at the food in his arms as he took inventory.

Then, he glanced up, suddenly aware of my presence in the room.

"You're back!" Manny practically yelled, pulling my attention from Tristan. The relief in his tone made me smile.

"I am. For a bit, at least. I wanted to check in with you guys, let you know I'm okay."

Marcela pushed past Tristan and Manny to rush toward me, arms already outstretched. She hugged me just as tightly as Toni had, making it hard to breathe.

"The girls were worried sick about you," Manny said from behind his sister, prompting Toni to shoot him a look.

"The *girls* ... were worried?" she echoed teasingly. "Says the guy who tried to scale the wall, and then got blasted off like it was an electric fence."

"It was those stupid sigils," Manny grumbled. "Accidentally touch one and it's a wrap. Had to learn the hard way," he added quietly. "Hurt like hell, too. Not that anyone cares."

I held in a laugh, imagining him flying from the wall, landing flat on his back as air sputtered from his lungs. Just for dramatic effect, I pictured singe marks on his cheeks and smoke coming from his hair.

"We made a *huge* scene," he added.

"Got so bad your girl Blythe even came over to help. She'd seen the whole thing, apparently — even your episode in the courtyard," Toni revealed. "So, she came over to where we were pitching a fit at the gate, *claiming* she wanted to help."

I felt my face twist into a scowl. "I doubt it. Blythe Fitzgibbons doesn't lift a finger to help *anyone*. It had to have been about something else."

"Maybe, but either way, she got in the guards' faces right with us, called them everything except a blessing," Toni added with a shrug. "She threatened to do some of that dark juju bull-crap, but they didn't budge."

Blythe getting involved was ... weird, but then again, last night had been anything but ordinary.

All of a sudden, my skin felt alive with electricity as the guys were signaling one another again.

'Blythe? Princess ever mention that name before?' Paulo asked.

'Nope, not that I remember," Kai responded.

"Hold up. Did I hear right a minute ago?" Toni asked, drawing my attention toward *her* instead of the guys. "I got sidetracked, but did you say something about not staying?"

It was going to be awkward explaining things in front of *everyone,* so I held back, giving as little info as possible.

"I *did* say that," I confirmed, glancing toward the Omegas before continuing. "There's, um … a lot going on with me that I haven't quite known how to talk about."

"Like what?" Marcela urged thoughtfully. "There's no judgement here."

That was so apparent. I only felt their love and concern.

"Well, for starters," I dove in, "I've been experiencing some strange things since arriving on the island. I've seen things, had weird dreams and experiences. None of it really made sense until the guys helped me understand, but I still have a lot to learn."

While my comprehension was limited for now, it was my hope that things would be different soon. With the Omegas acknowledging me as their mate, I imagined information would no longer be withheld from me.

"Weird dreams, like the one you told me about on our first day of school? The one I thought might have been something you ate?"

I nodded when Toni asked, recalling that one, and the many *others* I'd kept to myself. "Yeah."

"And … just what kind of experiences are we talking?" Manny chimed in. "Alien abduction type stuff, or is it more of a head-spinning-full-three-sixty, call the priest type deal?"

"Neither, but … maybe just as bad," I admitted with a nervous smile. "When we were at the lagoon, I sort of, I don't know … slipped away, someplace else."

That sounded so crazy, but I'd already said it, and couldn't take it back. The blank stares aimed at me made me a bit self-conscious.

"Someplace else?" Tristan asked, shoving his hands in his pockets when he leaned against my door.

"Yeah, like it was Sanluuk, but … not quite. It was dark and the surface was sort of scorched," I tried to explain.

Tristan's eyes narrowed when he thought about it. "I remember that, I think. You came out of the water looking dazed. I was on my way to help you, but someone got to you before I could."

That someone had been Kai, and I was pretty sure Tristan hadn't forgotten either.

"So, what does it all mean?"

When I shrugged, it wasn't that Marcela's question didn't deserve a better answer. This was just the only one I had for her.

"Honestly, your guess is as good as mine," I shared, "but this showed up last night and I believe it's all tied together."

There was a brief moment that I hesitated, wondering if it was really okay to put it all out on the table, but then I just went for it. Turning, I lifted my hair from the nape of my neck and revealed the symbol to my friends.

"What in the—" Toni's sentence cut off when she stepped closer. "This happened after you shifted?"

I nodded. "Yeah."

"Can I touch it?"

I didn't see any reason she shouldn't, so I nodded again. Her finger traced the outline of my mark and I stayed silent while they observed. Even Tristan pushed off from the wall to take a look.

"It's so weird," Manny commented.

"If it wasn't so scary that it just showed up out of nowhere, it'd actually be kind of cool," Marcela added.

"It is weird," I agreed, "but not so much that I have a mark, but because mine is different."

I breathed rapidly as all four of my friends' brows quirked in unison.

"Different from whose?" Marcela spoke up, likely asking the question on all their minds.

I glanced to my right, where Ori was still standing guard by the window—always seemingly on duty. He'd never struck me as the sensitive type, but I sensed so much warmth from him now, as that hard look he always wore softened just a little.

"Different from theirs," I confessed, turning back toward Toni and the others. "Different from my guardians, my ... *mates.*"

I was only weirded out saying it because I knew my *friends* would be weirded out. We did things quite differently on the mainland, so I didn't expect them to understand. Heck, I'd only accepted it myself a couple days ago—first kissing Kai, and then Paulo, Rayen, and Ori.

After that, I knew. I was undeniably theirs.

Manny tilted his head to the side, confusion creasing his forehead. "Uh, run that back, please. Did you say mates? As in, *plural*. And mates as in, like … 'bedfellows'?"

"Wow," one of the Omegas groaned behind me.

"Bedfellows?" Toni giggled. "Is that even a thing?"

Marcela slowly turned to face her brother, her expression becoming more disgusted by the second.

"I should slap you right now, in front of everyone," she warned. "Why on *earth* would you use such a stupid, *stupid* word, Manny?"

Unsure why his twin was so offended, Manny shrugged. "Well, what should I have said? The word 'mate' implies a *lot* of things!"

"You shouldn't have said anything, but definitely not that." Marcela, clearly giving up, rolled her eyes.

"Hold on a sec," Tristan scoffed, tossing an incredulous smirk toward the Omegas before his gaze returned to me. "*All* of them?"

My stomach did that weird sinking thing when the question was fired at me like a bullet.

"Why would I joke about that?" I answered reluctantly. That feeling of there being no judgment faded quickly, thanks to that look on Tristan's face.

He full-on laughed this time. "Noelle, be serious! Who the heck is filling your head with this crap?"

I went from feeling embarrassed by his reaction to offended.

'Know what would shut this kid up? A boot to the throat.' The voice inside my head was undoubtedly Rayen's.

'Stand down,' Ori said sternly. *'She can handle him.'*

His confidence in me nearly made me smile.

"One girl and four dudes? Who *does* that?" Tristan asked next, confirming that the judgment I sensed was officially alive and well. "So, you came here to learn, to get your foot in the door with The Guard, now you're giving that all up for *them?*"

"Wait, who said anything about giving up?" I asked, hearing the shrill tone of my voice as I frowned. "I haven't lost sight of anything. I'm still focused on school, but who says school has to be *all* I focus on? I can't have a life, too?" I asked.

Without realizing it, Tristan was speaking to an unspoken concern I held. That I would have to choose between fulfilling my purpose and the Omegas.

Tristan's only response was to shake his head as his gaze slipped from mine. Apparently, I was hard to look at now.

"Listen, I don't expect you guys to understand it, but this is how things are. I thought I was only coming here to learn. It wasn't until I got settled that I realized my mission might be bigger than that."

"Says who?" Tristan cut in. "You're barely twenty, Noelle, with your whole life ahead of you, and you're gonna just let these four piss on you and call you theirs? Laying claim to you for a lifetime? Nah, I call B.S."

The bed creaked behind me, and suddenly a massive shadow blocked out the trace of sunlight that remained. It meant the Omegas were all on their feet, and losing their cool.

Very quickly, I might add.

"Soooo... let's focus on what's important," Toni interjected, eyeing my guys as she positioned herself between us and Tristan. I guessed this was her attempt at keeping the peace. "Noelle is alive and she's safe. The other details aren't important, but no matter what, we should have her back," she added. "Because that's what friends do."

When she smiled at me, some of the tension melted away. "Thanks."

"Of course."

Tristan's expression hadn't changed. "Whatever," he sighed, beginning to grab the few things he'd left here overnight. "Noelle, glad you're okay. Now, if you'll excuse me, I just ... I have to get out of here," he announced, slamming the door as he exited.

Toni stared after him for a moment, and so did I.

'*Kid's a pussy,*" Rayen grumbled, speaking to the others in secret.

Well, kind of.

'*Chill. We knew he had feelings for her. Give him a chance to process that she's off-limits.*'

Hearing Ori speak on Tristan's behalf came as a shock, but it shouldn't have. He was always levelheaded, logical.

Toni turned to me again, tossing her braids back over her shoulder. "You know what? Forget that boy. He'll come to his senses once he's done pouting," she insisted with a forced smile. "Just know that the rest of us have your back. Regardless what Tristan, or anyone else has to say about it."

Having lost enough friends already, I hoped she was right about that. It meant a lot to return and find that she, Marcela, and Manny didn't share the popular opinion of my peers. Even after my freak out, even after news about my role within the Omega Hive, they were still with me when the dust settled.

These three were an example of true loyalty, and I wouldn't soon forget it.

CHAPTER SIX

NOELLE

One week in Ori's room and it already felt like mine. He made space for my things by clearing out a few drawers. I'd even been given my own blanket I was told to take with me when I left. It was one Rayen's mother made him when he was a kid, but by them all being so big, even *before* being called by Spirit, it was a perfect fit for me.

The guys made sure I knew nothing here was off limits, and they'd been keeping the house extra clean. No way that was the norm, so I appreciated their effort. They'd been so accommodating. If they weren't careful, this would start to feel like my home, too.

The place was quiet as three of the four prepared for patrol. Soon, it'd just be Rayen and I. We had plans to pass the time — snacks and a rousing game of Go-Fish. That was something my brother, sister, and I used to do when I got suckered into it. Now, I kind of missed those days.

I towel dried my hair, before slipping into a tank top and cotton pajama shorts. It was too hot and sticky for more clothing than that. Even with it nearing ten P.M.

I tossed my towel into the hamper and opened the door. The moment I did, three figures stopped in the dark hallway. They had a tendency to patrol wearing only their shorts. Apparently, "patrol" was less of a leisurely walk near the border, and more of the Firekeepers running at an unfathomable speed, stoking a continuously burning fire that marked a distinct line between the hemispheres. Although there were still occasional breaches, if it weren't for the work the Firekeepers did to keep Sanluuk safe, I imagined things would go bad quickly.

Knowing how dedicated they were to their duty only made them *more* irresistible as I gawked at each of the three — shirtless, brave, beautiful.

"We're headed out," Ori announced in a low voice. "If anything happens, Rayen will alert us and we can be back here in five minutes. Not a second longer."

I smiled up at him, although his features were merely shadows with little more than an array of candles lighting the entire bungalow.

"Relax," I laughed, pushing a hand through my hair. "Things have been quiet. I'm sure we'll be fine."

A few seconds passed and the length of his stare could be felt before he finally nodded. "Sure."

He'd been through so much, which left him with no idea how to loosen up. The ice between us had yet to be broken, but I was committed to helping it thaw. Placing my hand on his arm made him do a double take just before walking away.

"Be safe, okay?" I smiled, hoping this gentleness between us would eventually feel less like work, becoming more natural.

"Promise," he answered with a nod, and then I released the light hold I had on his bicep, allowing him to continue toward the door.

Somewhere deep down, he had a chill side. If given the chance, I'd do my best to help him find it.

Kai moved in closer and I peered up at him. "Stay up until we're done?" His request made me suddenly grateful he couldn't see that I most *definitely* started blushing.

"Um … okay."

His bright smile could be seen even in the dim light. "Good. We should be back in a few hours."

I felt giddy and anxious when I sank my teeth into my lip, nodding. He and Ori made their way out onto the porch, headed toward the dock, and my eyes followed them every step of the way.

Paulo still hadn't left, instead coming to stand before me. The feel of his hand slipping across my waist made the next breath I took seep from my lungs slowly. At first, I thought he only intended to speak before heading out. However, the next second, I was proven wrong.

With the difference in our height being so great, he craned his neck to reach my lips. Warm and soft, his pressed to mine, enticing my body to arch toward his. I breathed him in deep. In an instant, I was reminded of the experience we shared on the roof of my dorm. The power that ignited between us was unexpected and intense.

Then *and* now.

It wasn't lost on me that Paulo had made one bold move after another. The way he stood up for me at the dorm, and now, going against the strict guidelines set by his alpha. Eavesdropping on the hives inner-conversation, I knew Ori had warned the other three to keep their distance. It was important to him that I didn't feel pressured to get physical just because we were a unit. But, if anything … I was the one starting to burn up.

Paulo's hands rested at either side of my neck when he pulled away. There was a lingering sense of that one kiss not having been enough. For *either* of us. However, if there was one thing I knew about the Omegas, their responsibility to this island was second to none.

And I loved that about them.

"Guess you should get going," I breathed, fighting how my body rejected those words. The *last* thing I wanted them to do was leave.

"Yeah … I should," he acknowledged, but when his eyes met mine, I was certain he felt it too.

The heat.

The tension.

If I lasted here another week without exploding, it would be a miracle.

"Be good while we're gone." A smirk followed the playful warning, and I nodded before watching him walk away.

What stole my attention was a slight noise coming from the kitchen. The sound meant Rayen was likely preparing the snacks he promised to deliver, so I moved away from Ori's door and into the living room where I dropped down onto the couch.

Playing cards were set out on the coffee table — our mode of entertainment for the evening. The space was cast in soft, yellow light. Candles were everywhere — one in each window, one beside the cards we'd use, another on top of a small bookcase near the door. Somewhere, a radio played softly, filling the room with gentle music.

It was … perfect.

"I hope you like chocolate." Rayen's voice commanded my attention. "Probably should've asked that before I got started."

He came closer, carrying a tray lined with store-bought cookies and brownies. Beneath his arm, a bag of chips, a two-liter of soda, and cups.

I watched him place it all on the table before me. "Show me a girl who *doesn't* like chocolate."

One corner of his mouth quirked with a smile. "My sister, Leilani, hates it. So much so, she managed to convince herself she was allergic as a kid."

With everything set out, Rayen came to join me on the couch, causing it to dip with his weight.

"Paulo mentioned you all having sisters the other day, when we were at the dorm. Do you come from a big family?" I asked.

"Three sisters and two brothers," he shared. "I'm the oldest."

"Like me," I said with a smile, thinking of Lea and Evan, who were probably at home getting on each other's nerves at that very moment.

"It's a job, isn't it?" he chuckled.

"*Oh*, yeah. There's always a fight to break up, a mess to clean up—"

"A mistake to cover up before they get caught."

"That too," I smiled. "Like last year, when my brother was on this kick, trying to prove he wasn't just some sheltered kid who never colored outside the lines. He was stupid enough to convince some *other* idiot to buy him booze, so he could throw a party at the local reservoir. Mind you, he was fourteen at the time, and most of his guests were *my* age."

"Nice. I'm sure *that* went great," Rayen added sarcastically.

"Well, lucky for him, I found out about it before our parents. Which meant I got to be the un-fun sister who stormed down to the falls, busting up the party."

"Been there," Rayen said with a grin, reaching to pour us both a cup of soda.

"Of course, he didn't see the bigger picture—that I was trying to keep him safe, trying to save his skin before our dad found out. All he saw was his big sister ruining his life."

Rayen handed me a cup. "You talk about your dad a lot. You guys are close?" After asking, he took a sip.

It was hard to imagine I hadn't seen my parents in so many months.

"We are," I shared. "He's awesome."

My gaze lowered when I got caught in the grip of emotion. I missed them all, but there was something about knowing my dad was close by. There was never anything I could do or say that pushed him away. No matter what, he was always there, ready to protect me at the drop of a hat, accept me no matter what I'd done, and love me when I wasn't sure I deserved it.

"I'm sure he misses you, too."

It wasn't until Rayen said those words that a tear actually fell, and as soon as it did, he brushed it from my cheek with his thumb.

"I didn't mean to make you cry."

I peered up at him through my blurred, watery vision. "It's not your fault. I just didn't think it'd be this hard being away from home."

"I can't even imagine what that's like," he commented. "Which, I guess makes you the brave one between the two of us."

His smile drew one out of me, too.

"Yeah, right." I replied, dabbing my eyes with two fingers to dry them. "I can only imagine the things you've seen and done as a Firekeeper. I'm pretty sure others couldn't handle *half* of what you guys have been through."

He lowered his gaze with a smile, but neither confirmed nor denied.

"You've seriously never left the island?"

Rayen shook his head. "Never had any reason to. My family is here, my hive is here, and now that I have a job to do, I guess I *can't* leave."

He didn't seem sad about kind of being stuck here now.

All this talk about being with the ones we cared about caused my thoughts to take an unexpected turn. Now, I was thinking about *them,* the Omegas, and what the future held for us. Especially once I left to join The Guard.

But I didn't want to think about that yet. That opportunity was still months away and I preferred to live in the now. An idea came to mind and I reached for the cookies. When I handed Rayen one, I turned to get more comfortable.

"I know we made plans already, but … what if we do something different," I announced, facing him completely.

His brow quirked with the suggestion. "Like?"

"Like, something fun … something you're probably gonna think is a bad idea."

CHAPTER SEVEN

NOELLE

"You want me to teach you to fly," he guessed.

I grinned cheekily. "Well, you basically told me you would. Last week in the Jeep," I reminded him.

That sexy half-smile of his returned, but he didn't answer right away. I didn't miss how his eyes slipped over me. Nor did I miss how much I liked having his full, undivided attention.

"Come on," I begged. "Please? Wouldn't you prefer that I learn with one of you, instead of an instructor next term?"

He was quiet again, but this time I had hope I'd get my way.

Pushing off from the couch, Rayen caved. "Let's go."

I was giddy and practically squealed with excitement when he reached for my hand. He led the way out onto the porch, and then down onto the dock. It was pitch black out, but only for a moment. With the hand not holding mine, Rayen ignited a concentrated flame at the tip of his finger. He used it to lite the torches we passed, brightening our path toward the shore.

Beneath the slats, gently rushing water moved under our feet, and the roar of the waterfall cascading down the cliff wall added to the ambiance.

My gaze was set on Rayen. Observing him, it was hard not to gawk as his broad shoulders rolled with every step he took. Even his walk was a turn-on — casual, confident, mannish. Then there was the sheer size of him, and how the sleeveless shirt he wore left powerful arms exposed to my greedy eyes.

First, he stepped down, and then me, feeling soft sand squish between my toes.

"This is a good spot."

I looked around after he spoke, and then smiled. "Why? Because we're far from the bungalow and the trees? Because you think I might screw up?"

"All of the above," he quipped. The quick response turned my smile into a laugh. Dude didn't even worry that I might take offense.

"When you're ready, start by bringing your dragon forward."

At Rayen's command, I closed my eyes to focus my attention inward, until I identified her. The idea of having two new shifted forms lying dormant within me at any given time would take some getting used to, but it was a welcomed change. For one, the added power and abilities were convenient.

Warmth moved from the center of my chest outward, spreading down my arms to my hands, my legs to my feet. By the time I reopened my eyes, my entire body was engulfed in bright flames. Outlining my figure, my dragon form was significantly larger, even *before* considering my wingspan.

"Excellent," Rayen said with an impressed grin, not needing a moment to gather his thoughts before calling his own dragon forward.

Right before my eyes, with what seemed like zero effort, he shifted. Cloaked in fire, his eyes burned white as his wings stretched high and wide. He was beautiful.

Or rather, we were *both* beautiful, I guess.

I'd watched my parents do this a million times, but the thought of being miles above ground, relying on my own ability, made me just a tad concerned.

But the worse that could happen was I'd plummet from the atmosphere, smash every bone in my body, and then have to wait hours for it to heal itself. It would hurt like hell, but a fall wouldn't kill me.

Bright side, right?

"Okay, so the important thing to remember is that this is natural for you. It doesn't matter that you've never done it before. Just let your dragon guide you, let her take the lead."

I nodded, shaking off my nerves. "Got it."

"Taking off can be kind of rough, but don't let that scare you," he warned. "Let's give it a try."

My limbs felt heavy and it dawned on me that I shouldn't have been fixated on them, on anything having to do with my human form. This was all about my dragon.

Readjusting my focus, I concentrated on moving my wings. *You've got this. Just let go.*

A sudden burst of energy swelled within me and I did what my body told me to do, not what my mind tried to rationalize. Crouching when it felt like the power I contained would shoot from my body if I didn't move, the next thing I knew, I took off into the air.

My eyes were wide with amazement, watching as the ground seemed to spiral away from my feet, and the tall palms were eventually beneath me as well. Climbing higher, I could see a ways off into the distance. Flickers of orange light glowed sporadically, wherever there were other bungalows with life buzzing inside them. Eventually, the shoreline and ocean came into view as well, putting the height I'd soared to into perspective.

Shooting upward like a missile, Rayen joined me in the air as I peaked, feeling myself running out of momentum with gravity's pull.

"Now, move your wings," he instructed, yelling loudly to be heard over the atmospheric sounds.

I heard him loud and clear, but … my dragon didn't cooperate. I think Rayen realized that when I flashed him a panicked look, as I slowly came to a stop midair. That was the precise moment my worst nightmare began to come true.

Frantic, and now plummeting toward the ground, I turned head over heels. I tried commanding my wings, but I'd gotten it in my head that I couldn't do anything but fall.

So, that's what I continued to do.

Everything tumbled around me, and had it not been for Rayen spearheading toward me like a fireball, I might not have known which direction was up. A line of flames marked the dock, which meant I was coming dangerously close to the ground, and there was only one thing left to do.

Brace for impact.

Squeezing my eyes tight, every muscle in my body tensed as wild breaths puffed from my lungs. I could practically feel my bones breaking, my skin grating against the terrain.

Only, what I felt instead were arms. A large set that gripped my waist before flipping me toward the sky. Somehow, Rayen had caught up, and had me locked against him. He stretched his wings and the change in our speed was slight, but I felt it. The maneuver created a bit of wind resistance, likely his attempt to somewhat cushion our landing.

And quite a landing it was.

We toppled through the sand, rolling so far it felt like it went on forever. The only thing that brought us to a stop was my back slamming into a post at the entrance of the dock.

The impact knocked the remaining air right out of my lungs, and I was afraid to move. We'd just fallen miles out of the sky, and I had no idea how I screwed that up so badly.

Rayen turned onto his back beside me, spitting granules from his lip. Covered in sand just like I was, he let his eyes fall closed while his large chest rose and fell with each heavy breath.

"Yup," he groaned, now facing the stars above us. "It's broken."

"What is?" Concerned, I stared at him even more intently.

"Everything," he answered with a long breath.

Out of nowhere, a pained laugh left my mouth, despite being winded and in so much agony I could hardly see straight.

"Well, if it makes you feel any better, you're on my leg and I'm not completely sure it's still attached to my body."

He chuckled—a quiet, labored sound. "Yeah, well, I ain't moving anytime soon, so get comfortable."

One last puff of air left me, and I fell still beside him, staring skyward as we lie there, entangled with one another.

"What … the hell … was that?" he asked with a dim smile.

Somehow, my head found its way onto his arm while we recouped. "I guess I freaked out a little," I admitted, knowing I should feel embarrassed. Only, with him, I didn't.

"That was you freaking out … *a little*?" he groaned.

I ignored his question and asked one of my own. "Guess it's a good thing I didn't try it alone, right?" When I glanced over, he met my gaze for a moment.

"Yeah … good thing," he grunted, lightheartedly rolling his eyes. "For one of us."

Smiling when he added that *last* part under his breath, I turned to peer over at him. "I already said I was sorry."

He kept his eyes trained on me when I moved, managing to get up on all fours. Slowly, of course.

"This apology must have been given in sign language, because I didn't hear a thing," he countered, dripping with sarcasm. "But I'm all ears now if you want to give that a go. I'm always game for a good groveling."

I snickered and finally stood to my feet, deciding I'd help him into the house if I was able. "Mmm … maybe I'll get around to that later," I teased. "For now, just give me your hand."

After a deep breath, he did as I asked, pressing his palm to mine. "Ok, try to stand," I instructed next. "Use me to pull yourself up."

"I suppose this is the least you could do. You know, after landing on me," he joked, still sounding winded.

"Yeah, yeah. Your hands," I said with a grin. My heels dug into the sand as we worked together. I gave it all I had to help hoist him from the ground, and once he was on his feet—the giant composed of solid muscle—I tossed his arm around my shoulder.

He winced. "Easy."

"Sac up," I teased. "I'll get you inside and on the couch in a second."

He stepped gingerly, and while I gazed down at our feet, I took note of the purple bruise already forming on his calf—likely the result of a deep fracture, or even a break.

"I can do a spell that will take the pain away, too," I offered.

"Got a spell to make me forget that you landed on me?"

My side was sore, and only ached worse every time he made me laugh. "Stop being a baby about it. Most guys would have been overjoyed to have a girl on top of them."

"Trust me, had it been under different circumstances, you'd have no complaints from me right now," he chuckled. "And let it also be known that I wouldn't be the one limping away."

Hearing him say those words, I drew in a shallow breath, imagining that to be very close to the truth.

We shuffled across the dock, and once on the porch, I let go of Rayen for a second to open the door. He stumbled in beside me and I lowered him as carefully as I could manage to the couch.

"I'm sorry," I told him, hearing him wince again when I hadn't been able to support his weight all the way down.

"It's fine," he panted.

"Close your eyes," I instructed as I knelt at his side.

In time, he would've healed on his own, but I wanted to speed along the process. I recited an incantation over and over until I felt the healing light warm my hands. It brightened the room enough that it could be seen even through my eyelids.

When it faded away, I met Rayen's gaze. "Better?"

He looked skeptical, and I understood why when he moved the injured leg. He was still in pain. The bruise had faded, but apparently the break had yet to heal all the way.

"I probably just missed something because I'm still a little out of it. I can try again," I offered, but a hand on top of mine halted me.

"Don't worry about it. I'll mend on my own in a few," he reasoned. "For now, mind helping me to the shower? I'm ... kinda filthy."

He glanced down at his clothing, prompting me to look over my own. Like his, they were covered in wet sand.

But what did he mean *help* him? Like, get him there? Or help him with ... *everything?*

"If it makes you feel any better, you have my word this isn't a setup," he said with a grin, cutting into my thoughts.

It dawned on me that he must have read my expression and drawn his own conclusion as to why I hesitated.

"I wasn't thinking that," I answered in a rush when embarrassment began to set in. "Of course I'll help you."

The words came out sounding confident and casual, not at all like they'd just short-circuited my brain.

Reaching for Rayen's hands again, I hoisted him back onto his feet. One of his arms went around my shoulders and we hobbled down the hallway together. The bathroom door was already ajar, so I was able to nudge it the rest of the way with my foot. Two candles—one resting on the counter, another on the windowsill—lit this space, just like every other in the bungalow.

I propped Rayen's heavy frame against the wall for a few seconds. The showerhead sprayed powerfully when I turned on the water for him.

"Well, there you go," I announced, backing toward the hallway again. Part of me still wondered what he'd meant by his use of the word *'help'*.

"You're leaving?"

The question made me pause, so close to escaping. "Well, I thought … don't you … I mean, I just assumed —"

"I can't really put pressure on my leg," he cut in, pointing at the one I hadn't been able to heal fully. "Can you just help me with my shorts?"

He stared innocently, contradicting every single thought that fluttered through my dirty mind.

Your shorts? Sure! No big deal.

Clearing my throat, I pretended not to give his request a second thought. Pretended it didn't make me uncomfortable in all the right ways.

"Of course." That sounded casual enough, I think.

Rayen, still bracing himself against the wall, reached to grab the back of his shirt, removing it over his head and then down his arms. It fell to the floor while I held my breath, acknowledging the sheer size of him as he dwarfed me. Now shirtless, he lowered his shorts just to his hips, enough to reveal the black fabric beneath them.

Slowly, he dropped to the edge of the stool beside him. With his limited range of motion, it was on me to remove them from that point.

I leaned in and gripped his waistband, easing it the rest of the way down. Beneath them, black boxer-briefs that only covered his upper-thighs clung to the mounds of smooth muscle beneath his tan skin.

Clung … *everywhere.*

My pulse quickened with every part of him that was revealed to me, until the shorts were on the bathroom floor beside his shirt. He wasn't shy, and rightfully so.

My mouth felt dry, so I swallowed deeply, still staring despite myself.

"Well, I guess that's it." This time, I didn't move toward the door as quickly. Although, I had no idea why I stalled.

Rayen used the edge of the counter to lift himself again. "Thanks."

"No problem."

Standing close, he stared down on me in the flickering candlelight, and something within me stirred.

"I um … I think I should go," I stammered, pushing loose strands behind my ear.

Letting his gaze slip to my lips, Rayen nodded. "That's probably a good idea."

So, if we both agreed, why hadn't I moved?

Steam condensed on the mirror, matching the heat that swarmed within me. We stood close, but we only breathed one another's air as our charged surroundings nearly sent up a smoke signal. I stared with bated breath, listening as water pelted the tile beside us.

As I peered up at him, I was aware of our bond's strength, like an invisible chord linking my heart to each of theirs. It was stronger than any vows we could recite, more commanding than any piece of paper. Our souls were one entity, and in that moment, our flesh longed for the same.

I held Rayen's gaze and, behaving totally out of character, I took the hem of my shirt, pulling it over my head. When I tossed it to the floor, panting as I awaited a response, the look in his eyes was wild, conflicted. It was crystal clear he wanted this, but there was something else.

Something that made him hesitant.

Maybe this was a mistake. Maybe my timing was all wrong and…

A kiss quieted my reeling thoughts. Even more so when I was backed into the shower, into the warm water that covered us both. My back fell against the tile where Rayen's palms were flat at either side of me, boxing me in. His lips moved to my neck and I faded in and out of awareness, catching glimpses of him when I was able to open my eyes.

His jet-black curls clung to his back and shoulders, while water trails curved down his inked skin.

Impatient, I pushed my shorts down my hips and let them drop to the shower floor. Then, without asking, I slipped Rayen's boxers off as well. He stepped out of the soaked fabric when it fell to his feet, and then came closer, pressing his body flush against mine.

The Omegas burned me alive, from the inside out. I didn't stand a chance of resisting them, so the rawness of this moment didn't surprise me even a little.

My hands touched him everywhere they could reach, exploring without reservation. Because he was mine to explore. His body was like a foreign land to me, uncharted territory, and my fingers were on a journey of discovery.

Both palms slipped over the hills of muscle at his back, and then around to his chest, before trailing down his stomach where water rippled lower. Suddenly inspired, I reached lower too, gripping him, drawing a deep groan from his lips to my ear. It let me know how much he enjoyed being touched this way—by someone who wanted him in ways words could never express.

A strong tug to the back of both my thighs brought them higher, to Rayen's waist as his forehead pressed to mine. Wedged between his massive body and the wall, I sought his lips again, lulled into a trance by their fullness. However, the welcomed distraction left me unprepared.

With one impatiently powerful push, he groaned with relief as our flesh became one. My fingers wandered up, through the back of his soaked hair, and I held him closer. It almost terrified me how connected I felt to him. It was so natural it was … *unnatural.*

Alone, situated in the middle of the lagoon, no one could hear how our voices carried through the window, and out into the night air. As the minutes passed, I was aware of Rayen's full strength returning, aware of him being less focused on pain as pleasure took its place. There was so much we'd kept inside, it threatened to explode from us both now, every time his body crashed into mine.

Air puffed from my lungs and grazed his neck. Neither of us could hardly catch our breath as it became abundantly clear how well we fit together. In every way possible.

His hands tightened at my waist and what little self-control I still held on to slipped away. Within seconds, I rushed into ecstasy, and Rayen wasn't far behind. As the high began to fade, what remained was raw emotion, making it hard for us both to let go.

Our hearts beat wildly as the reality of what had just taken place seemed to take hold. I was left with a sense of wholeness I hadn't realized was possible.

My face cooled a few degrees when he pulled his cheek away from mine, and we stared into one another. I could have wondered if he felt it too, could have asked if he was aware our connection had just evolved once more, but I didn't need to.

It was so obvious from the way he stared, the way he held me long after I was lowered back to the tile.

Eventually, we turned off the water, and then stepped out onto the rug. A towel was handed to me, and I covered myself. Although, being honest, I felt so comfortable with him, I would have been fine without it.

I gathered my things from the floor and turned when I took the knob, expecting to find Rayen still in the moment, but instead …

"Everything okay?"

That seemed like a strange thing to ask him, considering what we'd just done. Yet, there was no missing that he was troubled.

He offered a dim smile when his gaze met mine. "Everything's perfect."

He brought me close after speaking to place a kiss in the top of my hair. Still, something seemed off.

"What is it?" I asked. "You can talk to me."

The forced expression finally left his face, and I prepared myself for the unexpected.

He kept his eyes trained on my arms where they folded across my chest, as if he couldn't look me in my eyes. "We can't tell the others about this," he sighed.

"But … I don't understand." And I *didn't*. From what I'd seen, there was no jealousy among them. Besides, it wasn't like I intended to plaster *'I had sex with Rayen!'* posters all over Sanluuk, but he seemed genuinely concerned about this.

"It's a … rank thing."

The explanation made my head tilt when I became even *more* confused.

"Excuse me?"

Rayen sighed, maybe realizing I was going to need more than that.

"Ori's our alpha. So, according to protocol, he's supposed to be with you first."

My brow tensed, hearing the word "protocol" again. Only, it'd been spoken out loud this time. The whole thing suddenly had a very strong animal dominance ring to it that didn't sit well with me.

"So, let me get this straight," I started, shifting to lean against the door. "There's some archaic rule that *actually* states Ori gets to 'mark' me first?"

Tristan's reaction to being told I was mated to all four Omegas came to mind, and I envisioned a dog peeing on a chair it believed to be his. In this scenario, I was the chair, and the idea disgusted me a bit.

Rayen's eyes slammed shut as he adjusted the towel around his waist.

"It's not like that," he tried to convince me. "It's not meant to imply ownership of you. It's about our place within the hive. Spirit gave us an alpha for a reason, and we're meant to uphold all the guidelines set in place when we were called as Firekeepers."

As much as I wanted to be upset, this was another instance of their homeland and mine being vastly different. I recalled being told by a guide upon arrival that the traditions of Sanluuk didn't have to be understood by outsiders. Only respected.

With that, I silenced that side of me that wanted to give someone a piece of my mind on behalf of feminists everywhere, and instead saw Rayen's side of things.

As mates, we'd done nothing wrong. It would have been unfair to hold something against him that was out of his control.

"So, what's it going to cost you?" I asked, not taking my eyes off him.

"I don't think anything," he answered, "as long as Ori doesn't find out."

I didn't like the feeling of not knowing how this worked, but we had no choice. We couldn't take back what we'd done, nor would I if that had been an option. So, for now, what happened with Rayen was our little secret.

CHAPTER EIGHT

NOELLE

As I lie there, staring at the gym ceiling, I had a moment to reflect on how this practice session had gone so far. To sum it up, I'd just blasted myself with my own magic ... again ... because I'm so effing smooth.

Before this, I thought the term *'seeing stars'* was just a saying, but yeah, it was a real thing.

A bright pulse of light had backfired, hitting *me* instead of my intended target—the black and white bullseye a mere twenty feet away. As I peeled myself off the mat, I tried to shake off the mounting frustration.

Three mother-lovin' weeks. That's how long we'd been at it, and my accuracy hadn't improved even a little. Our instructors this term were none other than our Domain Akaasha overseers—Sira and Claire from the revered Bahir Dar coven of Ethiopia. Knowing they were likely aware of my mother's lineage having stemmed from theirs, it only added to the pressure. I was supposed to be strong and graceful, not a walking, talking mistake of magic.

Some of our finals were being replaced with Domain evaluations. Hence the reason we'd been challenged to wield our magic in ways only the most skillful witches on the planet knew how to do. The last week of classes would be much more than filling in bubbles with correct answers, we had to *also* prove that we held a strong command of our supernatural abilities. Unfortunately for me, I had *three* Domains to impress.

Kill me now.

None of us had exactly nailed this assignment. However, while most of my classmates' version of a failure looked like dim puffs of magic barely lighting up their palms, mine manifested in the form of a blast so powerful I nearly blew myself right out of my shoes.

Imagining it might have gotten a laugh out of me, if I hadn't been so frustrated.

On my feet … *again,* I breathed deep and tried to ignore the fact that I had everyone's attention. Including hers—Blythe. It was unlikely she'd forgotten what a disaster I was back in the day, so if I had to guess, seeing me fail was like déjà vu.

Her latest stunt—pretending to help my friends at the gate the night I shifted—hadn't been far from my thoughts. Mostly because her intentions were super vague and sketchy. What could she possibly have gained trying to convince those guards that I was worth the risk of going into the unknown?

Whatever the case, she was up to something.

I just knew it.

"Again," Sira called out.

She passed behind me as I resumed my stance, and my focus. I couldn't see her, but felt her judgy stare all the same. Her long, heavy skirt made this unsettling *swooshing* sound as she paced the mat, back and forth, back and forth, grating on my nerves. Almost like it was just her and I in the room, only my performance under review.

I stared at my hands as they faced outward toward the target like I'd done before. Then, I envisioned myself blasting a hole right through it with a concentrated pulse of energy, just like Claire had done during her demonstration. No, it wasn't easy, but it was possible. Heck, I'd done it at the orphanage when Janet came at me. Should've been a piece of cake, then, right?

Wrong.

Air burst from my lungs when my back slammed to the mat again. Everything ached, and I swear I blacked out for a second. I hadn't had issues controlling my magic in such a long time, I'd forgotten what it was like to fail at it over and over.

Apparently, since transitioning, I was back at square one. Only, *new* me, me with the rage of a hybrid dragon inside her, didn't have the same measure of patience *old* me had.

Panting and gritting my teeth, I chose not to stand right away. Mostly because something didn't feel right. I was angry and frustrated, yes, but this felt more extreme than that.

As my fists tightened at my side the urge to slam them against the ground got the best of me and I gave in, feeling like I'd explode if I didn't dispel some of the rage somehow. The sound ricocheted off the hard surfaces in the room, causing those around me to quiet their chatter. They were probably staring too, but I was so consumed with anger I could have been in that room alone. My skin burned like a million tiny razorblades sliced through it, and that's when I saw the light.

A turquoise glow that seemed to illuminate the space around me.

My arms, my legs, *everything* glowed with blue-green sigils that covered every inch of skin I could see and feel. The sight of it made my breaths come quicker, remembering the Omegas saying they'd seen this the night I shifted. I believed it was a onetime event, brought on by the stress of transitioning, but … what did it mean this time?

And why did they show up as the negative energy swelled within me *now*?

"Look at her eyes!" someone gasped. "They're completely black!"

What?

Suddenly panicked, I sat straight up just as a figure approached from my right. It was Toni, and her brown skin reflected the bright light I couldn't seem to control.

"Don't come any closer," I rushed to say, unsure I wouldn't do something to hurt her. If that happened, I'd never be able to forgive myself.

"It's okay," she said reassuringly, kneeling beside me as she clutched my hand without fear. The moment I realized touching me wouldn't instantly kill her, I squeezed.

Because I was terrified.

"Do you want me to get Kai?" she asked, still managing to sound calm. "He was right in the hallway when I went to get a drink."

"No!" That word flew from my mouth quickly, because I did not want the guys to know things were still not right with me. The entire time I stayed with them at the bungalow, I didn't have a single weird thing happen, and seeing how much relief that brought them … I couldn't ruin it by letting him see me like this.

I wanted to be normal.

Wanted *them* to believe I was normal.

"Has this happened before?" I peered up when Sira asked. Her expression reflected both her concern *and* her intrigue as she observed me from a distance.

I nodded. "Only once. When I transitioned about five weeks ago," I admitted, hating that a crowd gathered around me now.

Including Tristan, who hadn't had much to say to me since break ended.

"Have you seen anything like it before?" Toni turned to ask.

Claire studied me more closely, and then shook her head. "Never. And I've been around a long time." She met my gaze then, filling me with a sense of dread.

"I … I think I can help."

The voice that spoke was familiar, and I looked left to confirm it was Blythe who came toward me. Her dark hair rested on top of her head in a bundle while we trained, wearing a Dragon Fire Academy logoed t-shirt and shorts like the rest of us.

She kneeled beside me, just like Toni to my left, but instead of holding my hand, she gripped my shoulder. I stared as her eyes fell closed, and she began to murmur an incantation barely loud enough to qualify as a whisper.

I kept my gaze trained on her — this girl who made my life a living hell, for reasons I still didn't know — and the longer she spoke over me, the more the rage faded. Her lips stopped moving and my breathing slowed, just as the sigils began to dim and the turquoise glow subsided altogether. I had no idea what she'd done, or how she'd done it, but I was happy to see my skin return to normal.

"I … thank you," I forced out. It was beyond strange saying those words to her.

The look on her face made me think it was equally as difficult for her to hear them. "No worries."

Her gaze flitted away from mine and she was quick to get to her feet, already starting to put distance between us as the rest of the class began to whisper. About me, no doubt.

Toni was still at my side, and the way her brow knitted together made it clear she was still concerned, too.

"What the heck was that?" she asked.

There was so much she wouldn't understand, starting with me having been marked by The Darkness. There was no explanation for why my magic was so wonky, no explanation for why I felt so … off.

"It's nothing," I answered, downplaying the truth. "Just a tri-hybrid thing, I guess." To lighten the mood, I smiled and shrugged it off as I stood to head to the locker room with everyone else.

Toni was a lot of things, but gullible wasn't one of them. She would undoubtedly have questions, and hopefully by the time she got up the nerve to ask them, I'd have answers.

***

I adjusted the lapel of my blazer, focusing on the three pins situated in triangle formation there, representing that I belonged to all three Domains. Whatever had just taken place in the gym still had me rattled. So much so, I lingered in the locker room long after changing, pretending to only be fixing my hair. When, in reality, I was trying to make sure I wouldn't cry the moment I stepped foot outside that door. Kai was waiting on the other side of it, and he couldn't know things had been so hard.

"I need to get to class, but … you're okay?" Toni's expression reflected her concern for me, and how much she cared.

Faking a smile, I nodded. "Yup, totally fine. Go. I'll see you back at the dorm later."

Even with my permission, she lingered a moment before touching my arm and going her own way. One more deep breath and I decided I could handle going out into the world.

The door opened and shut behind me, and Kai read me instantly.

Of course he did.

"What's wrong?" The question left his mouth sternly.

I peered up and smiled, pushing my braid behind my shoulder. "Geez! Nothing, Dad," I teased as I turned to face forward again. "Just a difficult session. They're really pushing us this term."

Our steps echoed in the hallway as we neared the exit.

It didn't surprise me that we halted then, and a set of heavily concerned eyes were now glued to mine. Having his full attention made me uneasy, mostly because I feared he'd see right through me. The pressure brought out a nervous smile.

"I said I'm fine," I assured him. "What about you? You seem ... stressed."

That was the best word I could find for the extra helping of tension he seemed to carry.

"It's the Chief. I asked to speak with him and the only time he has open is an hour from now," he revealed with a sigh.

It wasn't lost on me that he referred to his father in this way. Not Dad. Chief. It also stood out that Kai had to make an appointment to speak with the man who raised him.

Curious, I crossed my arms over my chest. "Speak with him about what?"

The one and only time I encountered the man was when he denied my right to leave the island.

"He needs to know we've found our mate. Technically, we should have informed him weeks ago, but … we had our reservations."

If by reservations, he meant he didn't trust the man further than he could throw him, we were on the same page.

"Besides," Kai continued with a sigh, "I've been thinking about what you suggested — that maybe he already knows? At first, we didn't think it could be, but it's possible one of his more intuitive advisors could have sensed it and informed him. Honestly, it's the only reason we could come up with for why he was so adamant that you stay in Sanluuk. Having you complete our hive will strengthen us over time, so maybe he feared what might have happened if you left before we all discovered the truth."

I didn't want to speak against Kai's father, but I wasn't so sure his motives had been this pure.

I smiled coyly and nodded, deciding against calling attention to his family's dysfunction. It wasn't my business, nor was it something I believed he wished to discuss.

"I see. So, what you're trying to say is that you're leaving me here to fend for myself today." My back fell against the bricks as my eyes flickered up to meet his. Most of the other students had cleared that area of the building, so it was just us.

"Only for a bit," he promised, smiling back.

He was the first Omega to soften and really see me for who I was — more than a princess, more than a burden. But a person.

For that reason, our connection was a bit different from what I shared with the others. Not stronger or more meaningful; there was just an ease to it that made it feel perfectly natural when I reached for both his hands, bringing him closer.

We hadn't kissed since the private moment in the grotto behind the waterfall. Tasting his lips again was both thrilling and familiar. It was also just what I needed to push the disaster in the gym out of my mind.

I placed his hands on my waist before securing mine on his shoulders. Being late to class wasn't even a concern as I got lost in him. Whenever I was close to *any* of them, the amount of passion, protection, loyalty, and steadfast devotion I felt was like nothing else I'd ever experienced. I looked forward to a lifetime of sharing those feelings with the entire hive.

Kai leaned in, letting his body settle against mine, locking me against the wall. A flashback of that night with Rayen in the shower came to mind, and I inhaled sharply, kissing Kai deeper. His hand slipped lower, gathering the side of my pleated skirt until his blazing-hot fingertips trailed my thigh.

A breathy laugh slipped from my lips when I pulled away slowly. "If we don't stop, we're gonna end up giving this school a show I don't think they're ready for."

There was hunger in his eyes as he lingered with his face mere inches from mine. "As much as I'd love that," he groaned, "I couldn't. Not even if it was just you and me."

I blinked hearing his response, but didn't speak. That night with Rayen, it was brought to my attention that there was an "order" to things.

"It's just how our hives function," Kai explained. "There's a delicate balance between us and Spirit that has to be maintained."

"What does that mean exactly?" I asked. Maybe he knew more about this than Rayen did.

"It means that, with Ori being our alpha, he's supposed to … *establish* you as our queen before anyone else."

"Establish me as your queen?" I echoed with a faint grin. He was practically squirming beneath my gaze. "That's basically just a nice way of saying he's supposed to screw me first." The words left my mouth as more of a statement than a question.

Kai flashed a quick smile that was gone too soon. "I guess that's one way of saying it," he answered, "but please don't be offended by how this all works. It's not like a … macho thing, or even Ori's decision. It's just the way Spirit ordained it."

"Why?" My eyes were fixed on him when I asked. "What would happen if we … I don't know … broke the rules?"

I honestly didn't mean to sound as though I was tempting him, or even *suggesting* that we went against this unspoken code. However, something came over me and the words *definitely* left my mouth sounding that way.

I could admit it; I wanted them all. Like, all the time. I'd never been this open, craving *any* guy to the point of feeling as though I might choose sex over food if forced to pick between the two. But there wasn't a second of any given day I wasn't on fire for them. Even Ori, in all his broodiness and buried pain. Regardless of *his* flaws and emotional walls, he was still mine.

I pulled Kai closer, until there was no space between us. Fantasizing what might have happened behind that waterfall if he hadn't been called away, very bad thoughts ran through my mind.

His gaze flickered up from where it had just been focused on my chest, and a deep, frustrated breath left his mouth. "I'm not sure," he answered. "None of the other hives have veered off course, so it's just one of those things we know not to do."

As badly as he wanted to, there was a sense of resolve about him that I knew wouldn't budge. He was steadfast where Rayen and I had both been weak—not that I regretted that weakness for even a second.

"I need to run," he said against my ear, right before craning his neck to place a kiss against my jaw. "I'll catch up with you in a few to let you know how things go."

Disappointed, I nodded. "Okay."

I followed him out of the building, and we parted ways at the end of the sidewalk. I would likely be the last one to class, but spending time with him had been worth the negative mark on my attendance.

'Headed to see Chief now.' Still not entirely used to hearing them speak inside my head, I stopped. Kai was trying to reach the other Omegas, but there was no answer.

'What's going on guys?'

I started walking slowly, only to avoid looking suspicious if he turned and saw me at a standstill. I glanced over my shoulder, though, cutting across the courtyard. He'd come to a complete stop when the only feedback he got from his brothers was silence. My body tensed, remembering they'd been on patrol. What if something went wrong? What if someone was hurt? What if *all* of them were hurt? It was insane how fast my heart raced even considering it.

'I hear you,' Rayen finally answered, *'but barely.'*

Barely? What did that mean? It wasn't like communicating by cell phone, where there was sometimes spotty reception. Their tether should have *never* been weak, only strong and solid. At least, that's how it always was for my parents. Maybe their connection was different, though, which I supposed could have been the case.

Kai was walking again, apparently satisfied to have at least gotten through, but to me, something felt off. The day, in general, had just been a weird one.

CHAPTER NINE

KAI

Sitting in Chief's office was always unnerving. Had been since I was a kid, forced to wait my turn to speak with my own father, just like the rest of our people. One thing no one could ever accuse the man of was showing favoritism for his own family. Even my two siblings who'd chosen to become members of our Council had earned their seats with no favors.

I glanced around his office, noting how he still kept no photos or personal effects visible. I'd only ever known him to be cold and distant, hyper-focused on work. While he kept my brothers, sisters, and myself at arm's length, it was a completely different story when it came to my mother. She'd always been his pride and joy. But then again, there wasn't a person who'd ever met her who didn't love her.

Where my father was cold and aloof, Mom was warm and accepting. Always. My grandmother liked to think they balanced one another out, but I saw things differently. When the time arrived for me to be a father, I would never leave room for my children to wonder if I loved them. A real man never should.

"Malakai." My name was uttered sternly when he entered the room.

"Chief." I stood as it was customary to do, not resuming my seat until he'd taken his.

"What brings you here today?" He clasped his fingers before him on the desk while asking.

A deep breath left my mouth. "It's about Noelle, Sir."

His brow quirked when I said her name. "I'm listening."

My mouth opened, but no sound came out. There was a plan the others and I came up with. Chief was owed an update that we had located our queen, and we agreed that I ought to be the one to deliver the news, but … the words wouldn't come out. It wasn't fear or intimidation that stopped me.

It was suspicion.

"She requested to leave the island several weeks ago," I forced out instead. "You denied this request. Why?"

There were several things Chief Makana did not tolerate. Just beneath threats on that list, was opposition. When his shoulders squared and his eyes narrowed, I knew he hadn't appreciated my question *or* my firm tone.

"Why?" he repeated. "Because it was my decision to make and the answer I saw fit to give was '*no*'."

He stared unwaveringly, as if he'd interpreted my question as a challenge. The deeper I considered it, maybe it had been just that.

"Is this why you requested to see me?" he asked. "Is this why you're taking up valuable minutes that I could be dealing with any number of pressing issues on my agenda?"

There it was. He never ceased to make it clear how low I fell on his list of priorities. But I wasn't a kid anymore. I stopped wishing he cared more a long time ago.

"As the ones you've put in charge of looking after her," I continued, "I think we deserve an explanation. What reason could you have possibly had for not letting her go? Her first transition could have very well been disastrous for all of Sanluuk, but I'm guessing you already knew that."

The look he leveled my way could have cut glass, and when he stood to stare down on me, there was no mistaking that I'd stricken a nerve.

"Has the small taste of authority granted to you by Spirit gone to your head, boy? It would be wise to mind your tongue and remember who *truly* rules over you," he seethed. "Questioning my decisions is *way* above your paygrade."

Heat rolled through me and I clenched my jaw. The flare of rage in my chest made it impossible to stay seated while he stared down his nose. Rising to meet him at eye-level, I didn't blink.

"I just pray no one means to do her any harm," I warned. "Because if that happens, the Omegas will rain down hell on this entire island and *no one* will be able to stop us."

Chief's eyes widened with surprise as silence filled the room. I'd never spoken against this man a day in my life, but I'd never been more certain of any promise.

"Is that a threat?" he asked with the hint of a smile. "I could have you arrested for treason so fast your head would spin."

"It's only a threat if you have something up your sleeve that's gonna put her in danger," I reminded him.

That wicked smile of his grew when he leaned in closer, placing both hands on his desk.

"My, my, look how my son has blossomed into a man," he grinned. "And all it took was finding his queen."

I didn't release the breath I held, and he seemed to notice.

"What's the matter? Didn't think I knew about that?" he asked with renewed confidence. "I'm Makana Sigo, long-reigning chief of the island of Sanluuk. *Nothing* takes place here without me knowing. I have eyes and ears everywhere, and you would be wise to remember this the next time you forget who's in charge."

"Who told you?"

"Trivial details, son," he answered dismissively. "What you *should* be questioning is whether it was even Spirit who gave this girl to you."

When he leaned away, there was a look of satisfaction on his face that sickened me.

"What are you talking about?"

A casual shrug lifted his shoulders. "Just look at history," he reasoned. "Never once has a hive been given a queen not born on this island—a woman unfamiliar with our customs, one who might not be readily accepted and loved by our people. How easily do you think your beloved Noelle will be brought into the fold by the tribe when you present her? Or, better yet, how do you think *she* will respond once she knows how our island has managed to co-exist all this time with The Darkness?" He crossed both arms over his chest. "The hard decisions we've had to make? The sacrifices? Do you think she'll still be as enamored by you four then?"

My gaze lowered and I considered it all, every dismal word he'd spoken.

"Spirit blesses, The Darkness curses. I suppose you'll know soon enough which she'll be to your hive—a blessing or a curse," he shared. "In the meantime, I challenge you to invite your betrothed to the Firelight Celebration next month. If she doesn't condemn us all for our sins after finding out the truth," he paused to shrug, "then maybe Spirit really *did* send her. But I suppose we'll all have to just wait ... and ... see."

He drew those last syllables out and each one grated my nerves.

"Now, if you'll excuse me, my guests have just arrived on the island, and they're waiting to be properly greeted," he announced casually as he rounded his desk, headed for the door while I stood in silence. "Have a good day, son. Ano-Luana."

CHAPTER TEN
NOELLE

"Who's up for a pop quiz?"

Ms. Audrina's announcement was met with a cacophony of groans and complaints. The day was so close to being over, so it stung a bit more knowing we'd narrowly escaped.

"Oh, come on," she grinned. "We've been back at this for seven weeks, and this is the first test I've given all term. Besides, I think you're gonna enjoy this one. Partner up."

With the only familiar souls present in Sorcery-102 being Blythe and Tristan, I decided to try my luck with a stranger. Smiling at the girl seated beside me, I gave it a go.

"Partners?" I asked.

She smiled a skeptical sort of smile that told me everything I needed to know.

"Ah, so you *have* heard of me," I joked when the truth became evident.

"Sorry," she said, shrinking into herself a bit as her freckled cheeks tinted red. "I didn't mean to cause any offense."

I lifted my hands. "None taken."

There was a brief moment that passed, and I thought I'd have to sit out on this lesson. However, the girl whose name I knew to be Jessica surprised me when she turned on her stool, facing me where we sat at our shared lab table.

"It's not that I don't want to work with you. It's just that … your reputation precedes you a bit."

This was true, and I was starting to get used to being the odd-girl-out. No, I didn't like being stared at, but the gossip had at least been kept to a minimum. Thanks to Paulo sending such a loud message through one Mr. David Sinclair Junior.

Or, as I still heard being whispered around campus, Sir Piss-A-Lot.

A warning like that wasn't likely one *anyone* would forget soon.

"It's fine," I assured her. "You can pair up with someone else. I'm sure Ms. Audrina has an alternate assignment I can do for credit."

I faced forward, silently encouraging myself to be okay with Jessica's honesty. Besides, I couldn't exactly blame her.

A heavy sigh stole my attention and I turned to meet her gaze again. "Know what? Screw it," she concluded with a grin. "I'm feeling brave today."

Apparently, Jessica had quite a set of balls on her.

"You sure?" I asked, giving her one more chance to back out. After all, we still didn't know what the assignment would be.

"It'll be fine," she said with newfound confidence.

So, with that, I had myself a partner.

I peered up, watching Ms. Audrina take slow steps around the room while we prepared. She got to Tristan's table, and that's when I noticed how he watched me. We hadn't had much to say to one another since break ended, and I kind of hated that he kind of hated *me*. But, like Ori said, he likely needed time to process the idea of me being with them.

I knew firsthand how strange it was to think of one woman being mated to four men. However, feeling so strongly for them all, it made perfect sense to me now. Hopefully, one day soon, Tristan would learn to accept it.

Realizing I'd caught him staring, he quickly looked away, resting his elbows on the stone slab surface. Ms. Audrina passed in front of my line of sight and I refocused.

"Okay, so today's quiz is relatively simple. In fact, you won't even be graded on your performance, so think of it as more of an assessment of your abilities," she explained. "You'll be casting positive emotion charms on your partners."

Jessica's long, blonde ponytail whipped through the air when her eyes left Ms. Audrina and were suddenly fixed on me. She forced a smile, but I didn't miss the look of panic that filled her expression. Apparently, the idea of me casting *any* kind of spell on her was terrifying.

Couldn't even blame the girl.

"This will be no different than the blissful charm I demonstrated on the class last week. The words are simple, and you need only focus your energy on evoking a positive mood toward your partner, and that should be it. Now, link hands, please."

The metal legs of our stools scraped the tile when we all adjusted ourselves to face the ones with whom we paired. Jessica took my hands and offered another one of those 'I'm-not-scared' smiles that didn't quiet reach her eyes.

"The words are right here on the board," Ms. Audrina announced as she finished the last phrase and placed her dry-erase marker on the ledge. "Take turns repeating them three times each, and report your emotional response when you finish."

"I'll go first," Jessica rushed to say.

I nodded. "Cool. Okay."

Confident, she smiled and did a quick shimmy on her seat to get comfortable. I stared when she closed her eyes and recited the spell. The third time she spoke it, a warm breeze passed between us and I was filled with an inexplicable sense of calmness.

"Did it work?" Jessica asked, her perky tone sounding hopeful.

I nodded. "It did."

"Yes!" she celebrated. When Ms. Audrina glanced her way, Jessica gave an enthusiastic thumbs-up to signal her success.

"Ok, now … your turn, I guess." That smile melted right off my partner's face, but it was obvious she was also being mindful not to hurt my feelings. "Remember, just say the words with the intent to evoke positivity," she reminded me.

"I know," I assured her. "Your hands, please?"

Large, brown eyes blinked at me, and then my partner finally gave in. With her palms flat on top of mine, I let my eyelids fall closed and murmured the words I had just committed to memory. I can admit, I wasn't quite sure how to intentionally 'evoke positivity', but I did my best, thinking happy thoughts and whatnot. When I finished, I had really high hopes that I'd done as well as Jessica.

However, upon opening my eyes, I realized that likely wasn't the case.

Jessica pulled her hands from mine, placing both on her stomach. There was a strange look in her eyes and—

"I think … I think I'm gonna be sick." The announcement—although spoken quietly—seemed to gain the attention of everyone in the room. At that moment, I realized this was because we were already being watched. They observed to see if I'd screw this up like I'd done so many other things.

And, from the way Jessica began to heave, my classmates wouldn't be disappointed.

Thick, green-colored vomit went all over the floor, covering my shoes and knee-high socks, too. I suppose I should have been grateful the girl at least had the wherewithal to aim down toward the floor.

Small favors.

Panting, and still holding her stomach, Jessica peered up at me with a scowl. "What did you do to me?"

Confused, I did sort of an embarrassed half-shrug, because I *thought* I'd done the spell correctly. However, the mess on the floor proved otherwise.

Suddenly, I no longer had her attention as she seemed to focus her thoughts inward. Tension creased her brow and she stabbed me with a look.

"My powers!" The words left her mouth frantically, like she'd go into a panic attack any second. "They're gone! You took my powers!"

My gaze widened with surprise. "No, I didn't," I shot back, feeling defensive as the many sets of eyes fixated on me darkened with Jessica's accusation.

She climbed off her seat quickly, taking several steps back, like she couldn't get far enough away from me.

Ms. Audrina rushed over just as I was getting to my feet.

"I didn't do anything wrong." I felt like my declaration would fall on deaf ears, but I was innocent.

"Then why don't I feel my magic?" Jessica wiggled her fingers, attempting to do a spell, I assumed, but when nothing happened, her fiery glare landed on me again.

Whispers fluttered all around me and I knew what they were all thinking. The same thing everyone *else* always thought.

"Ok, let's calm down, shall we?" Ms. Audrina said chipperly, trying to diffuse the tension in the room. With the wave of her hand, the pile of puke disappeared, as did the awful smell. My shoes and socks were even clean again.

"It's highly doubtful she's taken your magic, dear," Ms. Audrina reassured Jessica. "Syphoning or bestowing magic is an extremely complicated task," she explained. "It would require several highly-skilled witches, and a boatload of dark magic to perform a spell of that magnitude. So, let's just settle down. I'm certain this is just a ... glitch of some sort," she added, clearing her throat. "Ladies, your hands please?"

My lungs filled with air several times before I did as Ms. Audrina asked. Mostly because I was very much afraid I'd hurt her by accident. I spoke out against Jessica's accusation, but honestly? I wasn't convinced she hadn't told the truth.

Because ... there was a sensation I couldn't describe. Almost as though my hands buzzed with more energy than usual. Maybe ... that was what I'd taken from Jessica. Maybe that was the signature of her magic.

I was frozen in place as Ms. Audrina breathed deeply, and then murmured foreign words to herself. Jessica stared at me with the fury of a million suns and I knew she regretted trusting me. She wasn't alone, though.

I regretted trusting *myself*.

The room went silent again and, a few moments later, the delicate grip Ms. Audrina had on my hand released me completely. The next second, her eyes found mine.

"Are they gone? My powers?" Jessica asked in a shrill voice that could have shattered glass.

"Noelle, I ..."

"Did she take them?" Jessica interrupted, demanding an answer.

Ms. Audrina ignored the question and her gaze narrowed as she kept it trained on me. That's when I saw it, the moment I lost the one ally I had in this room.

"Noelle, what have you done?" The softly spoken words nearly broke my heart as they left Ms. Audrina's mouth. When I failed to come up with an answer, she turned to comfort Jessica. "I'm sorry," she said, "I don't know how this could have happened, but I won't rest until I find a way to fix it."

The next look Ms. Audrina cast my way was one of fear and distrust, joining the ranks of my peers.

Angry tears streamed down Jessica's cheeks as her bright red face contorted into a scowl.

"I knew I shouldn't have worked with you," she growled. "You're a freak, just like everyone says you are."

Snatching her bag from the table, she stormed from the classroom and I was left to bear the weight of my classmates' — and my *instructor's* — judgement.

If I knew how to take back what I'd done, I would have in a heartbeat, but the way they stared I was certain they all shared one thought about me.

I was certain that, in their eyes, I was nothing but a monster.

CHAPTER ELEVEN
NOELLE

The door creaked open, but I didn't move, just kept my eyes trained out the window.

Light footsteps preceded a body dropping down onto the mattress just behind my knees. It wasn't heavy enough to be one of the guys, so I knew it was Toni before she even spoke.

"Ready to talk about it yet?"

She had no idea how awful I felt—syphoning another witches powers away, having my classmates think I'd done it on purpose.

"No," I said quietly, feeling another tear race from the corner of my eye, toward my pillow.

A comforting hand rubbed small circles on my back. "Want me to go away?"

I shook my head 'no', but didn't speak.

"Well, would it make you feel better if I told you we got invited to something kinda cool?"

She had my attention.

"I'll take that as a yes," she chuckled. "Apparently, there's gonna be some sort of festival next month. Locals call it the Firelight Celebration, and it sounds like a pretty big deal. Tristan said some kid handed him this flyer in the hallway and Marcela and Manny are already on board. Should be fun, right?"

Again, I didn't answer.

"Okay … then I have *more* good news, and this time I'm *sure* you're gonna love it," she announced. "A couple hours ago, my History teacher slipped and told us something big. I mean *huge*."

My lack of an answer didn't seem to frustrate her.

"So, to make up for having those sucky evaluations at the end of this term, there will be recruits from The Guard on campus. Supposedly to scout new talent and issue early invitations to join. That means, those chosen would get to bypass the application process and tryouts."

Judging by her tone, I assumed she thought this was a good thing. However, all I felt was dread. The last thing I needed was for these recruits to see me flubbing up my magic and my application would surely get shoved right into the trash. Whatever was going on with me, it was starting to seem like the only things I could do … were dark.

"Noelle," Toni sighed, "whatever happened can't be that bad. I wish you'd—"

"I stole a girl's magic," I admitted, tired of holding it in.

My eyes blurred with tears and each breath was ragged as I wrestled with my emotions. Behind me, Toni sat in silence. The hand she once used to comfort me, went still against my back.

"The thing is, I don't even know *how* I did it," I admitted. "We were supposed to cast a positive emotion charm and I did exactly what Ms. Audrina told me to, but ..."

Shaking my head, I couldn't even finish.

Toni didn't jump off my bed and run as far away from me as she possibly could, so that was a good sign.

"Noelle, stop crying," she said gently, before grabbing my shoulder to force me to at least turn and meet her gaze. "You're not a monster."

She had no way of knowing those were my exact thoughts, so when she spoke directly to my fear, it only made the tears fall faster.

"I know your guys are working hard to figure this out, and I believe they will. But until they do, I've got your back. Even if no one else sees you for who you are, if they don't see that you've got the biggest heart in the world, never forget that *I* see it."

She leaned in to hug me as tight as she could, and I hugged her right back. I'd been so afraid to touch anyone, thinking I'd do the same to them as I'd done to Jessica, but my best friend couldn't have cared less about all that. Like she said, she saw me for me.

A sharp swooshing sound from near the door interrupted the moment, causing both of us to turn that way.

"Someone pushed an envelope under the door," Toni said, getting to her feet to grab it. She stooped and stared at the front of it while she straightened. "Looks like it's for you."

I sat up when she handed me what looked like a thin letter. Staring, she dropped back down on the side of my bed as I broke the seal.

I scanned the careful penmanship and the wetness in my eyes cleared a little.

"Who's it from?"

"I have to go." Toni's gaze lifted when I hopped off the bed and headed toward the door without answering.

The message was from someone who thought they could help me, and … I wasn't in a position to turn *anyone* down if they believed they might have answers.

Not even a sworn enemy.

***

I couldn't believe I'd stooped this low, but here I was.

Just as I lifted my fist to knock again, the knob twisted, and a second later I was staring into the eyes of the last person on Earth I thought I'd ever turn to for *anything*.

"I didn't think you'd come," Blythe said, letting out a deep breath. "Come in."

She stepped aside and gestured with her hand for me to enter. My feet didn't move immediately when my brain told them to. Apparently, they were conditioned to move in the *opposite* direction of wherever Blythe stood.

Smart feet.

The sound of the door closing behind me was a bit unsettling, but I hid how it unnerved me to be locked in such a small space with her.

"Where's your roommate?" I thought to ask.

"I told her to make herself scarce for a bit after dropping the letter off to your room."

I smirked while observing her space. Shouldn't have surprised me she still behaved like she was queen bee. Just like in high school.

Macabre paintings hung on the walls, and I knew they were pieces Blythe had painted herself. Likely since arriving on the island. She'd always been artistically talented, although her work always veered toward the dark side.

"You can sit if you want," she offered casually, pointing toward a chair beneath the window.

I sighed after lowering there. "So, I'm guessing this is about what happened in class today."

She nodded. "Yes. Well, that and in the gym a few weeks ago. And when you transitioned."

Apparently, she hadn't missed anything.

"How do you think you can help?" My tone was dry, but I didn't have much faith that I could be fixed, nor did I have much faith in Blythe.

"We'll get to that," she said quickly. "First, tell me about that … *thing* on the back of your neck."

Instinctively, my hand went there, to the symbol beneath my hair that was always just a smidge warmer than the rest of my skin.

"There's nothing to tell."

"Lies," she shot back with a smile, reaching for a bottle of black polish beside her on the nightstand. Her eyes flickered up toward me as she opened it and began touching up the chipped paint on her nails.

The savage didn't even take off the old coat before applying another.

"What do you think you know?" I asked.

"I think it happened when you transitioned, and I think it's the reason your magic has been all wonky. Am I wrong?" Her dark gaze found me again.

A sharp breath puffed from my lips. "Yes and no," I admitted. "It showed up when I transitioned, but I honestly don't know what's up with my magic. It never seems to work right."

Frustration set in when I relived the moment in Ms. Audrina's class.

"Correction," Blythe cut in. "The *dark* side of your magic works just fine."

There was a look of satisfaction in her eyes that rubbed me the wrong way.

"Look, if you just asked me to come here because you wanted to be nosey, I don't have time for this." I pushed off from the chair, but stopped before standing completely.

"Wait," she called out. "I'm sorry."

Those were words I hadn't heard Blythe Fitzgibbons utter since going dark years ago.

"I do want answers, but only so I can fully understand what's happening to you," she clarified. "But … I should have known better than to think you'd just open up to me after all this time."

"Time isn't the only issue between us," I reminded her.

She didn't meet my gaze as I stared at her, pretending to be absorbed in the action of fixing her nails.

"I owe you an apology for all that, too, but I hope you understand why I can't get into that right now," she said coldly, which didn't surprise me. "Getting into our past issues would make you think I was only bringing any of it up to prime you for some nonexistent ulterior motive," she rambled in that know-it-all way of hers. "It'd become a whole … thing, so let's just skip that part for now, and get right to business."

My arms folded over my chest. "And what does that mean exactly, Blythe? What business?"

"You have a ton of dark energy," she shared. "There's light energy in there as well, but honestly, I can't tell which side has more of a hold on you."

My heart sank hearing those words and I shifted in my seat. "You can sense that?"

She nodded. "I can, and it would be remiss of me not to say that you could go either way at this point. So, whenever possible, avoid dabbling with negative energy."

"Well, that should be easy," I said. "I don't intend to use dark magic. Like, ever."

Blythe blinked up toward me for a second as she blew over her nails. "That may be," she answered, "but that doesn't mean it doesn't intend to use *you*."

I didn't know what to say to that.

"In the gym, in class today—did you choose for either of those things to happen?"

Her question didn't require time to think of an answer. "No." I lowered my head, seeing where this was going.

"Exactly. So, that's where I come in. I'm gonna help you learn how to get rid of that dark energy and embrace the light."

A laugh slipped out. I couldn't help it. "You?"

She didn't seem offended. Actually, she smiled a bit. "Believe it or not, I still remember how to be good. I simply choose not to be."

Shaking my head, I guessed that was true.

"So, from one freak to another," she smirked, "do you want my help or what?"

This seemed the equivalent of making a deal with the devil himself, so I had to ask.

"What's in it for you?"

Blythe flashed me a look I didn't expect, one of the most sincere I'd seen from her in years.

"Redemption," she breathed. "I suppose you're not the only one who needs to know there's still some good left in her."

My heart thundered inside my chest as I weighed her words, watching carefully. If I hadn't been so desperate, I might have turned her down, but ... I was slipping toward the darkness faster than I realized.

"Okay," I agreed.

Blythe smiled up at me, giving a small nod to seal the deal. "Okay."

CHAPTER TWELVE

NOELLE

It felt like forever since *all four* had a night off from patrol. Usually, there were at least a couple members of the hive missing, or *I* was the one with a full plate.

Mostly, what kept me away was the crap-ton of studying I had to do, but I'd also managed to sneak in my first meeting with Blythe a couple nights ago. It was far less awkward than expected, so I agreed to her suggestion that we start getting together regularly. Once that started, I would be stuck at the dorm a lot more in the near future.

However, for this evening, I had the Omegas all to myself.

With my head kind of all over the place lately — like on how I'd stolen a witch's power and *still* hadn't figured out how to give it back — I needed this night with my guys.

We had nowhere else any of us needed to be.

No distractions.

Lucky me.

Soft music lulled in the background while I chilled beside Paulo, resting on top of his comforter. My eyes followed the football he tossed into the air repeatedly, watching him catch it with ease every time. Kai had been laid out across the bottom, holding my feet in place on his thigh. The bed shifted when he readjusted to get comfortable, and his gaze stayed fixed on the ceiling. I wondered where his thoughts had taken him, wondered if it had anything to do with the meeting that took place with his father a few days prior.

A meeting he hadn't talked about since.

From the window where he sat staring out, Rayen stretched. With the sleeves of his t-shirt cut off, I'd gotten caught up in how his biceps flexed with the movement, making the veins there more pronounced. When I finally stopped ogling his physique, and my eyes settled on his, he flashed a loaded smile.

One that made my teeth sink into my lip.

I'd been caught staring but didn't care a whole lot. Mostly because, with us being so in sync, there was no doubt our thoughts were aligned. I knew that, he too, had traveled back in time, to that night in the shower several weeks ago.

How I hadn't pinned him down and had my way with him since then was beyond me. It had taken a measure of self-restraint I didn't even realize I possessed.

"I'm gonna check in with Ori, see if he needs help finishing up dinner," Rayen said to us all, but when he eyed me, I swear we were alone in that room. He had a way of making me feel exposed under his gaze.

Just as he readied himself to stand, I stopped him.

"No, stay put. I'll go," I announced. He didn't have a chance to speak before I eased my feet from Kai's grasp and jumped down off Paulo's ginormous bed.

The guys stares could be felt as I left the room, headed for the kitchen.

Ori seemed to be softening toward me a little more every day, and I did my best to help things along. I know some girls have a thing against being the one to pursue a guy, but it was different with us. For starters, he wasn't just some guy. Also, there was the fact that he'd experienced something tragic, and it changed him. As his mate, I'd become inexplicably sympathetic, making it my mission to help him move forward.

"Need some help?" I asked when I reached the kitchen.

Leaning against the counter, Ori turned with a look of surprise that made my heart flutter. I loved that he seemed to not only be getting *used* to having me around; he seemed to *enjoy* it.

"Thanks, but … it's mostly just simmering now," he answered.

When he first offered to prepare dinner, I wasn't sure I shouldn't get the medic on speed dial. My dad was a good cook, but I hadn't known many other men who were. However, with the incredible aroma coming from the three pots on the stove, I guessed Ori was another exception to the rule.

I took slow steps closer, shoving both hands in the back pockets of my shorts. That warmth and softness in his expression were both addictive, partly because I believed I was the only one he looked at that way. An indiscreet glance passed over me, starting at my thighs until finally reaching my eyes. If the thinning ice and burgeoning sexual tension between us were any indicator, I'd say we were making progress.

"It's nice out tonight," I commented, shooting a look toward the open window. It hadn't gotten cold by any means, but February in Sanluuk meant mid-eighties in the day, and low to mid-sixties at night—perfect for the combo of jean shorts and loose-fitting cream sweater I wore, and Ori's sweats and tank.

"Miss the snow? I'm sure your hometown is covered in it by now."

He wasn't wrong about that. Michigan winters were notoriously harsh, but there was something picturesque and serene about this time of year. Smiling, I envisioned it—my family's property blanketed in white, dotted with large evergreens that made it feel like the holiday season hadn't quite left us.

"A bit," I admitted.

His smile matched my own. "Maybe one day I'll get to see it for myself."

It hadn't dawned on me until he spoke that he'd been here on the island all his life and *couldn't* have ever experienced snow.

"We'll have to visit my family one Christmas, which is also around the time of the twins' birthday," I told him. "You'll get the full effect—plenty of snowball fights and igloo-building contests. Trust me, you'll be *sick* of snow by the time it's all over."

"Looking forward to it."

During the quiet moment that followed, I envisioned a future with the Omegas—one we'd build once the dust settled. Although things with us were fairly new, our connection was permanent, strengthening every day. Despite how we felt when we first met, these four were an important staple in my life. They were family.

"Oh, and just be prepared," I chuckled. "My siblings are annoying as heck. I didn't have a moment's peace from the age of five, until I came here. They're loud, they bicker all the time, and—"

"And … you miss them," Ori cut in, stirring my soul with the half-smile he gave.

"Is it that obvious?"

"Completely," he snickered.

"I just wish I could talk to them. It's so hard to get through to the mainland."

Ori nodded in agreement. "Bright side is, you're almost on your final term, so … I guess it won't be long before you get to head home and see them. At least until you leave to join The Guard."

The air of sadness in his tone wasn't lost on me. It hadn't been there before conversation shifted to us discussing my future plans. Namely, the possibility that I'd be leaving the island for quite a while once classes concluded.

"Yeah … guess so."

Silence crept in then, and I felt my stomach tighten in knots. Before meeting them, my path had been so clear. I knew exactly what I wanted, what it would take to get there, and what I was willing to give up to achieve it. Only, those plans were made before my heart had been divided four ways.

My desire to do something more hadn't been quenched, so that meant I had some tough decisions to make in the coming months.

That is, assuming I could re-learn how to control my magic.

"Come here. I have something to show you." There was sort of a gleam in Ori's eye when he spoke. It was akin to excitement.

A little skeptical, and super intrigued, I waited the few seconds it took him to turn off the stove, and then followed him back into the living room. We didn't stay there, instead heading down the dark hallway to his bedroom. On the way, we passed by Paulo's room where he and the other two were still sitting around, laughing and arguing all in one conversation.

The second we crossed the threshold into Ori's space, and the door closed behind me, it was like we entered a cone of silence. The background noise and chatter lowered considerably, and it was just us.

We hadn't had very many moments like this, moments alone. That may have been intentional on both parts, to avoid any awkward lulls where we sometimes ran out of things to say.

"Have a seat," he offered, gesturing toward his bed after turning on a dim lamp.

I did as he suggested, keeping my eyes trained on the ink-stained skin on his back where his tank didn't cover. He moved to the dresser and reached for the shelf above it. The small, blue box trimmed in gold I noticed before was taken from its place. I hadn't pried, but curiosity had definitely left me wondering what was so sentimental that it had its own case.

He came toward me again, and something about the way he clutched it in his hand told me whatever it held was of great value. Even if only to him. The fact that he thought enough of me to share it made me breathe deep when he joined me on the bed.

"I uh … I don't talk about myself much," he admitted, keeping his eyes trained on the ground while I stared only at him. "It's not because I don't want to let you in, it's just the way I've gotten accustomed to being, but … I'm working on it." A faint smile touched his lips, but left too soon. "I lost my dad when I was a kid."

A breath passed between my lips as I listened, unable to speak when the conversation took an unexpected turn.

"A man came into the store my parents owned one night — a dragon, enraged and possessed with The Darkness. He lunged for my mother, but my father intervened so she could get away," Ori shared. "He … didn't make it out of there alive."

I exhaled again, feeling Ori's pain as my own as I tried to imagine how this must have torn his world apart, at such a young age.

"We didn't have much, so there was no fortune or property to inherit," he continued with a small, humorless laugh. "There was only this."

The box creaked open and my gaze went there, to a silver necklace. At its center, an oddly beautiful, smoke-colored crystal hung from the end.

"It's incredible," I practically whispered, staring at the unique piece.

"Dad found the crystal himself," Ori shared. "Apparently, he believed it brought him luck. In a way, I suppose it did. Within a week of wearing it, he met my mother."

This time, when Ori smiled, it was steeped in sentiment.

His gaze shifted toward mine and I don't think either of us meant to stare so deeply into the other, but we did. Something about this man made me want to pull him into my arms and never let him go. He held so much love within him, although he didn't readily show it. He cared intensely for those he kept close, and it made me want to be the one to care for him.

"I, um … it's customary for an alpha to present his queen with a token of his loyalty," he finally forced out, tearing his gaze away. "And this is mine to you."

My heart skipped an entire beat hearing these words. "Ori, I can't accept this. You can't part with something that belonged to your—"

"Noelle, giving it to you doesn't mean I'm parting with it," he said gravely, daring to look into my eyes again. "*You're* with me forever, so *it's* with me forever."

My breaths came quickly as he slipped the necklace over my head.

"Instead of hiding in a box … it'll be worn by my queen."

He stared where the piece rested gently on my collarbone, likely noticing how my pulse throbbed just beneath the skin. A tsunami of emotion rushed in, reaching to the hidden parts of my heart I hadn't yet let Ori into, but there was no keeping him out now.

The feel of my hand at the side of his face made his body go rigid. He wasn't used to being touched, but he'd get past that in time. For now, I was okay being the one who chipped at the wall between us, removing the debris that encased his heart a little at a time.

His gaze slipped to my lips and I knew he wanted to kiss me, but I also knew his iron-clad will would never allow it. My body gravitated closer to his and the desperation in his eyes only became more apparent. With the others, touching and kissing had become our state of normalcy, leaving me to burn with curiosity about Ori.

What did he taste like?

When would the beast inside him finally take what it wanted?

How would it feel for there to be nothing between us but shared breaths and sweat-dampened skin?

The space keeping us apart disappeared when I leaned in, unable to resist at least feeling his mouth against mine. A broad hand gripped the side of my neck and I breathed out at the feel of it, at the realization that he was just as tired of fighting this as I was.

There was no impatience, no rushing, only long, tender strokes of his tongue slipping over mine. The hand not already on my skin moved to my hip, bringing me closer as the kiss deepened. So close, his scent was potent and dizzying — a strange frenzy of smoke, earth, and testosterone that drove me crazy. It didn't take long to realize why it was so different, so much more potent than the others.

It was the scent of an alpha.

My bottom lip was drawn between his, and then released just quickly enough to make me long for more. But then another deep plunge of his tongue inside my mouth made me forget my own name, and all was forgiven. My waist tingled with the sensation of warm fingertips working the button of my shorts, and the hunger inside me swelled with the lowering of my zipper. The shorts — and then the thin cotton beneath them — were pulled away from my stomach.

Allowing just enough room for a hand to slip inside.

Air passed from my lips to Ori's when the relief of being touched by him swept in like a hurricane. His silken strands shifted between my fingers when I moved my hand through the back of his hair, keeping him close when I lost concentration, ending our kiss. How could I possibly focus on his mouth, when his ... fingers ...

"Should I stop?" The deep rasp against my ear made me shiver.

I only panted against the side of his face at first, finally finding words a few seconds later. "No, please don't," I answered with what little breath I had.

His lips found mine again, and soon electricity radiated from someplace deep, causing my body to quiver. Wrought with pleasure, every part of me cried out for him. I squeezed the back of his neck where I held him, and he swallowed the series of soft moans that forced their way up my throat.

Tension drained from my limbs and I rode a slow wave down from ecstasy, practically melting against him. Without hesitation, I reached to place my palm against the front of his sweats, feeling the evidence of his need. My mouth grazed the side of his neck. Dazed, and still not sure of my name, I placed soft kisses on colorful art that told a story I had yet to unlock.

He seemed both reluctant and desperate, so I chose to only focus on the latter—his desperation. I'd barely loosened the drawstring and tugged at the elastic waistband when ...

"Wait ..." he panted, the single word laced with so much frustration. "Someone's here."

"Can't the others take care of it?" I sank my teeth lightly into his collarbone with the question. "While I ... take care of *you*?"

"It's one of the alphas," he explained with a sigh. "Might be important."

Although I deemed this between us to be important, too, I knew better than to interfere with Firekeeper business.

So, matching Ori's frustration, I backed off, putting my hands up in surrender when I let his strings fall from my grasp. "Okay."

Several deep breaths later — and probably quoting baseball stats to send blood racing back to the rest of his body — Ori stood and leveled a look my way. One I read loud and clear.

"Rain check?" he asked.

I looked him over before answering, accidentally letting my stare linger on certain parts of his anatomy longer than others. I hadn't meant to, and was also certain I'd been caught, but who was I kidding?

The Omegas had me open, and I was no longer afraid of what I felt for them. So, I answered Ori truthfully.

"Just say when."

CHAPTER THIRTEEN
NOELLE

Ori and I got to the living room last, for obvious reasons. He needed to … calm down before facing his brothers, and the one who'd stopped by at nearly eight this evening.

It was Ty — the Solaris Hive alpha.

All eyes shifted toward Ori and I when we entered the space, and the collective expressions were filled with concern.

"What's up?" Thick arms crossed Ori's chest after asking. He didn't sit, just stayed posted beside the sofa while waiting for an answer.

"We need to talk," Ty spoke up. "I'll get to the real reason I'm here in a sec, but possibly an even bigger issue is the fact that I'm standing here at all."

The statement seemed to confuse the guys, and me too.

Ty tapped the side of his head. "I can't remember the last time I've had to stop by to deliver a message," he explained. "Should've just been able to reach you in thought."

Now, I understood. Well … kinda. It sounded like Ty had tried to access the guys via their tether—which I hadn't realized before now extended into the other hives—but he hadn't been able to get through.

I glanced left, to witness the grave look on Ori's face as he stood beside me frowning. "What are you saying?"

"I'm saying we're somehow disconnected. And it's not my hive, or even my connection to the others." His eyes slipped toward mine, unintentionally I believed. "It's just you all."

There was a stretch of silence that felt loaded. Like, there were so many unspoken thoughts that the air seemed thick and heavy.

"What's going on?" Ty's inquiry made the silence even more apparent.

"Nothing that I know of," Ori expressed, staring at the ground while he thought. The deep crease between his brow was an indication of confusion.

My thoughts shifted back to a couple weeks ago, when Kai seemed to have trouble getting through to the other Omegas while they ran patrol. Maybe Ty being locked out was the same thing.

"Have any of you noticed anything strange?"

The four peered up when Ty asked.

"I've felt weaker," Paulo spoke up. "When my dragon steps forward, I should feel the surge of power at least tenfold, but it hasn't been that way lately. It's like …" He paused to find the right words. "It's like how a lightbulb starts to dim and flicker, just before going out."

The analogy made my heart sink. Just the *idea* of him — or *any* of them — losing their abilities was terrifying. Especially considering how danger lurked a little too closely for my liking.

Ty let out a deep sigh, keeping his stare trained on Paulo. "That doesn't make sense. You've located your queen. If anything, you should all be at peak performance now, functioning more efficiently than ever before."

Hearing this made me extremely uncomfortable. I was aware that me being added to the hive should make the Omegas reach their full potential, but … why hadn't that happened? Why did it seem like — based on this conversation — me being linked with them had actually been a setback?

My hand wandered to the back of my neck, feeling the warm symbol just beneath my hairline.

"I hadn't said anything," Rayen spoke up, "but the other day, I had trouble shifting. I thought it was just me, just a onetime thing, but … now I'm starting to wonder if it's more than that."

Their growing concern was unnerving. So much of who they were was connected to their role on this island as FireKeepers. If something was wrong, I had no idea what that would mean for them, this unit of four who were real brothers except for the fact that they didn't share blood.

"None of this is a coincidence. The issue seems specific to your hive, so you can't ignore it. Seek counsel," Ty advised.

Agreeing, Ori nodded once.

"I'll get in touch with Maureen as soon as she returns," Kai chimed in. "Even if she wasn't my aunt, I'm not sure I'd trust anyone else with this."

"I think that's wise," Ty concurred.

The sensation of static prickled my skin before unspoken words filled my head.

'Maureen's away?' Ori's voice faded in with the question.

'Mount Panluah,' Kai answered. *'She's due back soon, though.'*

'I hope you're right about that.'

Ori hadn't come right out and said it, but his sense of urgency made it clear he wasn't taking any of this lightly.

"Well, I suppose this brings me to why I needed to speak with you all in the first place," Ty shared. "I just left Chief Makana's chamber and was given a very peculiar assignment."

"And what's that?" Ori's tone was fittingly suspicious.

"We were asked to keep close watch on you five, and to report back any strange findings." When he finished speaking, Ty smirked. "However, while I will always be loyal to my island, I'm loyal to our brotherhood."

A look of mutual respect passed between Ty and Ori, and I swallowed hard. Why on Earth would Kai's father want him—want *all of us*—surveilled?

"I have no interest in secret missions, nor will I betray my brothers. So, I'm doing what Chief wouldn't," Ty added. "I'm bringing my concerns to you directly. Man-to-man."

There was another breadth of silence, but then Kai stood. "I might know something about that."

All eyes darted toward him when he spoke up.

"When I visited him," he said, "we spoke about Noelle. Chief shared his thoughts and, if I'm being honest, he wasn't exactly thrilled."

Well, there's a shocker.

"To start, he isn't convinced it was Spirit who sent her to us," Kai forced out.

And I say he forced the words, because the strain behind them made it seem as if he wished he could have kept them to himself.

"He seems to think she … might serve a different purpose than what we think," he continued.

"Like?" Rayen asked gravely, his expression hard and suspicious.

Kai's gaze met mine before he said more, and there was no missing the remorse behind them.

"He thinks she's a curse," he breathed. "He thinks … The Darkness sent her to infiltrate our hive, and tear us down from the inside."

"That's ridiculous." It surprised me that Ori was the one who spoke first, defending my place within the Omega Hive. "We all felt the connection when Noelle was given to us. That can't be faked."

My gaze lowered to the floor, and I had no choice but to think about what Chief said. I mean, really think about it.

From the symbol on my neck, to the way my magic had been behaving, to the hive being off kilter ever since I was added to them was … one huge coincidence. Still, the look on Ori's face told me he wasn't willing to accept it that easily.

Maybe because he'd been so reluctant to let me in, and now that we were getting closer, he couldn't imagine undoing it all.

"We'll consult with Maureen," he said harshly, "and until then, nothing has changed. We've all seen how Chief's conducted himself lately, and I'm not even sure he's on our side anymore. The last thing I'm willing to do is take his word on this matter."

And there it was. The alpha had spoken.

The other three seemed to linger in their thoughts, likely still processing what Kai had just shared. None seemed to readily believe that I was their hive's curse, but … it was only normal that they'd at least consider it now.

I certainly was.

"If anything should arise, you know the Solaris have your backs," Ty promised. "And rest assured, nothing I see or hear regarding this matter will ever be reported to the chief."

Ori stepped forward and placed a hand on his comrade's shoulder. "Thank you. We'll be in touch."

Ty gave an earnest nod, and then we were alone again. The night had started off so well, and now, as we stood in silence, I wondered if their thoughts aligned with mine.

I wondered if they were thinking I was their downfall.

CHAPTER FOURTEEN
NOELLE

It was nice coming back to this place. For more reasons than one.

Seeing that the kids and staff had recovered from the ordeal months ago was mostly why, but also because I believed the guys and I needed a change of scenery. They'd been here to visit several times, but this was the first I'd been able to join them.

It felt like I'd barely had time for anything other than studying lately. By day, I kept my head down and tried to keep focused on school—and *not* the fresh whispers floating around about me. By night, I was sneaking off with Blythe, to the basement of the dorm.

Our sessions were *nothing* like I thought they'd be. When she first led me down to the small room tucked away deep in the dark corner, I half-expected to walk in and find potions in a cauldron. However, aside from candles and the smell of sage, there wasn't much else to speak of. There were no spells and incantations. Only yoga and meditation.

At first, I laughed at her new-age approach to *fixing* me, but I was starting to understand. Because my magic was a part of me, I needed to first ensure that my mental and emotional health were in balance. As much as I hated to admit it, being around her had been kind of helpful.

For instance, as I sat with ten girls ranging from the ages of five and eleven running brushes through one half of my hair, while awkward braids stuck out on the other, my blood pressure didn't even spike. Nope, I was completely Zen.

Soft giggles and chatter fluttered into the air, and I knew I needed this — to get off campus and just hang with folks whose biggest decisions they faced were whether to wear Velcro or lace-up shoes. Those were my kind of people.

"Done," Sydney announced, beaming from ear to ear.

The last time I'd seen her she was huddled in a bathroom, terrified of the raging Darkness. Tonight, she was all smiles.

I accepted the mirror I was handed, and observed the girls' work.

"Oh!" was my initial reaction, but I curbed the shock. "It's … beautiful!"

Their hands were back in my hair as each one wanted to show which braid she did, hoping to take credit.

"Well, I think you *all* did a great job," I assured them. "Thanks to you, I'm more beautiful than ever. Maybe one day, I'll even be as pretty as all of you."

So many warm grins came my way, my heart just about melted.

Standing from where they had me sitting for the last hour, in the middle of their shared bedroom floor, I moved toward the door.

"Wait! What about makeup?" one called out, holding a small kit with brightly colored eyeshadow.

"I … why don't we save that for next time," I suggested, hoping I'd successfully maneuvered my way out of that idea.

The girl nodded and closed the case, before shoving it back inside her nightstand drawer.

"Go show the boys," Sydney suggested with a grin. "I'll bet they'll love you even more like this."

I chuckled, nodding in agreement. "I'll bet you're right. Wish me luck."

They rushed me with hugs, and I could hardly make myself let them go. When I did, they went back to playing—some with the dollhouse near the window, others forming a huddle at the foot of a bed to color together.

There was so much love and light in this house. It made me grateful for the work the guys all did on the island to keep them safe.

My thoughts shifted back to a conversation I had with Ori, when he shared that *they* were the reason the Firekeepers fought so hard to restore order. Seeing the kids all happy and safe, I completely understood why my guys were so driven.

The steps creaked as I made my way down them, intent on finding at least one of the four, but I stopped at the front door, peering out onto the porch through the screen. There, perched on the steps, was Malu. In my head, he was more affectionately known as Malu The Brave. His heroics the night of the attack had earned him that title.

Kai had told me his story, about how he lost both parents to The Darkness several years ago. Even through that, having seen firsthand what the dark presence could do, he still enacted a plan to save his friends.

If that wasn't bravery, I don't know what was.

"Mind if I join you?" I asked, stepping out onto the porch.

Large, brown eyes peered up from his seat on the steps, and then came a smile.

"Sure. Just watching the stars."

Dropping down beside him, I faced the sky, too. The night was clear, and here on the island, the twinkling lights seemed so much brighter than at home, where the lights of surrounding cities dimmed them.

"You doing okay?" I asked, glancing at him for a moment.

In my peripheral vision, I saw him give a small nod. "Yeah. It just gets crowded in there sometimes, so I sit out here where it's quiet."

A small laugh left my mouth. "I can relate. Living in a dorm is kind of the same way."

"You share a room?" he asked.

"I do," I nodded. "With my best friend, Toni."

His eyes flitted toward me a sec, full of curiosity. "Toni? The Omegas don't mind you sharing with a guy?"

This time when I laughed, it was a big one. "While I'm sure they wouldn't like that a whole lot, they have nothing to worry about," I shared. "Because Toni—spelled with an "I"—is a girl."

Malu gave a look as his mouth formed an O, but no sound came out.

"How many of your friends are in *your* room?" I asked next.

He held up his hand, with all five fingers spread apart.

I nodded. "Cool. I'll bet they all look up to you."

A proud smile crossed his face. "Maybe a little."

"I figured. Especially with how you look out for them."

His head bobbed and a mop of shoulder-length curls swayed with the motion. "That's what family does," he said. "They look out for each other."

I turned to face him—this kid who was wise beyond his years. "Couldn't agree with you more."

His gaze was set on my hand. "Cool tattoo. Does it mean anything?"

I glanced at it. "It does. My dad has one just like it. Reminds me that I can always find my way home, no matter what."

Malu peered up. "You miss them? Your family?"

The sting of emotion that hit whenever someone asked that question still hadn't faded. "So much."

"Your sisters and brothers?"

"One sister, and one brother," I corrected with a smile. "And yes, I miss them a lot, but how'd you know I wasn't an only child?"

Malu shrugged. "I just know things," was the only answer he gave. "Like … I know you're really sad right now, and a little scared."

My heart lurched with those words, and his eyes found mine. He wore a look that made me believe he wasn't sure he should have said anything, but there was no taking it back.

"I'm—"

"It's because you think there's something wrong with you."

Again, I stared, speechless.

My gaze followed Malu when he stood, his silhouette outlined in moonlight. Slowly, he lifted his hands, placing one on my forehead, the other on my shoulder. Then, to my surprise, words left his mouth, but they were spoken over a beautiful melody.

As much as I wished I understood the lyrics, it didn't matter. It was perfect even without interpretation. After a couple verses, Malu went silent, and my skin cooled when he removed his hands.

I peered up with a smile. "What was the song?"

"A traditional Sanluuk blessing," he explained. "It's to keep you safe."

He sat beside me again and a feeling of gratitude washed over me, that this child thought enough of me to bless me.

"Thank you. I need it." A humorless laugh slipped out.

"No matter what happens, never forget who you are," were the last words he spoke before one of the staff came to the screen.

"Time to turn in, buddy," the woman announced.

Malu stood, and then headed inside. I sat there a bit longer, thinking about what he said, about not forgetting who I am. That hadn't been so easy lately, and the statement was surprisingly fitting, especially coming from a kid.

I eventually went in, too, set on a path for the sunroom off the back of the house. There, the Omegas had been hanging out with a few kids who roped them into a night of board games and bad knock-knock jokes.

They meant more to me than I ever realized they could — a fact that was driven home even more as laughter fluttered into the corridor where I now stood listening. These children loved and depended on them for so much, and knowing the guys' hearts were big enough to love them all made me even more grateful for my place within the hive.

Only, in the few weeks that passed since Ty's visit, I was beginning to feel distant. Not because they froze me out, not because my feelings had fizzled, but rather because I wasn't sure Chief Makana hadn't been right. There was no guarantee I wasn't the Omega Hive's curse.

A warm tear slipped down my cheek at the thought of it, the dread in my heart contrasted by the happy sounds coming from the sunroom. I wanted to be a part of the guys' world more than I realized, and the idea of this time with them only being temporary broke my heart.

There was only one thing I could think of that would be worse than having to separate from them, and that was the idea of being responsible for their demise.

As effective warriors.

As a hive.

Soft conversation came from the opposite direction, stealing my attention. One voice was male, the other female. Seeing as how they were both adults, I knew they were members of the staff. Their hushed tones made me curious, so I leaned in.

"I've heard two will be chosen this time," the guy said. "I guess that's the Council's way of seeing if doubling the lottery selection will somehow restore balance."

My brow quirked hearing that word — lottery. I had no idea what it meant, but the two discussing it seemed distraught, which made this … *lottery* … seem like a bad thing.

"I don't think it'll make a difference," the woman said. "I can only pray they find a better solution, one that's not so hard on the people."

They piqued my interest, and I tucked this information away in the back of my mind. Whatever this lottery was, it sounded like the inhabitants of the island were unhappy with it, and felt it was time for change.

Maybe the guys knew something about it and wouldn't mind me prying in island business. Once things between us weren't so tense, I'd ask.

CHAPTER FIFTEEN
NOELLE

"Don't stop! Right there!"

I popped one eye open and stared at Blythe. Was she really going to pretend she didn't hear that?

Somewhere in the basement—our makeshift dojo—a couple had been screwing for the past twenty minutes.

"Faster. *Faster!*" A strange sound followed those words, when the girl who uttered them lost control.

Naturally, I snorted a bit.

"Ignore them," Blythe said drably, still sitting with her eyes closed.

The laugh I held in slipped a little. "Ignore them? It sounds like she's getting teeth pulled over there!"

Blythe stayed stone-faced for about three seconds, before I saw the corner of her mouth twitch. The girl screeched again, and Blythe sighed with frustration.

"Seriously, dude! Just bust a freakin' nut and keep it moving!" she yelled. "Some of us are trying to get in touch with our spiritual side over here!"

"Blythe!" I whispered, mouth gaping open.

"What? They're rude," she reasoned. "And someone's really bad at his job if it's taking this long to get the poor girl across the finish line." That last part was *also* yelled loudly for the lovebirds to hear.

I didn't muffle my laugh this time, seeing as how it was no longer a secret we were unintentionally eavesdropping. Needless to say, the serene vibe we hoped to achieve was nowhere to be found today, but it was okay. We'd been at this a couple weeks and I could honestly say the meditation was helping. I hadn't lost control or experienced anything weird since we began, but this was just our starting point. She had a plan, and we would eventually involve magic. For now, it kind of just felt like hanging out.

Which, needless to say, had taken a little getting used to.

Blythe and I hadn't been friendly in years. However, I was starting to look forward to meeting with her. Mostly, our interactions had been surface-level, nothing too deep, but dare I say we had fun. Maybe it was her dry sense of humor, or her outspoken nature, but it was kind of cool being around someone who knew what it was like to be an outcast.

The couple had gone quiet, so either they'd taken Blythe's advice and finished quickly, or they took off when they realized they weren't alone. Either way, they successfully ruined our session, like I guessed we had just ruined theirs.

I stood and checked the time.

"Shoot, I should run," I announced, not realizing it had gotten so late.

"Got a hot date?" she asked, teasing with a smile.

"Eh … something like that." If you called hooking up with the Omegas to meet Kai's aunt a date. Apparently, they thought she might have some answers for us.

Blythe moved around the space gathering her candles to place them in a bag.

"Oh, I was kidding," she chuckled. "Didn't realize you'd met someone since coming here."

While, yeah, the wall between us was starting to weaken a bit, I wasn't willing to spill all my secrets.

"Uh … yeah," I admitted. "It's fairly new, so—"

She nodded, stooping to grab the blanket we'd been sitting on to fold it. "Well, you should hurry before he comes looking for you."

I smiled at that, substituting the word *'he'* for *'they'* in my thoughts—*they* would come looking for me.

I took a step toward the door once everything had been gathered, but I didn't turn the knob. Glancing back, Blythe raised a brow.

"Isn't your dude waiting for you?" she asked.

She was right, I needed to take off, but there was a huge elephant in the room, and I couldn't go another day without addressing it.

"Hang on a sec," I sighed. "We can't keep doing this."

She quirked a smile. "Can't keep doing … what?"

"Acting like nothing happened, like there's no bad blood between us."

Blythe lowered her head, but she said nothing.

"Listen," I said breathily, "I'm not trying to start anything, but I need to know why? What did I do that was so bad that you made my life a living hell?"

I stared at her long, dark hair when she set her things down and pushed a hand through the strands. My heart hammered inside my chest and I prayed there were no tears as I allowed myself to relive all the hurt and torment.

"There really *is* no explanation," she admitted. "Not one that serves as a valid excuse anyway."

"Well, I'd still love to hear the reason."

The side of her lip clamped between her teeth as she took a breath, seeming to search for the right words.

"Jealousy?" The word left her mouth as more of a question than a fact. As if she wasn't quite sure that had been the right term to use. "You had it all—the loving family, so much potential with your magic," she listed. "There were things going on with me that you didn't know about at the time. And I can admit I let it get the best of me, let it change me."

My brow pulled together. "Things? What things?"

Blythe settled back on her heels, shoving both hands in her pockets.

"Mostly emotional abuse," she sighed, "and some physical."

When she finally peered up at me, I didn't know what to say.

"You never told me anything."

"Because I didn't want to talk about it. Time at school, time with you … that was when I was able to forget, pretend none of it was happening."

My arms settled across my chest when I folded them, feeling some of the tension leave my body.

"I'm sure you remember my mom and I didn't have the best relationship."

The statement made me recall a number of nights she begged to sleep over with my family, and how my parents had taken her under their wing.

I nodded. "I remember things were tense between you two."

"Yeah, well, it was a little deeper than that. There were things I could never quite find the words to say."

I wasn't sure what that meant, which made my stomach tighten in knots.

"Mom was violent, and she was powerful. So, imagine trying to contend with a witch who's mean, and nasty, and not afraid to use her magic against her own daughter." A humorless laugh slipped from Blythe's lips. "I knew I'd need to defend myself against her one day, knew I had to learn to be stronger than her. So, that's what I did," she admitted. "That's why I turned to dark magic."

Her eyes slipped from mine again and I didn't miss the shame that filled them.

"It changed things. Changed *me*," she sighed. "Dabbling on that side made me more powerful, yes, but it also made me angry, and mean, and capable of doing things I never thought I'd do," she added. "Things like hurting my best friend."

Water pooled in the corners of her eyes, but she still wouldn't look at me.

"It got out of hand," she admitted. "And once I was in it deep, I couldn't find my way out. It wasn't until maybe this past year that I've pulled back a little, slowly working my way back toward the light, but it's been hard," she said with a nod. "Dark energy is like a drug. You get addicted to not feeling, not caring. Because that's what I needed back when I was with my mom — not to feel or care."

So much animosity had been trapped inside me for so many years, it was almost hard to find sympathy within my heart for her. A small part of me wondered if this story was even true, because it wouldn't be the first time she manipulated me. It would have been so easy to take this opportunity to be mean and vindictive, tossing her explanation aside.

But …

I didn't think this was fake. Mostly because I knew the relationship with her mom had been rocky, and it wasn't a stretch to think she'd been abusive as well. So, for a young girl whose father was never around, and who was ashamed to tell the world what she endured at home in private, I could understand her decision. She turned to dark magic to gain strength, but it cost her something, changed who she was.

"I'm so, so sorry for how I treated you," she choked out, struggling to hold in tears. "I was awful to you, and I've wanted to apologize for years, but couldn't quite figure out how. I mean, what do you say to the girl you dropped like a bad habit, and then tormented?"

My own eyes were watering now, feeling her pain—past and present.

"You already said it," I assured her. "And I forgive you."

She didn't wait for me to embrace her, instead she locked both arms around my neck first, holding on tight.

"Thanks for trusting me," I said into her ear. "And I'm sorry you felt so alone back then."

"I should have been a better friend," she sniffled.

"It's okay." I said, squeezing her tighter. "There's still time."

CHAPTER SIXTEEN
NOELLE

Surprisingly, there was no pressure to explain why I exited the dorm with red-rimmed eyes. The guys seemed to accept my answer, that I'd simply had an emotional conversation with a friend.

… A friend.

I hadn't referred to Blythe in that way in quite a while, but she'd been a big help to me the past few weeks. We still had a long, *long* way to go, but if I learned anything from what I'd gone through lately, it was to be more forgiving and less judgmental. I was a walking, talking billboard for a person who sometimes needed those closest to her to understand that things weren't always so black and white.

Seemed my entire life had become one big gray area.

Wedged in the backseat between Rayen and Ori, I barely fit—their broad bodies taking up most of the space as the Jeep bounced and swayed. We'd driven about fifteen minutes from the academy, mostly silent. That was happening a lot lately—quiet spells that left me feeling awkward and wishing there was some way to fix what doubt had done.

Doubt concerning my place within the hive.

It felt strange even saying this because of what I felt for them. Since the first time I kissed each, realizing I was their mate, our connection had been strong, and it had only grown with the time that passed.

Still, according to Chief Makana, I could just as easily be the hive's curse as anything else.

A small house came into view, nestled among dense greenery in a segment of the rainforest the guys hadn't yet taken me to. The engine died and it seemed birds sang all around us. The incredible sights and sounds of the island were among the things I loved most about this place, but it was … *different* here.

Paulo noticed how my steps slowed as my gaze lifted toward the trees, searching for the source of the beautiful sound.

"Crazy, ain't it?" he said with a smile.

Words would do it no justice. It was almost as if, here in this space, nature performed a symphony, harmonizing to a degree of perfection that defied reason.

"It's Maureen," Paulo explained. "The energy around her is always like this."

I was astonished. "Always?"

"She's deeply connected to Spirit," he explained with a nod as we neared the porch. "Every generation, an individual is chosen to commune with Spirit, and it's usually a member of the Sigo bloodline. For *our* generation, it's Kai."

I'd heard that mentioned before, but didn't really know what it meant.

"He's not as in sync as Maureen yet, but in time," Paulo shared. "Part of it is her spiritual journeys to Mount Panluah. She visits around two to three times a year to restore clarity, and once, she came back with this sweet gray streak in her hair."

"Wow, that's crazy. How long does she usually stay gone?"

He shrugged. "Depends. Sometimes a few days, sometimes months. She just returned from one yesterday, which is why we had to wait to bring you by."

My gaze shifted back toward the door as we approached it, and I swallowed hard as I climbed the short staircase. It sounded like this Maureen was quite intuitive, and I could admit to being a bit nervous what she'd find when she read me. Already, Malu and Blythe had *both* detected my energy was off. Who's to say Kai's aunt wouldn't find even *more* wrong with me?

"Please, tell me she's nice," I whispered, which brought a laugh out of Rayen this time, and he peered up. The sun behind him darkened his handsome features.

"Maureen's always chill," he assured me. "You'll love her."

A strong gust of wind swept past, moving a song into the windchime that hung above our heads. I glanced there for a moment, and lowered my gaze when the door creaked open.

There, staring back at the five of us who darkened her doorstep, was a small woman with gray weaving its way through one of two long French braids that hung over her shoulders. I observed her, how that gray contradicted the youthfulness of her skin. No doubt, she was much older than she looked.

A row of beaded bracelets shifted on her wrist when she extended a hand to greet me.

"You must be Noelle."

My heart raced, and I was terrified to touch her, fearing what she'd see or feel when I did.

But it would have been rude not to, so …

My palm pressed to hers, and I half expected her to snatch away, but she didn't. Instead, a thoughtful smile curved the corners of her mouth.

"Ano-Luana," she welcomed me. "Come in."

Two entered in front of me, two in back, and then the door closed behind us.

I peered around Maureen's space while each of the guys hugged and greeted her warmly. Where the outside had been painted white, with colorful flowers growing around the perimeter, inside was quite different. Walls painted beautiful shades of turquoise, purple, and yellow made her home feel just as bright and vibrant as the sounds that fluttered in through the open windows. Photos showcased in white frames lined the mantle, and I recognized several of Kai and the other Omegas right away — the awkward teenage years, ones with big grins with teeth missing, Christmas mornings in ugly pajamas. They were close to her, spent a lot of time here as they grew over the years.

"Have a seat, dear," she said sweetly, gesturing toward an armchair angled toward the one she took.

Feeling a bit more relaxed about this than I did originally, I lowered to the cushion.

Maureen's gaze shifted to Ori and her smile broadened, warming as words left her mouth.

"You look well," she told him.

"Thank you. You look very rested," he answered. "I take it your time on the mountain was peaceful."

"Like always, but I'm happy to be home," Maureen smiled, smoothing the length of her flowing, white skirt down her legs. "It's always nice to see my boys."

Ori gave a small nod and I noted the mixture of contentment and worry behind his gaze. I guessed Maureen noticed it too, because her head tilted as she observed him.

"You're troubled," she said evenly, keeping her piercingly dark eyes trained on the poised alpha who clearly meant to conceal his thoughts.

"I ... there's a concern," Ori eventually stated, clearing his throat right after.

I took a breath and clasped both hands in my lap.

"Hm …" Maureen said thoughtfully. "The moment you stepped inside, I could tell the hive's energy was a bit off. Has anything changed?" Her gaze shifted toward me after asking. "Aside from locating your queen."

My brow twitched and the guys had similar reactions.

"How did you—"

"I just know," she answered, cutting Kai off before he'd even had time to finish his thought.

There was silence in the room, and I could only account for my own speechlessness. Before this, I had honestly started to question whether I even still deserved that title, fearing I was merely a pawn in The Darkness' scheme to weaken—and eventually break—the Omegas. Only, according to Maureen, I was right where I belonged.

Ori breathed an audible sigh of relief.

Maureen turned to face me again. "Have you begun to prepare for the ceremony, dear?"

My lips parted and then snapped shut again before I was finally able to ask, "What … ceremony?"

Maureen glanced around the room toward the guys, questioning them with her eyes, and then met my stare once again. "Did no one tell you? There will be a ceremony, making your union with the Omegas official within the tribe. That's not to say it isn't official now," she clarified. "It's mostly just a tradition. The tribe will be delighted to meet their newest member, *and* your family."

The statement overloaded my brain. Not only was there some big ceremony — of which I'd be the center of attention — but my entire family was expected to attend as well?

"You haven't told them yet." Maureen's intuitiveness revealed what I hadn't shared.

"No, they ... not yet," I stammered.

Her eyes narrowed inquisitively. "You're afraid?"

She was practically reading my thoughts, so there was no point in lying. "I'm not entirely sure how my father will feel about me being with ... well ... "

A quiet laugh left Maureen. "You think he'll blow a gasket when he finds out his little girl has been mated to four strapping young men, am I right?"

I nodded and smiled a bit. "Yeah, basically." I peered up at the guys as they watched with content expressions, listening to my conversation with Maureen.

"Well, you just get them here, and let Spirit do the rest. A father's concern is only that his daughter be loved, respected, and protected." She paused to nod toward the Omegas. "He'll soon learn that you've got all that and *then* some, right here with my boys."

Warmth spread within me, hearing her speak of them this way.

"I'd love to assist with the planning," she offered, "seeing as how the four knuckleheads didn't even *think* to give you a head start."

Paulo scratched the back of his neck. "Things have just been a little crazy lately," he explained, summing up the last couple months pretty accurately. "Plus, Noelle still has another term at the academy and—"

"You're a student?"

I nodded, answering Maureen's question when she interjected.

"How lovely," she smiled, before her gaze returned to Paulo. "But that's still no excuse for not letting a girl know she's approaching one of the biggest events of her life."

"It wasn't just that," Ori spoke up, sounding as though he didn't quite know how to explain things. "We've had some ... difficulties lately."

"What sort of difficulties?" Maureen's brow quirked with concern.

Ori was thoughtful for a moment before answering. "Trouble communicating through our tether among ourselves, with the other hives. Rayen's had trouble shifting, Paulo's noticed he's weaker. We thought having our hive finally complete would strengthen us, but ... that hasn't been the case."

Maureen studied his face, intrigued. "Did you experience any of this before establishing protocol."

There was my favorite word again. She may as well have asked if he'd *performed his duty* yet.

A slight twinge of redness in Ori's face told of the heat that flashed beneath his skin.

"Well, we ... I ..."

"Relax. It's fine if you haven't gotten to that part yet." Maureen's laughter put Ori out of his misery. "I didn't mean to pry. I only asked because I sensed in your queen's energy that things had progressed a bit further, but … perhaps I'm mistaken."

A look flashed my way and I cleared my throat discreetly. At that precise moment, Rayen lowered his gaze to the floor. At first, we thought the only issue that might arise would be a slight scolding from Ori for our impatience, but … maybe it was bigger than that.

Maybe doing things out of the order Spirit established had caused the hive to break down? But that didn't make any sense? I mean … did it?

"Could that be what the issue is?" Paulo chimed in. "Maybe Ori needs to seal the deal to make the connection more solid?"

A cold stare flashed Paulo's way when Ori seemed to get annoyed that he'd been discussed like he wasn't in the room. Or better yet, like intimacy between us would be some sort of transaction.

Maureen shook her head. "No, once Spirit has bonded you, it's done," she clarified.

The Omegas were all quiet after that, maybe racking their brains like I was. It wasn't until Maureen's gaze shifted to me again that I looked up. The way she studied me so deeply, like I had my life story written on my skin, I knew she was doing what I feared she would.

Reading me.

I squirmed a bit in my chair, wondering what Spirit would say.

"You're … different," she finally commented. "The term *'old soul'* comes to mind."

The smile I gave was tight and forced. "I've heard that before." And I had, mostly because my soul *was* old.

"May I see your mark?"

Again, I stalled. From what I'd been told, the Omegas hadn't given Maureen any information about me, about us as a unit. So how could she know there was anything about my mark that would make it worth seeing?

When I hesitated, she laughed a bit. "Don't be afraid. Chief Makana may be my brother, but we're nothing alike. You can trust that whatever is discussed here today will not leave the six of us sitting in this very room."

When she nodded, the kindness in her eyes reminded me of Kai, so I turned with my back to her. Lifting my hair, I revealed the odd symbols.

"Interesting," she said to herself.

"Do you think you can help us?" Ori sounded desperate when asking.

"Not exactly," wasn't the answer I think *any* of us were hoping Maureen would give. "I'm not entirely certain there's anything *anyone* can do except Noelle."

My heart sank and despair crept in.

"You've been marked by Spirit *and* The Darkness," she confirmed. "You're a unique vessel. A vessel *either* entity can use—one for the greater good of humanity and supernatural beings alike, the other … for unimaginable destruction."

I wasn't sure she meant to sound all doom and gloom, but that was definitely the impression I got.

"We need to know what we can do," Ori commented, the words leaving his mouth harshly.

Maureen continued to study me when I turned to face her again. "Well, *you* can't do a thing," she answered. "It's like I've already told you. Only Noelle can decide."

"Then, that's simple, right?" Ori jumped in. "She'd choose to follow Spirit."

Maureen's head tilted ever so slightly. "There may be a finer line between good and evil than you realize," she explained. "Sometimes, it's a matter of perspective and intention. An action one may deem right and necessary, could bring you to the tipping point—the line that, once crossed, there's no going back."

There was a long breadth of silence following this revelation.

"I don't accept that," Ori's voice boomed. "Give me facts and actionable steps. That's what I can work with. Not parables and leaving things to chance. Tell me what we need to do to ensure she's safe."

My chest heaved with the heavy breaths that followed his statement.

Maureen, unfazed by the outburst, eased back in her chair, keeping her eyes trained on me. "I can't do that, but the advice I *can* offer concerns the state of your hive." Her gaze shifted to Ori. "Something has disrupted the balance, and as alpha, you're responsible for figuring out what it is."

Frustrated, Ori turned to face the window. "Is that all?"

Maureen seemed to sympathize with him when she nodded. "I'm sorry, but yes. There's nothing you or I can do beyond trusting Spirit. In this war over your queen's soul, as much as it pains me to say this … your only role is to watch, wait, and pray she lets Spirit guide her."

CHAPTER SEVENTEEN
NOELLE

They were troubled.

Complete silence during the ride back to the bungalow, followed by *more* silence while we sat around the living room, were clear indicators.

A heavy arm tightened around my shoulders and I leaned deeper into Paulo's side. Maureen had eased my mind with one breath, and then troubled it with the next. Sure, we at least had confirmation that Chief Makana was wrong. His suggestion that I wasn't the true mate to the Omegas was false, but we *also* knew I could slip over to the dark side in the blink of an eye.

Apparently, the line between the two was finer than I realized.

The floor creaked beneath Ori's weight as he slowly paced in front of the window. He, in particular, had been upset by

Maureen's vague foretelling of how our lives together would play out. There was also something that had been shared with only him, when Maureen called him back inside alone. He had yet to reveal what this additional information was, but based on his sullen mood, it couldn't have been anything good.

The thigh not pressed against Paulo had been kept warm by Rayen, so when he stood, my gaze followed his impressive height into the air. He took slow steps toward Ori and I watched curiously.

"I think we need to talk," he said quietly. Something about the weariness in his voice, and the guilty look he flashed toward me, left me suspicious.

Ori's brow quirked a bit when he looked his brother in the eyes. "Okay. My room," he answered, just before their heavy footsteps echoed across the floor.

My heart fluttered and I felt torn. On one hand, fear of the unknown left me content to let Rayen confess what I *thought* he wanted to confess on his own. But on the other, he certainly hadn't acted alone that night in the shower. It didn't seem fair he'd be forced to have this difficult discussion with Ori, without the support of the other guilty party.

Me.

"Excuse me for a sec," I said quietly to Paulo. He passed me a curious glance as I used his thigh to push myself up on my feet.

He nor Kai asked where I was headed when I trailed behind the two who'd just walked off.

I reached Ori's door the moment he'd begun to close it. Feeling resistance when I pushed it open again, he let me slip inside. I caught Rayen's eyes, and he appeared to be both confused and relieved. I was pretty sure I knew the cause of both.

"What's this about?" Ori's tone was only curious when he asked, letting his gaze volley back and forth between Rayen and I.

Beside me, Rayen's shoulders tensed and we both breathed deeply.

"There's something you should know," he exhaled. "Something I believe may be the cause of our hive breaking down."

"...Okay," Ori said skeptically, crossing both arms across his chest. His brow pulled together, too, as concern filled his expression. Studying him, my stomach began to swirl with worry.

Rayen's eyes shifted down toward his own feet. "Noelle and I... We... I violated protocol." He forced the words out like he'd lose his nerve if he didn't.

Dead silence followed, and I imagined the many ways things could play out from here. All of which involved Ori hulking out on us and making me regret following Rayen into the bedroom.

Only, the rage and pissed off expression I expected ... they never came. Instead, Ori's gaze lowered to the floor and he didn't lift his eyes again.

"I knew there was a specific way things were supposed to take place," Rayen rushed to explain, "but I wasn't thinking as clearly as I should have been."

Hearing him take the heat on his own, I had to speak up.

"Actually, I came on to *him*," I confessed, recalling the sexual tension that mounted between us that night. When I could have walked away, I pushed the limits, which resulted in a night I didn't regret, but I certainly didn't understand the consequences of it. Actually, I still didn't.

"At the time, I thought the worst thing that could happen would be that it'd piss you off to know I'd broken the rules, but now I see it's bigger than that," Rayen sighed. "I had no idea it would affect us all."

Ori still hadn't said a word, which made him impossible to read.

And also made me a little worried.

"I won't stand before you and lie," Rayen continued. "I wouldn't take back what happened, but I would at least tell you sooner."

My heart squeezed hearing him say this, because I felt the same way. We'd done nothing wrong. As his mate, there were no limits or boundaries. But, apparently, there were rules.

"You're pissed, but say something," Rayen pushed, staring as he waited for his brother to reply.

At first, Ori only shook his head, still keeping his gaze trained on the ground. But then, his hazel irises met Rayen's. "I'm not angry," he said. "If anything, I take responsibility for what's happened."

My brow quirked with confusion.

"How is any of this your fault?" Rayen clearly shared my thoughts.

Ori dropped onto the edge of his bed when emotion weighed him down. He seemed … disappointed. Although, it was still hard to tell where the feelings were directed.

"I wasn't as receptive to this new bond as all of you seem to be. I've been slow to thaw, so it's not hard to understand how something like this could happen." He still wouldn't make eye contact with either of us while he spoke. "You three and Noelle had a connection before discovering she was our mate, which is why there was already chemistry between you, fewer obstacles to overcome."

Listening to him speak, I knew exactly where the disappointment was aimed.

At himself.

His eyes lifted to Rayen suddenly. "I've been late to come around to the idea of having found our queen, and for that I apologize," Ori said, shocking me yet again. Not only was he *not* angry, he felt he was at fault. "You did nothing wrong."

With those words, he freed his brother of the guilt I'd seen riding his shoulders since the night it happened.

"Whatever it takes to make this right, I'll do it," Rayen promised. "I'm heading over to see Ty. Maybe he'll have answers."

With that, Ori nodded to give Rayen his blessing to go, and then it was just us.

The room was silent, and Ori's words weighed heavily on my thoughts. He seemed to hate how long it was taking for his heart to warm, but coldness wasn't what I saw when I looked at him.

I only saw devotion, conviction and passion. He worked hard to conceal them all, but as his queen, I was beginning to see right through him.

"Please, understand that this … protocol has nothing to do with me. It's not my rule, not some manifestation of my ego," he explained. "I take no issue with *you* being the one to decide which of us you should be with or when. This is simply the way Spirit established order within each of the hives."

I already knew this, but appreciated him making it clear that his pride hadn't come into play here. The Omegas were all important to me. Although, I wasn't completely sure Ori understood that.

I took a few steps forward, to where he still sat perched on the edge of his mattress. The closeness brought his eyes to mine.

"You think I don't feel as connected to you, but you're wrong," I admitted, feeling the way my soul ebbed toward his as I confessed. "I love that you don't give everything to everyone, reserving what matters most for those you know won't hurt you. You're selective who you trust, selective when it comes to who's allowed to know the *real* you. Because you lock the rest of the world out, honestly, I'm honored that you're starting to let me in."

Long dark lashes closed over his eyes for a few seconds before he reopened them. "I wasn't sure you could feel the change," he rasped. "I know I'm hard to read, hard to understand, but—"

"I want you just the way you are." My statement brought his to an abrupt end, and he seemed relieved to hear me say the words.

I took another step closer, until I stood between his parted knees, staring down at him.

"You're just as important to me as the others," I shared, believing he needed to hear me say it. "You four are my mates and my future, but … you're my alpha—the one Spirit saw fit to protect and lead us *all*."

My heart thundered inside my chest when his stare deepened, seeming to pierce straight through me. Not so long ago, I made it a point to tell him he didn't rule over me, wasn't "*my alpha*". The only thing that had changed between then and now was that I'd gotten out of my own way, stopped thinking his position would make him drunk with power, thinking he could lord over me. Ori wasn't that type of leader, and with how graciously he handled Rayen, I was now even more certain.

There was more I wanted to say, but wasn't sure how the words would come out. So, I did away with them altogether, choosing action instead.

Ori's silken strands slipped through my fingers when I lightly gripped the back of his head, bending to lower my mouth to his. Taken by surprise, he drew in a long surge of air that lifted his shoulders where my arms rested on them. Hot palms moved over my skin when he touched me, his hands sliding up the backs of my thighs. The contact ignited what felt like small fires wherever his fingertips trailed. The chemistry that sparked between us before, was rekindled now, as my need for him swelled greatly.

My stomach quivered when one hand left my thigh and moved to the front of my shorts. First, he undid the button, and then lowered the zipper. With a slow, gentle tug, the fabric moved down my hips and then quickly fell to my feet. Thin, wispy silk that matched my black bra followed, and I stepped out of both. The lips I craved were taken away when Ori paused to push my shirt up my torso. Once it was lifted over my head, and then dropped to the floor, I was almost completely exposed to him. While he stared with unmasked appreciation, I pushed thin straps down my shoulders, and then reached to the center of my chest to undo the small silver clasp.

Naked.

Nothing hid any part of me from him, and the look he wore made me think I'd go up in flames.

A primal groan rumbled from his chest to his throat—a sound that made goosebumps dot my skin. Taking his hands, I made him stand, towering over me like the formidable dragon warrior he was. He didn't flinch when I pushed both hands up his abdomen and chest, gathering the material of his shirt. At his shoulders, he removed it the rest of the way.

Thick muscle sheathed in magnificently flawless skin met my eyes wherever they roamed, and I feasted on every inch of him. It amazed me that my guys were the total package — kind, honorable, and freakin' beautiful.

My hands lowered to undo his shorts, and I pushed the waistband down his toned hips, revealing tempting divots at the apex of his thighs that drew my attention toward more.

And by *'more'* I mean the evidence of how the sexual tension between us had reached its peak.

Evidence of this moment not arriving a second too soon.

Evidence of the unfinished business between us.

With my stare returning to Ori's hungry eyes, I lowered the shorts, and then the boxer briefs that barely contained him. Now, we were both completely exposed, both at the mercy of the other.

We spun slowly, switching places until my back faced the bed and I was made to lie on top of the mattress. The solid mass of Ori's body covered me — a buffet of smooth, tan skin and rigid muscle, of which I would never have my fill. As I wantonly dragged the sole of my foot from his calf to the firmness of his thigh, I writhed beneath him. That maddening aroma of his seemed to only be present when we were close like this, turned on. It grew stronger and filled my senses, and I breathed it in deep like before, knowing exactly what it was — the scent of an alpha.

My body was practically vibrating with need as my craving for him deepened. His weight could be felt when his waist wedged between my thighs, pushing them further apart, impatience brewing in his gaze. Fire raced through his veins in short bursts, scattering up his forearms and biceps like peculiar lightning. When he craned his neck to kiss me again, his flesh heated against mine.

Emotion seemed to swirl around us like a cyclone of warm, sultry air. My breath stilled when he briefly lifted his weight, and then ended my suffering by slowly pressing himself into me.

Ori groaned and a quiet, whispered gasp left my mouth, disappearing into his dark hair when he leaned close again. The tips of my fingers pressed into him when I gripped his back with both hands. It was all I could do to stay somewhat composed, feeling like each flex of his hips would pull a moan from within me. Holding it in only made the hunger I fought to suppress grow more intense.

Just like Ori's impatience.

My hand blazed a slow trail down to his waist and he drew in a sharp breath through his nose. The reaction confirmed a theory that had begun to form in my thoughts. I believed that the mighty giant who had kept others away for so long, hadn't been touched in this way in a long time. His body—like his heart—had been off limits.

The other Omegas hadn't said as much, but with how girls threw themselves—and their panties—at them, they'd taken advantage of their status as local celebrities on the island. I couldn't say how *many* they had in their beds over the years, but I knew there were enough. But … I didn't think that was the case with Ori.

The thought of being the first one he'd gotten so close to in a very, *very* long time … I don't know … it excited me.

The invisible wall between us was shattered into a million tiny pieces in an instant.

As my volume rose carelessly, carrying up into the air.

As Ori revealed to me the full breadth of his power.

I briefly wondered if his bed — and my body — could withstand the pleasurable assault. But then, just as quickly as the thought came, it left again because I lost focus.

My voice grew louder still, and my limbs tightened around him as we both came undone in one another's arms. Soon, once our sated panting slowed to normal, the only sound to be heard was the gentle rain that had begun to fall outside his window at some point. We hadn't quieted down enough to hear it before then.

Soft kisses placed on my neck and chest lulled me deeper into a daze, and I didn't even think about leaving him. Staying the night hadn't been in my plans, but now I couldn't imagine spending it alone.

Somehow, the dynamic between Ori and I — between the *entire hive* — had just shifted again, and it came with a deepening sense of loyalty and belonging. Now that order had been restored, and I'd established a proper connection with our alpha, our unit felt more solid than ever.

Unbreakable.

CHAPTER EIGHTEEN
NOELLE

Ori fell to the side of me, and I turned with him, unable to let him wander too far. I'd never been one to cling to a guy, but I was beside myself at the moment, feeling crazy possessive over this one. It was almost like he'd marked me in some way, like our souls were even more entangled than they'd been before.

Maybe this had something to do with why Spirit meant for him to be the first.

A massive hand landed gently on my hip, tugging me toward him, and I didn't hate it. My breasts pressed to the firmness of his chest and, so close, you could hardly tell where one body started and ended.

I stared at Ori—beautiful, sexy, mine—waiting with bated breath when I realized he'd speak.

"From this day forward," he declared, running the back of his hand down my cheek, "you're my responsibility."

My eyes fluttered slowly. "Don't you mean I'm the *entire hive's* responsibility?" I asked, thinking he'd misspoken. However, when he shook his head, I realized that hadn't been the case.

"First, you're to come to me," he made clear, the depth of his voice shaking my soul. "Then, if I need reinforcement, the others will step in, helping to ensure that you never want for anything."

The hand that warmed my cheek slipped lower, unintentionally grazing the side of my chest while Ori held my gaze.

"Also, I believe it goes without saying, but we're all at your disposal," he added, "for anything you need. For anything you want."

The intended double-meaning wasn't lost, causing me to draw in a breath.

A girl could get used to this life.

The tone shifted from hot and heavy to sweet when he reached behind me to pull the comforter over us both. Despite this being the first time, it felt like we'd been here a thousand times before — comfortable, natural.

Who knew the king of icy glares and cold shoulders was capable of showing such warmth.

"I hope Maureen didn't make you uncomfortable today," he said, pulling me from my thoughts. "She brought up the ceremony before any of us had the chance. I guess we were just waiting for things to settle down a bit before we overwhelmed you with something new."

With a faint smile, I shook my head. "She didn't scare me, but … maybe she did freak me out a little."

His broad chest vibrated against me when he laughed. "It's nothing to worry about. Honestly, it's more for the people than it is for us. Our bond is already solid, already complete. The ceremony is simply to present you to the tribe, and give them a chance to acknowledge your place within our hive."

I swallowed hard with the word that came to mind. "Is it like a … *wedding* kind of thing?"

Ori laughed louder this time. "No, more like a reception. Seeing as how Spirit took care of the actual union."

I nodded with my head leaning on his arm.

"So, what about bringing your family here? Ours will all be present."

My stomach sank at the very idea of it. "I suppose it'll have to be done eventually one day, so … why not."

"Don't sound so enthusiastic," Ori joked.

My hand moved beneath the blanket, coming to rest on the side of his ribs. "You know I'm in this one-hundred-percent," I reminded him. "It's just that … well, you saw how my friends reacted. Or, more specifically, you saw how Tristan reacted. Who's to say others won't do the same? And while Tristan's a cool guy and all, I *definitely* care more about what my family thinks than him."

"I get it," Ori nodded. "It's tradition, but if you'd rather not do it, then that's how it will be. No one can make you do anything. Not with us having any say in it."

I loved the sound of him asserting himself, making it clear that he'd move heaven and Earth for me.

I peered up and couldn't hide my smile. "No, I'll do it. I'm not ashamed of what I have with you all."

A kiss to my forehead put my mind at ease, and I shrank into him even more.

"In the meantime, I *do* want to have something a bit more casual," he said. "We're thinking about a gathering here at the bungalow, Firekeepers and their family's only. Figured you'd enjoy hanging out with the other queens again."

Actually, I perked up just at the mention of them, the three exceptional women who'd been so kind and wise — Kalea, Lehua, and Nayeli.

"I'm definitely in," I smiled. "When are you thinking we'll do it? Keep in mind, I've got finals in four weeks."

And the big evaluation.

And rumors that scouts from The Guard would be dropping by campus.

No pressure, right?

Ori nodded thoughtfully. "Then, I'll leave that up to you."

I visualized the calendar, and did a little calculating. "How about two weekends from now?"

I hadn't expected any objection to the date, so it surprised me when Ori's expression seemed to shift, becoming solemn.

"Um … any weekend but that one," he said.

Curious, my brow pulled together. "Okay … Why?"

He breathed deeply, and I wondered why he seemed to have such a hard time answering that one, simple question.

"Because," he sighed, "there's a tribal … thing the guys and I have to be present for. Another tradition."

He was unnervingly vague about that, which only made me more curious.

"Well … can I come?" I asked chipperly, staring with expectation. Only, Ori's gaze wasn't so welcoming when it met mine.

"I'm sorry, but … no." The words hit me like a ton of bricks. How had we gone from me being told I could have anything I wanted, to having the door shut in my face when I asked to tag along.

"Okayyy …"

When I shifted to pull away a bit after the awkward exchange, Ori caught my waist and brought me back.

"Noelle, wait," he breathed.

I wouldn't look at him because I was inexplicably offended. Maybe because I was just starting to feel like I belonged, just starting to feel like I was really a part of the hive.

Ugh … it was so stupid being upset about something so small. I mean, I didn't mind them going off and doing things without me. It wasn't that. I just … I guess I just wanted to be around them.

"It's fine," I objected, deciding to be a big girl about this. "If it's not okay to tag along, I'm okay with that. I have friends,"

I reminded him. "I'm sure we can get into something on our own."

It was then that I realized the date I'd suggested to Ori.

My eyes closed and I smiled a bit. "Actually, I *already* have something going on that day. It completely slipped my mind."

His brow quirked. "Oh … well, that's perfect," he said. "What's the occasion."

"Something called the *Firelight Celebration?* A kid on campus was handing out flyers and my friends got a hold of one."

"Handing out flyers?"

I didn't know what to think when he pushed up onto his elbow, suddenly staring with a hardened look within his eyes.

"Uh, yeah," I clarified. "Apparently, it's supposed to be some big party and—"

"You're not going."

The firm assertion left me to stare at him, mouth gaping open.

"The Firelight Celebration isn't some … party," Ori practically growled. "And as soon as I find out who this punk kid is handing out invitations, I'm gonna beat his—"

"What's the big deal?" I cut in, finding it hard to believe he'd gotten so worked up over this. "Is this the thing you had going on? The reason you weren't available to have the party that weekend?"

"It is," he answered coldly, "but the celebration is a sacred event. One not meant for outsiders."

… Outsiders.

That word rested heavily on my heart, stinging in ways I didn't expect it to. An old wound that wasn't really closed to begin with was suddenly reopened. And by my mate, no less.

"I get it," I sighed. "I'm not from here. Therefore, I'm not welcome. Duly noted."

Frustration marked Ori's tone as he dropped an F-bomb quietly to himself. When I sat up, fully intent on leaving him there alone, my arm was taken.

"You know that's not what I meant," he protested, holding me in place.

My stare met his. "Then what did you mean? If I'm not forbidden to go because I'm an outsider, then what's the reason?"

His hazel eyes volleyed between mine, and no further explanation was given.

"Exactly," I sighed, feeling his grip on my arm loosen. This time, when I moved to stand, he didn't stop me.

***

RAYEN

I hated having to drop by and interrupt their evening, but I supposed it was a bit of an emergency. Ty and I sat on his front porch as the rain poured down all around us, rolling off the awning into the flowerbeds below.

He bounced the newest addition to his family on his knee—his great granddaughter.

The outside world would never believe that a guy who didn't look a day older than *I* did could have such an extensive lineage, but Ty was old. In fact, his entire Solaris hive — as well as the Tritons — were among some of our island's oldest dragons. It was his knowledge of hive politics, and the time he'd spent with Spirit, that brought me to his door.

I needed answers. Needed to know how to fix what I'd broken.

"So," he sighed, still processing the details I'd given — starting with how I'd broken protocol with Noelle. "Ori knows you were insubordinate, and your head is still attached to your shoulders. That's a pretty good start," he chuckled.

I smiled a little, but felt too weary to relax.

"Well, this is a first among Firekeepers, but there is a procedure intact to make atonement to Spirit."

"Atonement?"

He nodded. "Yes, you've broken rank, and the result is that your hive is no longer functioning as it ought to. However, lucky for you, you'll get to keep all your limbs and appendages. Including the one that got you *into* this mess," he added with a laugh.

I hated that his words lifted my mood a bit, because I still hadn't heard what my slipup would cost me.

"You need to make arrangements to go before the Council," he said. "There, you must make a formal statement admitting to your transgression, publicly expressing your apology to your alpha, and then your debt is paid."

My brow quirked. "That's it?"

Ty nodded. "Lucky for you, Spirit loves us and doesn't wish to do us harm. In fact, the only reason you even had this breakdown within your hive was to get your attention. To force you to make things right with Ori."

My head lowered hearing this, noting that my only regret was that my actions forced me to keep a secret from my brothers. I'd said before that I wouldn't undo what happened between me and Noelle, but it wouldn't have killed me to wait.

Wouldn't have killed me to trust Spirit.

Standing, I shook Ty's hand. "I'll see when I can go before the Council. Thank you."

He nodded and the brotherly tie between us was present like always. "Anytime."

I stepped down from the porch with a renewed sense of hope, looking forward to telling the others order would soon be restored. As soon as the Council had time to see me, I'd go before them and make things right.

With any luck, this would all go as smoothly as Ty seemed to think it would.

CHAPTER NINETEEN
NOELLE

"We shouldn't be doing this."

I hated that the only reason those words just left my mouth was because a certain alpha had planted them there. The sting of Ori's words—his forbiddance—had cycled in my head on repeat for two weeks.

They were the reason I hadn't had much to say to him.

The reason I made excuses to put space between me and the hive altogether.

All because of one word he uttered when explaining why I couldn't attend the Firelight Celebration—outsider.

Toni smoothed lip gloss over her lips before popping the tube inside the pocket of her jeans.

"*Of course* we should be doing this," she retorted. "Finals and evaluations are in two weeks. If I don't go do something fun for once, I swear I'm gonna lose it."

A breath left my mouth and I glanced down at my outfit — a casual black dress that barely hit my knees, matching sandals. I grabbed my jean jacket last-minute and clutched it in the bend of my elbow just in case it got chilly later.

Toni stood before me and braced both my shoulders. "Noelle, we're doing this. You know why? Because we were invited."

"Yeah, but then we were *uninvited* once I told Ori about it."

She popped a shoulder with a casual shrug. "Maybe, but this was already the plan. I mean, I get it if you choose to hang back, but the rest of us are going, and you'll be missed if you don't."

She did this puppy dog thing with her eyes and I rolled mine.

"Fine," I gave in, which made her squeal with satisfaction. "But you have to be on the lookout with me. If we spot one of the four, I can't be seen."

"Deal. Now, come on. Everyone's waiting," she said quickly, pressing her hands against my back to move me toward the door. "Besides, you invited that girl to tag along. No way I'm getting stuck entertaining her tonight."

I laughed, hearing the undertone of frustration in Toni's voice as she acknowledged that I'd told Blythe she could hang out with us for the evening. I still had reservations when it came to trusting her, but with the couple times we got together each week, I was starting to feel the walls crumbling between us. Which was why I wanted my friends to get used to her being around.

I could only hope things would go smoothly.

***

It, legit, seemed like the entire island had come out for the festival. All around us, colorful decorations had been carefully arranged. Kiosks where vendors sold local cuisine, hand-carved trinkets, and clothing were situated along torchlit pathways that branched off from a two-mile stretch of road. The entire length of which had been blocked off for the celebration.

Sanluuk natives had come decked out in traditional garb—human and dragon alike. The women in brightly colored sarongs of varying styles—some worn as dresses tied around the neck or across their chests, others as skirts with bikini tops. Most men were shirtless, with similar fabric tied around their waists like sarongs—vibrant colors with tribal symbols stitched into them. Elaborate jewelry and headdresses were worn to ring in the occasion, making my friends and I stand out like sore thumbs.

Collectively, the people of Sanluuk were beautiful.

Seeing so many natives, and only my friends and I from campus, I wondered how far word had spread. The answer to that seemed to be 'not far'. You would have thought the other students would have *jumped* at the chance to get off school grounds, get a taste of local culture. However, there really seemed to be no one but us, although my friends were too stoked about being free for a change to notice.

So, I stopped overthinking things and relaxed.

Well, I *sort of* relaxed.

Every few seconds, I was scanning the enormous crowd for the Omegas. They could have been anywhere for all I knew, which meant I needed to lay low. A small group of around eight to ten men and women were stationed beside the road with loud drums. I'd seen a vendor selling a ton of this style a few yards behind us. The sign posted above the booth said they were called pahus—a new word I committed to memory.

Those without drums had small flutes they played from their noses, or large hollowed out gourds they beat in alternating rhythm with the heels of their palms and their fingers. Watching them, I smiled, seeing the pride they held for their culture, their island.

We waded through the mob forming around the musicians. Marcela was definitely feeling the music. The point made clearer when she took Tristan by the hand and twirled beneath his arm. A smile slowly spread across his face, too, when she made him dance with her. Toni grinned so big it made me happy I hadn't missed this. Even Blythe seemed to enjoy herself. The heaviness she tended to carry was nowhere in sight.

Then again, Manny may have had something to do with that.

Maybe noticing she was on the verge of loosening up, he reached for her hands, turning her toward him, showing her his footwork—weird and uncoordinated as it was. Watching him wind his arms in odd slithering motions, while his hips swiveled like a broken washing machine, Blythe tossed her head back with a laugh. In response, Manny's eyes lit up, having thoroughly thawed the ice princess.

Toni and I shared similar looks, wondering if there might be something brewing between the two.

Soon, I forgot about being made to feel like I was too much of an outsider to attend this celebration, because I only felt welcomed. No one gave funny looks because my friends and I were mainlanders. Everyone we encountered had only been kind.

A small, elderly woman had been dancing her way through the audience, handing out leis. She eventually got to my crew, stopping at each of us with a smile, placing the same vibrant greenery with purple flowers around our necks. Now, thanks to her, we blended in a smidge more than before.

'Am I the only one free-balling under this thing?'

The sound of Paulo speaking in my thoughts made my feet stop moving instantly, swiveling my head to check that he and the others weren't too close. So far, I didn't see any of them, but casually tucked myself beside a nearby palm tree just in case.

'Nope,' Kai answered. *'For some reason, boxers seemed like overkill. I've just been praying there aren't any strong gusts of wind, so the people don't get an unexpected eyeful tonight.'*

Despite fearing I'd be caught at any moment, their private conversation made me crack a smile. It wasn't until a moment later, when four large, bronzed bodies came into view, that I understood their concern about the wind.

Hard, muscled shoulders glistened as they walked through carrying torches—each one in matching, burgundy sarongs that covered them from their waists to the middle of their calves. Large, white tribal markings decorated the fabric. Their chests and ripped arms were completely exposed, including the peek I got at their solid thighs as they took steps, moving with a slow, unhurried gait. Their strides were cocky in a way, but naturally so. No arrogance about them. Leafy headdresses sat atop their heads, and each one appeared so unwaveringly confident it overwhelmed me.

Their ink covered various portions of each one's body and, by now, I knew the patterns by heart, knowing what it felt like to trace my fingers over them. This was a strange time to get turned on, with all those people around, but it really wasn't up to me. Something about seeing them in this light, honoring their history in the traditional clothing so many others wore, just really got to me. Even Ori overwhelmed me—despite the recently renewed animosity between us.

They were past me now, so I came from behind the tree just a bit. Toni eyed me with a curious grin. "You good, girl?"

I nodded toward the guys. "Yup, just avoiding confrontation."

She followed my gaze and it became clear why I hid. "Oh snap! That was close. Good eye." Toni leaned in with an excited smile.

I didn't mention it, but it wasn't so much my *eyes* that were good. More like my finely tuned antenna that only tapped into the guys' internal thoughts.

Toni was still beaming beside me.

"You love this, don't you?" I said, laughing.

"Maybe just a little," she admitted. "But, while I've always been a bit of a drama-whore, I think all the pressure with our evaluations coming up has me desperate for entertainment."

I turned from her and looked to the guys again. Following closely behind the Omegas were the other four hives, dressed similarly, but with different colored fabric tied at their waists — dark blue, forest green, black, and a deep shade of purple. They were all headed in the same direction, toward a huge mound just beyond the performers.

'Let's get this over with,' Paulo said this time, his frustration contradicting the otherwise upbeat vibe the night held.

'Agreed,' Ori replied. Listening to them speak, I wondered why their mood didn't seem to match those of others who still danced and cheered the musicians along.

My gaze followed the four, even when all I could see were the flames of their torches as the crowd parted. Of course, being revered the way they were on the island, the procession of Firekeepers quickly stole everyone's attention.

Watching as nearly every eye turned toward them, I got the impression all the guys wanted to be *like* them, and all the women wanted to be *with* them. Seeing the way they responded to the Omegas didn't send me into a jealous rage. It only made me proud to be theirs, proud they were mine.

A large, grass-covered mound up ahead was the guys' destination. All twenty Firekeepers circled it until each one was in position at the base. On top of the hill, one man stood, his silhouette only visible now that their torches brightened the space. Long, stringy hair covered the man's face, and his dark clothing made him seem ominous, out of place.

Without anyone signaling those who attended, the entire festival fell silent. The only sound to be heard was the occasional chirp of nearby insects and quietly shuffling feet as others gathered closer.

For some reason, my heart began to race with excitement. The huge grin on Toni, Marcela, Blythe and Manny's faces seemed to mean they felt it, too. The only one not quite swept away by the festivities was Tristan. His eyes were almost glazed over with boredom, like he felt he had better things to do than hang out with us.

The distance between us made me kind of sad when I thought about it, so I tried not to. It was on him if he couldn't accept my decision.

Or, better yet, if he couldn't accept my fate.

My thoughts tore from him when the man who stood front and center on the mound finally lifted his eyes to the sky, stretching his arms outward.

"Spirit, arise!" The first tone of his loud, booming voice sent my heart leaping to my throat. "You have called forth the soul of your greatest warriors, given them to us to defend our island."

A burst of embers from behind the mound illuminated every face, as we watched the performance in awe.

"You will one day deliver us, your people, from the grasp of evil. We still believe you will bless us to triumph over our adversary," he added, smiling toward the stars. "Because we are not forgotten."

I didn't even blink as I listened, knowing this adversary they sought to defeat all too well.

Six with tribal headdresses and painted faces climbed either side of the mound, quickly joining the storyteller, holding props behind their backs.

"On the night of the great eruption, the enemy that dwells within the mountain of lava and brimstone revealed its vile face to us for a second time. The first manifestation being our island's great war millennia ago. While, on *this* occasion, it came in the manner of a wolf, one cloaked in flames, proving that this wicked entity can present itself in many forms. Observers reported that it stalked to and fro, watching as our ancestors' beloved land was consumed by fire and ash."

His words brought two of the actors to life, reaching toward the sky, their expressions showing their agony.

"Thousands of lives were lost, a tragedy that would have left our people broken for many generations," he said, emotion straining his voice when more of the embers burst from behind, clearly depicting the volcano he spoke of.

"It was then that you sent the first from your chosen bloodline to restore order. It was a valiant Sigo warrior who arose from the ashes, once dead, but suddenly brought to life by your might. In his hands, you bestowed the power of the mighty and treacherous dragon."

An eighth performer appeared as a slowly stalking silhouette, trudging up the hill, slowly placing his hands on the shoulders of the others, prompting them to rise and join him.

"He bravely walked the scorched earth on your command, searching for his fellow brethren to fill with this same fire, a peculiar flame that could not be quenched."

A chill ran down my spine, having heard a similar story told about my grandmother. She, like their Sigo warrior, had arisen from the ashes to awaken others who had fallen victim to an attack in her tiny village in France.

"Those who walked with this great warrior were able to force The Darkness back from whence it came, and for centuries this island was filled with peace and prosperity. This was so, until a series of great earthquakes and large eruptions made us quickly aware that our adversary had awakened yet again, eager to wreak havoc on our homes, our loved ones, our hard-won sense of peace," he explained. "Spirit could have left us defenseless. However, instead, the Firekeepers were called forth by name."

The crowd was starting to get amped up in participation.

"Triton," The man called out. A second later, the four wearing dark blue raised their torches.

"Solaris," the man said next, and the four in black lifted their torches as well.

"Eros and Aurora." The two hives in green and purple did as the others before them.

"And our newest hive," the man said with a proud smile, "the Omegas."

My heart pounded, seeing four more flames raised high into the air. People exploded with cheers and applause, causing the pride I held for them to swell even more. I heard each of their names on the lips of those who adored them, and I couldn't blame anyone for loving them.

Holding up a hand, the man quickly quieted the crowd. "This same fire still burns in our hearts," he continued. "And at the hands of these hives, the evil that plagues us has been forced into submission time and time again, allowing the sun to rise and set on our faces day after day. We believe that, one day, we will again reclaim the entirety of our land from The Darkness, declaring Spirit's goodness as we dance in celebration," he announced.

Still in awe, I hadn't turned away to even glance at my friends. Judging by their silence, they were just as engrossed in the performance. So much emotion bled from those depicting their island's history, it seemed to spill over onto the rest of us.

The circle the Firekeepers formed around the hill tightened, moving closer to the storyteller. My eyes were on my guys, of course. They'd been silent in thought since the initial conversation, leaving me to wonder if they were as moved by this presentation as I was. Or, perhaps having seen it before, or being on the frontline of the battle, they were numb to it all.

"There have been great sacrifices made by the few, to protect the interest of many," the man stated, lowering his head toward the ground, letting his arms fall as well. I couldn't take my eyes off him. "It is with great shame that we give of ourselves to appease our adversary. Our hearts are repentant and grievous for the blood on our hands, but with how you have continued to smile on us, we are certain your affection is never far away."

For the first time since he began, I shifted to glance at my friends. Their expressions reflected the same confusion I felt.

What ... sacrifices? What blood was on their hands?

"It was the father of our great Chief Makana who, several centuries ago, discovered a way to keep The Darkness sated, a way to lessen the number of attacks, a way to lessen the spread of it's sickness."

My stomach dropped, despite not having heard a full explanation. It was at this very moment that the word Ori used rang inside my head.

Outsider.

I was an outsider, not meant to be privy to all their ways, their traditions.

Their secrets.

"Soon, a new offering will be made, commencing with our next sacred lottery," the man stated.

Lottery—I heard that word before, but never with an explanation attached.

"Those nominated to be handed over to The Darkness will never be forgotten, and their names will forever be honored, memorialized on the Weeping Stone."

The Weeping stone—Rayen had once nearly slipped and said too much, settling on the explanation that the stone was a memorial. But now ... I was pretty sure I knew what—or should I say who—it memorialized.

Those chosen in the lottery.

Sacrifices.

My stomach rolled and I thought I might be sick. "I need to go."

Toni, having just heard the same explanation I did, didn't fight me on the decision.

"Come on, guys." The rest of our group fell in step when she suggested that we leave, and if it wouldn't have called undue attention to us, I would've run.

My head swam with all this information, with all the revelations, and I found it so hard to believe that the Omegas were a part of this. Did they really allow their own people to be sacrificed to The Darkness? I'd seen so much warmth and compassion in the four I couldn't even comprehend it.

Only, now, when I envisioned my mates, I only saw blood on their hands.

For the first time since being referred to as an outsider, I didn't reject the idea. If this was a tradition embraced on Sanluuk ... I didn't want any parts of it.

CHAPTER TWENTY

NOELLE

Devastated.

Sick to my stomach.

How could they let this go on right under their noses?

A body shifted beside me in the bed, and I was comforted by Toni's presence. She hadn't left my side since we got in a while ago. There hadn't been a single word exchanged between us yet, but I knew she understood all the same.

"You have to talk to them," she eventually said, breaking the silence. "They're not just some dudes you'll get tired of and move on from. Which means you guys have to fix this."

The child in me wanted to pout, reminding her that I wasn't the one who'd done something wrong, but I quickly put that thought to bed. Because she was right. I'd wait until I found the right words, until my emotions weren't so high, but I would bring it all to light soon.

"They just … hand their own people over to this thing, Toni," I said out loud, shaking my head. Maybe I just needed to know I hadn't misheard, hadn't imagined it all.

"I know," she assured me. "It's something they've practiced for a long time, before your guys were even born. And if there's one thing you know from your mom's situation, it's that change doesn't come overnight. Wolves and Dragons were under The Sovereign's thumb for centuries before she rose to power, so keep this all in mind."

Again, she was right, and I knew it, but I still hadn't quite wrapped my head around this. I suppose it was partially because, in my mind, they were these valiant heroes, infallible. Now, to hear that they knew what was going on, and hadn't done anything …

"Do you think they participate in this … lottery?" I asked. "Do you think that's one of their duties? Hauling innocent victims to their deaths?"

Toni shook her head. "Honestly, I don't know any more about this than you do, but I feel confident enough to say that I highly doubt it," she answered. "Why? Do *you* think that?"

Being honest, I wasn't completely sure *what* to think. "No, but … with my feelings toward them, I'm liable to give them a pass on *anything*. I guess I just needed to hear it from someone else," I sighed. "There has to be more to this."

"Which is why you need to put on your big girl pants, fess up to going to the celebration, and asking your guys flat-out what the deal is. I'm positive they'll tell you whatever you need to know."

"Not sure about that," I rebutted. "After all, had I not crashed the festival, I might not have *ever* known."

"You don't believe that," Toni cut in. "Think about it. Would *you* be jumping at the opportunity to tell someone you care about that your folks were into something like this?"

She was so level-headed, and I needed that more lately than I ever had in my life.

"No," I admitted with a sigh.

"Exactly. So, give them the benefit of the doubt and lay it all out in the open. But do me a favor," she added. "Wait until you can talk about it without sounding all judgey." There was a laugh in her voice and it brought one out of me, too.

"Agreed," I answered. "Besides, I'm kind of the last person to judge *anyone* right about now."

She rubbed my arm reassuringly. "Well, look at the bright side. You got all up in your feelings today and you didn't go dark on anyone. That's progress, right?"

I laughed again, only now thinking about it. "True that. I guess my time with Blythe has been helping more than I realized."

"Mmm hmm. I guess."

There was no missing the shade she'd just thrown, making me crack up for a third time.

"She's not so bad," I said, lightly defending Blythe.

"I already told you, you won't hear a peep from me about it as long as she doesn't cross you. If she does, the claws are definitely coming out."

I didn't doubt that for a second. "Understood."

We settled into the silence again, resting together in my tiny bed meant for one. Our talk had helped me see things more rationally. I'd be mature about this and talk things out with the guys, but not before I was ready.

Soon.

Or at least soon-ish.

***

RAYEN

Sleep was a no-show. Mostly, I tossed and turned all night, being serenaded by fireworks from the celebration that went on well past three this morning.

Now, here I stood beside my brothers, waiting for the Council to see us.

"Are they really going to drag this out?" Ori grumbled, deciding he didn't care enough about being heard to have this conversation in thought.

"Who knows?" Paulo sounded equally frustrated.

Yet, none of them could have been as on edge as me. Ty seemed confident I'd only be required to make a formal, public apology to Ori and the rest of the hive, so I was trying to hold on to that, but I felt unsettled.

"My guess is that my father's behind the delay," Kai added with a sigh. "He never misses an opportunity to show his power, remind people they're under his rule, on his schedule."

Anxiety had me pacing the entire forty-five minutes, glancing over at the clock every few seconds. When the door leading to the conference room finally opened, my gaze darted in the direction of the woman now standing there — Helene. She wore a polite smile, but I saw through it. They'd been discussing me, my infraction, and weren't pleased.

"Come in," she beckoned, stepping aside so the four of us could pass through. Once inside, six more sets of eyes landed right on me. Only, these Council members weren't as discreet about their feelings as Helene.

We each took our seats on the opposite side of the long, wooden table. I'd been in this room twice before, but never because I'd committed an offense.

Seated front and center, was Chief Makana, wearing a smug grin as usual.

"Ano-Luana, Omegas."

"Ano-Luana," we each responded.

He glanced around the table at us all, lacing his fingers on the surface before him. "Rayen, can you please explain to me, and the Council, why you're seated here with us today."

As if they didn't already know …

Glancing toward Ori, I cleared my throat before speaking. "Well, upon locating our hive's queen, I … broke protocol."

Explaining why I'd been intimate with my own mate left a bad taste in my mouth.

Chief Makana nodded. "I see." He lowered his gaze to the tabletop. "This is the first time in the history of the Firekeepers that we've experienced such a devastating transgression. You've disrespected your alpha, while also shaming and crippling your hive. So, forgive me for asking this question, but … what on Earth were you thinking?"

His eyes narrowed in my direction and I felt venom race through my veins.

'You don't have to answer that,' Ori said, cutting into my thoughts.

'It's fine,' I answered. *'I'll play along if it gets us out of here faster.'*

Meeting Chief Makana's gaze, I took a breath. "I was thinking I felt connected to our queen. I was thinking it wasn't anyone's business that we, two consenting adults, decided it wasn't necessary to wait for permission to do what felt natural."

As soon as the words left my mouth, I knew I should have chosen them more carefully.

Chief's mouth tightened into a hard line. "Hm."

He stared, unwavering.

"Chief, I—"

"I expected you to arrive this morning with a bit more remorse. A bit more … humility. However, it seems you feel justified in your wrongdoing."

"It's not like that. I—"

"Ori, what are your thoughts on the incident?" Chief asked, cutting me off midsentence."

My jaw clenched, knowing I had no choice but to let the man over-talk me.

Ori breathed deep before answering. "I wasn't upset by it. My only concern was that we needed to take care of this matter to atone with Spirit."

Chief Makana narrowed his gaze at my brother, leaning in to rest on his elbows. "Those were your only feelings? You weren't angry Rayen took it upon himself to lay with your queen before you'd had the chance to establish your *own* connection with her?"

He was *trying* to push Ori's buttons, attempting to light a raging fire between us that didn't exist.

"No, sir," Ori sighed. "As I stated before, I was only concerned about our obligation to uphold protocol as Spirit ordained it."

Chief's glare burned through Ori. "Very well then. I suppose we ought to get on with it." His gaze snapped toward me again. "Turn to your alpha. Make your formal apology and Spirit will forgive your disobedience."

My jaw gritted at his choice of words, but I turned toward Ori nonetheless. He stared back with not an ounce of animosity within him. It was only Chief who was angered by my actions.

I cleared my throat and blocked everyone else out of my mind.

"You have my sincerest apology, brother. I stepped out of line," I admitted. "You've been nothing but a fair and honorable leader, and I should have held your position as my alpha at a much higher regard. My judgment was clouded by my emotions, and I acted without considering our hive above all else. And for that, I am truly sorry."

Ori gave a tight smile that didn't quite reach his eyes, and I knew it was because he didn't think this display was even necessary. "I'd say I forgive you," he said, "but there's nothing to forgive."

I nodded his way, promising myself I'd never put him, myself, or our hive in this predicament again.

The four of us turned to face Chief once again.

"Very well then," the man grumbled, letting his stare volley between the two of us. "I suppose that concludes this meeting."

Happy to have it all behind me, I braced the arms of my chair to stand with my brothers, but halted when Chief cleared his throat.

"Just … one more thing," he added with a smile. "You've paid your debt to Spirit, but there's the small issue of repaying your debt to this tribe."

My brow tensed, staring at him. "What are you talking about?"

That sick smirk of his was still visible. "You will be detained for an undisclosed number of days, released when we — myself and my constituents — feel you have learned your lesson, and learned your place," he revealed, shocking me into silence.

But Kai had plenty to say.

"You'd put this tribe at risk, weakening our hive by removing a member all to prove a point? Because that's exactly what this is—a power play."

Chief narrowed his gaze toward his son. "Should I be condemned for weakening your hive? Or should your beloved brother bear that burden?" The question was followed by silence. "Now, I'm a fair man. I'll allow you a small window of time to get your affairs in order, and at an appointed time, we shall come to collect you," he announced. "And I should advise you not to flee. I'm granting you this opportunity because, despite your recent actions, I believe you to be a man of honor."

"But, sir ... this isn't right," I reasoned, doing my best to bridle my growing anger. "It's not like I've hurt anyone."

"And that's nothing but a stroke of luck," Chief snapped. "Any *number* of incidents could have occurred to endanger your hive when you crippled them. So, consider *this* portion of your punishment insurance. Insurance that you will never cross your hive or this tribe again," he added. "I believe that once you've served your time, you will have a newfound appreciation for those who have rule over you."

"How long?" Ori called out, the tension in his posture blatantly obvious.

Chief shrugged casually. "It's too soon to tell."

'Kai, how offended would you be if I dick kicked your father?' Paulo grumbled inside my thoughts.

'You'd get no objections from me,' was Kai's honest answer. *'There has to be a way to get around this, go over his head.'*

The suggestion was fine in theory, but I think we all knew we didn't have much choice in the matter.

My thoughts were interrupted when the door we'd just come into crept open. Long before turning to see who entered … I smelled them.

Witches. The evil ones.

There were no magic wielders on our island, except those attending the academy, but these three were far too old for that. Which meant Chief brought them here. For what purpose, I wasn't sure, but I had a terrible feeling now resting in the pit of my stomach.

When I glanced toward Chief, that smirk was back. "Which brings us to the final point of our meeting. The three standing before you are the latest additions to our island, and in this instance, they're also my backup plan," he shared before letting his gaze fall to me again. "Should you try to run, should you try to fight, you will be dealt with in a far less civil manner than you have been today. From now, until we come to collect you, you will be watched," he warned.

Ori stood. "You *have* to know this is overkill, right? Rayen's been nothing but good to you, to our tribe. Are you trying to make an example out of him?"

"That's *exactly* what this is," Chief admitted, slowly standing to his feet to meet Ori's glare. "I see how our people revere you four, bowing before you like gods here in the flesh. It's high time they realize the four of you are mere men," he spat.

A spark of something unexpected flared in his eyes.

Envy.

"Our people need to see that even the mighty can fall," he continued, anger spreading through his expression. "They will know that there is only one on this island who answers to no one."

My shoulders rose and fell with each furious breath I took.

"So, that's what this is about?" Ori seethed. I glanced his way just as fire began streaming through his veins, spreading upward from his fists. "You think your title protects you? You think seeing you strongarm Rayen will earn you the people's respect?"

Chief's expression tightened. "I have their respect," he forced out through his teeth.

"No, what you have is their fear. Respect is something you earn by showing you're worthy of it." Ori leaned away from the table his hands rested on, standing straighter. "I suppose I get it, though. It can't be easy seeing the man your son has become, and having to live with knowing you had nothing to do with it."

Chief Makana's nostrils flared as he struggled to hold his composure.

"How is it that I lost my father as a kid and he was *still* more to me than you've ever been to Kai?"

"Enough!" Chief's fist slammed the tabletop. The atmosphere in the room had suddenly changed, becoming far more hostile than before.

The Council members shifted uncomfortably in their seats while each observed, serving as little more than props in this meeting. None had said a word to speak against Chief. If they disagreed, we would never know it.

"I'm tempted to lock you up right along with him, but we'll chock this little outburst of yours up to … displaced emotions," Chief spat. "After all," he crooned, "it can't be easy knowing your beta appealed to your queen more than *you* did."

Ori breathed deep and smoke rolled off his skin, precisely at the moment a trace of his dragon's outline began to form around his frame. However, the three who had only stood in observation before now, lifted their hands. Immediately after, a searing-hot pain shot through my head and I couldn't move. My brothers growled in agony as well.

"What you feel right now is only a *fraction* of what they can do to you," Chief said loudly to be heard over our groans of pain. "Please, I beg you not to make me show you their full strength."

He let it continue a few seconds longer before nodding a command to his new pawns. As soon as they obeyed, the pain began to fade. Once I was able to focus again, Chief stared at the four of us with a smug grin.

"Take heed, Omegas. Today you should have been reminded of your place," he said with pride ringing in his voice. "That place is now, and will *always* be … far, far beneath me."

CHAPTER TWENTY-ONE
ORI

That couldn't have possibly gone any worse.

Not even in a nightmare.

Chief had shown us a side of him we'd never seen before, but it was one we were not completely surprised to discover existed. It was more than clear that he resented our positions — and the affection our tribal members held for us. He seemed to think it had gone to our heads, making us think we were greater than him, but the only one *any* of us revered as great was Spirit.

We, like Chief, were imperfect and capable of screwing everything up, just like the next guy.

"I can't believe he's doing this." Kai hadn't moved from his place on the couch, where he sat holding his head for the past half hour. "He's always been cold, but … this is even a bit much for *him*."

I couldn't have agreed more.

"Once he comes for Rayen, we'll be at a fraction of our strength. Yet, he'd rather prove a point than see to it that his people are adequately protected," Paulo griped.

"We're overlooking an even bigger issue," Rayen cut in. "The witches."

I breathed out, unsure where to even begin with that one. "Historically speaking, leaders only surround themselves with powerful witches for two reasons—for protection from great danger or impending evil … or to fulfill some wicked plan. The fact that I can't nail down which of the two holds true with Chief Makana says a lot about how hard it is to read his intentions these days."

"He used them against us, so I think it's safe to say it's about more than protection," Paulo pointed out. "Whole thing is screwed up."

Rayen released a heavy sigh before dropping down into an armchair beside the window, and I was reminded how all of this must have been ten times as difficult for him to process.

"You holding up okay?" I asked.

He didn't answer right away, simply staring off into space. "I just wish there was something I could do to stop him."

I briefly placed a hand on his shoulder, sympathizing. "I'm going to check with the other alphas to see if they can help us come up with a plan. There's no way we'll let you sit in some cell, for *any* length of time."

Rayen was shaking his head before I even finished. "Don't. The last thing we need is more of you getting caught up in this, crippling the hive even more," he reasoned. "I'll do my time."

It was hard to say which would have been worse—having Rayen taken from us the moment Chief declared his punishment, or having to sit and wait for him to be apprehended. Having to sit here, day after day, wondering when Chief and his minions would show up would be torture. Then again, that may have been exactly why he ordered it this way.

"I need to tell Noelle," Rayen said next, interrupting my thoughts. "She won't understand."

"Hell, I don't understand," Paulo scoffed, seeming to get angrier by the second. He held his position, leaning against the wall, but then suddenly pushed off. "I can't let Chief do this."

Rayen was on his feet the next second, blocking Paulo just as he reached the door. "You can and you will," he asserted. "If we keep our noses clean, it's possible he'll end my sentence sooner rather than later."

"I might believe that," Paulo countered, "if we were dealing with a fair man."

Rayen's gaze slipped to the ground for a moment. "Being a Firekeeper has never been about controlling the actions of others," he stated. "That goes for Chief and *anyone* else. His behavior doesn't change who we are, nor does it lessen our responsibility to represent Spirit with integrity."

The rims of Paulo's nostrils flared with his temper.

"You have to keep your head clear and look out for our girl," Rayen insisted, holding Paulo's furious gaze. "She'll need you all to reassure her that things are still okay."

The two stared at one another for a moment, and eventually, Paulo breathed deep and the harsh look set on his face began to soften.

"Life as we know it is shifting," Rayen sighed. "Our people were once led with love and grave conviction. However, I think it's time we face a hard truth that's been breathing down our necks for some time now. We need to accept that ... The Darkness is no longer our only enemy on this island."

CHAPTER TWENTY-TWO
NOELLE

"Class dismissed."

Miss Audrina flashed a smile toward my classmates as they moved toward the door to exit, and the expression turned weary by the time it reached me. Once, her class had been my favorite to come to, but since I'd accidentally taken Jessica's powers — and had yet to figure out how to return them — things were different.

Not only in *this* classroom, in *all* of them.

It wasn't so much that I'd been forbidden from using magic, but my instructors had begun to alter my assignments. For instance, when others were encouraged to demonstrate their abilities, it was requested that I sit out and observe.

Like today, for instance. The rest of the students were asked to perform a small charm to grant their partners with confidence. I, on the other hand, was only asked to memorize a simple incantation.

One Aunt Hilda had taught me when I was twelve.

Basically, no one trusted me, and therefore no longer wanted me here.

I would have thought it a miracle that I hadn't been kicked out by this point, but after one meeting with Chief Makana, it became clear that my leaving the island wasn't an option. I had a hunch this was something a few of my instructors discovered, assuming they'd gone to the administrators to recommend that I be removed from the academy.

Did I have proof of it? No, but having everyone except my friends suddenly afraid to walk within a ten-foot radius of me was a pretty clear indicator.

Passing Ms. Audrina's desk, it felt strange not speaking. I'd gotten used to her at least asking how my day had been, but now all I got were sideways glances that told me all I needed to know. As much as it sucked to admit it, the woman was downright scared of me.

I suppose that was understandable.

"Ignore her," a whispered voice said. Then, an arm looped with mine and I turned to meet Blythe's gaze. Normally, her witchy scent would have told me it was her long before my eyes did, but it was slightly less potent than usual.

"She hates me now," I said quietly.

"Meh, she doesn't hate you," Blythe said with a casual shrug. "Problem is, she can't figure you out, and *that* is definitely not your issue. It's hers."

Forcing myself not to take a second glance toward Ms. Audrina, I exited, pouring out into the hallway with the others. Blythe clung to me like Toni always did, both unafraid of what havoc I might wreak on their magic. Between the two, I felt less like a walking, talking disaster.

Bright light flooded into the building when we pushed the bar, unlatching the door that led us outside. We took the steps slowly, and I felt a tug to my left—the non-physical kind. The kind that told me my dragons were nearby. So, I glanced that way, finding Paulo's gaze set on me.

It was strange having him just keeping watch from a distance, seeing as how we'd all gotten considerably closer. However, I suppose the separation between them and me had been my own doing. Because I still hadn't figured out how to address the not-so-small issue of knowing one of the island's darker secrets, my way of coping was avoidance. If I cast up walls between us, I wouldn't have to pretend everything was okay. Wouldn't have to pretend I understood why they'd allowed this to go on.

Apparently, I gawked at my mate a few seconds too long, prompting Blythe to squeeze my arm a bit.

"Sooooo … managed to bag all *four* of 'em, huh?" she asked once she had my attention.

I glanced over to find her bouncing both brows at me.

"I don't know what you're talking about."

A hard eye roll came before she turned away, wearing a knowing smirk. "Those dudes. You're messing around with all four of them, aren't you?"

When I didn't answer right away, the smirk broadened into a full-blown grin. "Hey, no judgement, I just thought I'd ask instead of playing the guessing game. You're playing with fire, though, aren't you? Assuming they're all as close as they seem."

I took a breath, lowering my gaze to where my fingers toyed with the stone on the necklace I'd been given. "What makes you think I'm involved with *any* of them?"

"Ohhhh, I don't know. Maybe it's how I've seen you hugged up with, and/or kissing *each* of them in various 'hidden' places around campus." She said that word with air quotes, making it more than clear we hadn't been as inconspicuous as we thought.

"I guess your lack of an explanation means my hunch is pretty solid then?"

I smiled a bit. "Maybe, but … it's a little more than that."

We reached our dorm and went inside, headed toward the stairs that would take us to the basement, instead of up to either of our rooms.

"Well, call me crazy, but if I had four smokin' hot dragons falling all over me like you do, I don't think I'd even know Ms. Audrina was alive. Much less care what she thought of me."

The comment made laughter bubble in my throat.

"Just sayin'," Blythe added.

We made our way down the dark stairwell, not bothering to turn on lights, now that we knew our way without them.

"Listen, if it's okay with you, I really don't want to talk about any of this right now. Things have been … *complicated* lately."

I couldn't see Blythe's expression all that well, but felt the mood between us shift. "Gotcha," she answered, "but I'm here if you change your mind."

I smiled as we entered our *'study space'* and removed our identical blazers. I took the box of matches from on top of the hot-water heater and handed one to Blythe. She struck hers against the cinderblock wall, and I did the same, moving through the space to light the ten or so candles we'd left lying around last time. Once finished, we both took a seat on the pile of blankets in the middle of the room, careful to keep our pleated skirts in place.

Today was going to be different. The plan was to finally move on from meditation and yoga—which had helped with self-control tremendously—and now focus on using actual magic.

Blythe mentioned an incantation that should draw small amounts of the dark energy from me, releasing it into a jar sealed with the magic of a powerful spell. Currently, it rested beside us on the floor, ready for use should this actually work. We hoped that, if we tried this enough times, whatever traces of The Darkness that dwelled within me might disappear for good. It wouldn't be the one-stop fix I hoped for, but it was something.

Being honest, a small part of me still held out on giving Blythe my total trust, but we had made progress. With how she'd stepped up to help me, continued to hole up with me in the basement like it was the safest thing in the world, I couldn't help but to see her. She was trying, she was willing to help me. For that, I was certainly grateful.

"K, close your eyes," she instructed, and I followed her lead, placing both hands palms up on my knees.

"You're gonna repeat after me, but fair warning," she continued. "When this starts to work, according to research, you'll feel … uncomfortable."

My brow quirked. "You mean I'll be in pain, right?"

She lifted one shoulder, as if to say *'sort of'*. "Maybe, but based on what I read, it won't take long. Actually, you should probably open the jar and hang on to it in case this goes faster than we think."

I moved out of position only long enough to place it in my lap. "Ok," I sighed, closing my eyes again.

I heard Blythe let out a breath, and then the next sound I heard was her voice filling the room. Words I didn't understand flowed from her lips, and I was pretty sure she didn't know what they meant either. From what Aunt Hilda told me, magic had more to do with your intention when stating the words, than it did with your comprehension of them.

My shoulders rose and fell when I inhaled, wondering when this feeling Blythe mentioned would finally kick in. Then, no sooner than I could release the same breath, my stomach began to roll. It was like that feeling you get at the peak of the hill on a rollercoaster. That one that's kind of your body's way of alerting you that something really freakin' bad is coming.

I shook it off, trying to focus only on the words that filled the quiet space.

Tightening in my chest made it hard to breathe, and I did my best to hide it until I couldn't anymore. First, a single cough left my mouth, causing Blythe to pause for a second. But then, it was like I'd swallowed water that went down the wrong way, nearly hacking up a lung.

Blythe, having been prepared for this, didn't stop again. She simply spoke the words louder, while I coughed and choked, rivaling her volume. It felt like something was trying to claw its way up my throat, but my body fought it, trying to hold it in. My focus was completely broken now, and I was on all fours, hoping whatever blocked my airway would somehow dislodge itself so I could breathe. There was a strange sense of being detached, and also the awareness of my dragon retreating. It was almost like my soul had somehow separated itself from my body, but hadn't left it. Not quite like how I imagined death to feel, but close.

With my eyes wide as I panicked, I noticed the moment the space around me began to glow with the strange turquoise light I'd seen before—the sigils. They were beginning to show through my skin. I still couldn't breathe, and for some reason the lack of control that had once bread a sense of terror, was beginning to shift to anger.

Rage.

Only, it didn't feel like my own, or even that of my dragon.

It was something else.

A swift breeze swept through the sealed room, blowing out the flames that once flickered all around us. Illuminated in the blue light of the sigils, smoke wafted eerily toward the ceiling. My body went still, no longer struggling for breath or control, and while I *should* have been relieved the terrifying moment had passed, I was anything but that.

My nerves were on edge, and the urge to tell Blythe to run swelled within me. It had become commonplace that I'd lose control in the blink of an eye, and this felt like one of those moments.

Brave, she continued screaming the words as the now constant cyclone that filled the room whipped her hair across her face. A sudden surge of calmness swept over me, and it only alarmed me more.

Without commanding my limbs to do so, they were now bracing the floor, positioning themselves to stand. It was like … I wasn't even in control of them anymore. It was like something *else* had taken possession of my body, moving me into place like a doll. It seemed to fit the feeling of my consciousness being shoved aside within me.

Maybe sensing that I stood over her, Blythe finally peered up, but her lips never stopped moving. The word 'RUN!' screamed from within me, but I couldn't seem to make it leave my mouth. Instead, I felt the corners of it curve upward with a wicked smile.

"You can fight this, Noelle!"

When her words ceased, the wind pushing around debris and knocking over the candles gained strength. Blythe, no longer focused on the spell, stood to her feet, but showed no signs of leaving, which I couldn't understand. Clearly, things were not going as we hoped they would, and her best bet at this point was to save herself.

However, instead, she took two steps closer, and then did the stupidest things she possibly could have.

My hands warmed when she took them, holding my gaze. It was then, in her eyes' reflection that I saw my own—solid black—as we stared at one another.

"You can fight this. You're strong," she reminded me.

Only, I didn't feel so strong then. I felt small, powerless as something within seemed to have more say-so in my actions than I did. Hence the reason why, the next second, I snatched both hands from hers.

"She's whatever I say she is."

My heart raced with the sound of the voice that exploded from my mouth—deep, menacing … *not mine.*

Blythe's lips parted when she drew in a sharp breath, unable to hide how the tone startled her, too. So much that she finally began to back away.

Only, it was too late.

The being within me fed on our fear—Blythe's, mine—gaining strength with each passing second. My hands wanted to reach toward her, but I fought it, clenching both fists as tightly as I could to stop it. This thing inside me, it wanted to cause her pain. It wanted to end her … *for trying to help me.*

"Blythe, get out of here!" I managed to force out. The Darkness didn't like that I'd been able to break through. And to punish me, to show me it wouldn't stand for being suppressed, it took control with a vengeance.

Before I could stop it, my hand shot outward, locking firm around Blythe's throat. As much as I hated being in tune with this thing, its emotions bled into mine.

When it enjoyed the feel of Blythe's windpipe being squeezed in my palm, a part of me enjoyed it, too.

Lifting her higher, only the tips of her shoes touched the floor, and I hated how it delighted me seeing her struggle.

"You … can't … help … her." The voice that hissed from my mouth was again dark and terrifying.

My bicep tightened, bringing Blythe's weight closer. Then, before I could guess what was coming, she was tossed to the wall. She sank to the floor like a stone in water, drawing dark laughter from my mouth, in that voice — deep, ancient, raspy.

I'd heard it before, when I crossed over into its realm somehow at the lagoon.

My feet carried me toward Blythe again — slow, intentional steps that made my stomach sink with each one. Because I knew what it had planned once I reached her. Although we were not one being, I sensed its intentions.

It wanted her dead.

Centering my thoughts, I focused on keeping my feet still, keeping them in place instead of moving toward Blythe. The first few seconds, it felt like a lost cause. Only, the next, it didn't. Somehow, I'd been strong enough to hold my stance, forcing the entity to know what it was like being a prisoner in this body.

A dark, guttural growl rumbled in my chest first, before spilling from my lips in protest. It didn't like being forced into the background, but Blythe was right. I had to fight.

She was coming to in the corner, and I felt relieved seeing her move.

"Noelle, fight," Blythe repeated faintly, still groggy.

The Darkness pushed again, and I was forced to take a step when my own strength waned. The sound of a hollow glass cylinder rolling across the aged cement floor drew my eyes toward it—the jar.

It was somehow still intact, unbroken despite the state of things in that small room as The Darkness showed its power. The entity forced me to take another step, then another, and I allowed it. Because the jar was nearly within reach.

If this was what it was like just having a *portion* of this being working inside me, I didn't want to think about what would happen if it took over completely.

Groaning, I stooped to take the jar, feeling the tug of war within me. It took a few seconds, but I managed to remove the lid.

My stomach burned from the inside, bringing with it a wave of nausea as I pushed myself to limits I didn't even know I could reach. Still, it wasn't enough. I wasn't overpowering this thing, despite giving all I had.

From a mere ten feet away, Blythe began to recite the incantation again, barely being heard over the strong gusts that moved between us. She wasn't giving up on me, wasn't running despite this being her only opportunity to do so.

"Use the jar!" she paused to yell, going right back to uttering the spell.

I gripped the wide, glass container, and held it to my mouth. Another labored cough left my throat, and the feeling of being choked from the inside returned. Only, this time I didn't fight it. The first puff of what looked like black smoke leaving my mouth and nose alarmed me, but it was Blythe's scream of victory that made me brave.

Gagging, the dark vapors continued to pour from my body, settling in the jar.

"Yes! Keep going!" Blythe shouted.

Pain spread through my limbs, but I kept my attention on expelling as much as of the sinister energy as I could. One final choked cough left me and the sound in the room shifted, as if the noise had been reversed, sucked right out of the space as the swirling debris fell to the ground. Blythe's hair wisped into the air one final time, and then slowly settled into a tangled mess.

A low growl from the jar I held prompted me to clamp the lid on tight.

The only sound that remained was that of us panting in disbelief. My skin dimmed as the sigils faded from beneath it, and I shot a look toward Blythe.

"Are you okay?" I asked in a rush, recalling how she'd been hurled across the room.

She gave a wide-eyed nod. "Yeah. At least, I think so," she panted. "You?"

I glanced down at the jar as the small portion of The Darkness we captured swam within it. "Think so."

Blythe slowly lowered back to the floor, pushing a hand through her black, tousled strands. "Dude, just … whoa."

That was one way of putting it.

I glanced around at the mess I—or it—had caused. I'd known before that I was getting out of control, but what I experienced there in the basement stirred my soul.

Blythe must have seen me trying, and failing, to process everything. Because the next second, she patted the floor beside her.

I eyed the spot, and then her. "I should … I should probably keep my distance," I warned.

She had no idea how close I'd just come to hurting her. I mean *really* hurting her. If she did—

"I'm not afraid of you, Noelle," she said, cutting into my thoughts.

"But maybe you should be," I countered.

She didn't even bat an eye when she pointed toward the ground again. "Sit," she insisted.

Taking slow, cautious steps, I did as she asked, sliding down the wall to rest beside her. Now hip to hip, we both peered at the jar I held, evidence of just how effed up this all was.

How effed up *I* was.

"What the heck am I supposed to do with this?" A humorless laugh slipped out.

"You break it," was not the answer I expected.

"But won't that just release it again?"

"Nope. Opposite," she revealed. "Dark energy—no matter how powerful—is only as strong as its host. So, now that this dumb bastard managed to get itself trapped in our special little jar," she added, patting the top, "once you break it, that's the equivalent to killing it."

My brow narrowed, admittedly nervous it wouldn't be quite that simple. I suppose because nothing *else* had been simple.

"And you're sure this will work?" I asked one last time, blowing a strand of hair from my lip.

Blythe nodded. "Yup. Trust me."

My gaze shifted to hers when she said those two little words. Trust me. I hadn't fully trusted her in a very long time. However, I'd just seen her stay in this small room with me while I wigged the heck out on her. She could have left me to figure this all out on my own, but she didn't do that.

Trust her … that's what she said I should do.

I turned to the jar, seeing how The Darkness moved inside it.

"Screw it," I sighed. Lifting my hand into the air, I chucked the thing right at the wall, watching it shatter into a million tiny pieces. And contrary to how I envisioned it, the darkness evaporated with a ghastly hiss, trailed by a dual-toned scream that filled the entire room.

Just like Blythe said, it was gone.

"Sweet, right?" she asked with a grin.

I laughed a little. "Yeah, I guess you could say that."

She grunted, using my shoulder to stand. "Now, we just need to do that a few … hundred more times, and you should be all cured." The smile she flashed right after made me laugh.

"Oh, simple," I teased, knowing how far that was from the truth.

Getting to my feet, I brushed dust from my shirt. Blythe moved around the room, picking up the fallen candles, straightening the pile of blankets.

"Listen, I … I don't know if we should meet anymore," I admitted. "We have no idea how many more times we'll have to do this, nor do we know how much it'll piss this thing off, so … I think we should end it."

Yes, I knew this meant I wouldn't have her help anymore, but I couldn't let her sacrifice herself to save me.

"Noelle, I already told you. I'm not scared of you," she reiterated, stooping to hunt for scattered matches.

"Maybe not, but I'm scared *for* you," I countered. "We've both seen how unstable I am, and I can't let you do this anymore."

Her head whipped my way. "Let me?" She stood straight. "Last time I checked, *I* was the one who came to *you* about this."

"I know, but—"

"I'm not letting you down again, Noelle."

The abrupt statement was hard to comprehend at first, but then I caught the look in her eyes.

Remorse.

Guilt.

I settled down a bit. "Is that what this is about? You think you owe me?"

She didn't answer, which was all the answer I needed.

My gaze lowered to our matching shoes, unable to fight the onslaught of memories of us that flooded my thoughts—good and bad.

"You don't have to prove anything to me, Blythe." I met her gaze again. "This isn't some small thing, like repaying me a dollar you borrowed, or helping me with homework. It's life or death," I reminded her.

Her vague expression made me wonder if she understood.

"I knew what I was getting myself into," she rebutted, squaring her shoulders as she stared blankly.

I didn't know what to say to that. Once again, she wasn't taking the out I offered. All I could do was lower my head, thinking I'd just have to distance myself to help get my point across.

"People give up far too easily for me." Her words made me peer up again. "My dad when he left, our instructors because they aren't sure how to help you, just … people in general. So, I'm making the conscious decision to be different."

Her declaration made my brow quirk, but I said nothing.

"I'm in this with you, until you beat it." The steadfast way she spoke made it clear she meant every word and wouldn't be easy to talk out of it.

She was determined to stick with me, and I wasn't sure what I could do about that.

I shook my head at her. "Well, just so you know, this makes you incredibly, *incredibly* stupid," I informed her, laughing.

"Guess that's why we get along," she said with a smile and shrug. "Birds of a feather and whatnot."

CHAPTER TWENTY-THREE
NOELLE

"Go. I'm fine!" I said with a laugh, waving my friends toward the lagoon. "And have fun!"

Four weary smiles came my way—my friends, minus Tristan, plus Blythe. They'd been hovering over me since arriving at the start of the barbeque roughly thirty minutes before. Manny and Marcela eventually stalked off, stripping down to the clothing they'd swim in along the way. Toni and Blythe, however, lingered beside me longer. They, themselves, weren't exactly friends, but they had a common interest.

Me.

I smiled up at them both and raised a brow.

"That includes the two of you," I clarified. "You're here to hang out and have fun, so go do some of that." They didn't buy it when I laughed right after, probably sensing I wasn't quite myself today.

When Ori first mentioned a gathering at the bungalow, and told me that the Firekeepers, their queens, and my friends were all invited, I imagined it going much differently than this.

For starters, I didn't envision I'd still be avoiding the Omegas so blatantly. Just thinking about it, I did a quick scan to make sure none were close. I spotted them offshore, engaged in an intense game of football with the other hives, divided into two even teams—minus Ori and Ty, who both manned the grill.

My gaze flickered back to Toni and Blythe. "Seriously, I'm okay," I insisted.

"Maybe we'd believe you if you hadn't been glued to this spot while everyone else is having fun. I mean, isn't today about celebrating you?"

Toni's words saddened me for whatever reason.

"It is, but … I'm just a little out of it, I guess."

She knew exactly what was going on with me – the info I unearthed at the Firelight Celebration – but I didn't want to get into talking about that in front of Blythe. Granted, we were working through our differences, but … baby steps.

"We'll go, but only if you promise to join us once you're up to it," Toni bargained.

I narrowed my eyes at her, pretending to be deep in thought before a smile broke through. "Deal. Now go."

My promise had been enough to convince them, and then it was just me, sitting on the porch steps, watching everyone having a blast on the Omega's little slice of Sanluuk.

I glanced down for half a second to smooth my dress over my knees, and when I peered up, Rayen was suddenly coming my way. If I didn't move quickly, all the work I'd done to avoid him, and the others, would have been for nothing. He'd mentioned twice already that we needed to talk, and I knew he'd try again if I let him, but I just wasn't in the mood to pretend.

Pretend I didn't know what secret they kept.

Pretend I didn't know what they allowed to take place on this island.

Pretend I hadn't wondered why nothing had been done to stop the practice of humans being sacrificed to appease The Darkness.

Thinking quickly, I stood from the porch to walk toward the side of the dock where Nayeli, Lehua, and Kalea sat with their feet dangling in the lagoon. On my way to them, of course I had to pass Rayen, and it didn't surprise me when he caught and lightly gripped my arm.

Our gazes locked and I hated being like this, hated that I couldn't just come out with what was on my heart, without fear of what would happen next.

An argument.

Excuses.

Lies.

That last concern was, admittedly, a baseless one, seeing as how the guys had never been dishonest with me that I knew of, but I wondered if this would be the time. If this would be the thing that was big enough for them to decide the truth was too difficult to tell.

"Mind if we talk a sec?"

Hearing Rayen's request, I nearly faltered.

Nearly.

"Um … I was actually headed to chat with the queens while my friends swim. Don't want them to think I'm avoiding them," I added with a forced smile.

"*They're* the ones you're concerned might feel slighted?" he countered, referring to himself and the Omegas.

My stomach sank and I wished I had more of a poker face. Then I'd be able to look him and the others in the eyes without fear of them seeing straight through me. Only, that wasn't me. I tended to wear my heart on my sleeve, revealing everything with my eyes.

"It's not like that."

"Then tell me what it *is* like, so I can understand," he shot back, leveling a hardened stare my way.

"School just has me kind of frazzled," I explained, knowing that was only a very small part of the equation. "Finals are in a couple weeks, and I'm feeling every ounce of the pressure our instructors are putting on us."

Again, I sprinkled a heap of truth on my excuse, finding it made me feel just a tad less guilty for what I held back. A silent moment passed between us, and in those short seconds, the pull toward him strengthened, just from standing in his presence.

A slow, intentional gaze slipped over me, eyeing me in the strapless white dress Toni helped me pick just for this occasion.

"So … it's stress?" he asked evenly, as if he only sought clarity.

I answered with a quick nod as I took a breath. "Yes."

He was hard to read for a moment, but then I sensed his thoughts so clearly.

"Tell you what," he spoke up, his tone suddenly deepening as it moved over me like warm silk. "Come inside with me. Just for a little while," he beckoned. A few steps brought him closer. "I think I can help loosen you up a bit."

It was shameful how fast my pulse thrummed at the base of my throat. He'd gotten to me just that quickly, and my body's response to him was all the proof I needed. His hand slipped lower, dropping from where it held my arm, to intertwine with my fingers. Next, his gaze turned heavy, suddenly dripping with need.

His proposition made it clear the rest of the hive knew Ori and I had *'established protocol'*. It meant we were all free to do as we wished, without jeopardizing our rapport with Spirit.

It had been weeks since any of us had gotten laid, and yeah, I felt the pent up frustration just as powerfully as *he* did. Only, too much went on inside my head, and I knew I wouldn't be able to let go and be free with him.

"Everyone will think we're rude if we disappear out the blue," was the only excuse I had for turning down such a tempting, *tempting* offer.

Rayen's disappointment was apparent when he released a breath. "Fine," he conceded, "but we still need to talk once this is all over. It's important," he added.

My brow quirked when he said that last part, but I had to take the out I'd just been given.

"Okay. Sure," I answered, wearing a tight smile as I side-stepped him to head toward the queens, like I originally planned.

Nayeli spotted me first, then the others followed her gaze to meet mine. Huge smiles came next, which I fully expected. These three were among some of my favorite new people. I'd never forget the pep talk they gave during our last gathering. Their encouragement had been the sole reason I tried breaking the ice with Ori, had been the reason I was open to the idea of being mated to the Omegas.

Basically, they had a way of gently placing my feet on the right path and setting me straight.

"Well, if it isn't the reluctant queen herself," Lehua teased. "How's school going, co-ed?"

I laughed a bit. "Ask me again in two weeks, when this term finally ends." I lowered to the dock, taking the seat beside Kalea. She peered up, wearing a huge grin. "What?" I asked.

The expression brightened her face even more. "Nothing. I'm just astonished by how good queendom looks on you. You wear it well."

Warmth spread through me, hearing her say such a thing. Being honest, I hadn't felt like much of a queen lately.

More like a monster.

"Thanks," I said shyly, turning to face the water where the hives' children all swam.

"So, tell us how it's been," Kalea inquired. "Anything … *interesting* to share? Like, maybe how you and the Omegas were the first hives *ever* to break protocol?"

The three laughed and I felt a little embarrassed that they knew, but I guessed there weren't many secrets among them.

"Yeah, about that …" I could feel my cheeks turning red, if the heat that flashed through them was any indication.

"Relax. Kalea's just giving you a hard time," Lehua cut in. "We can see how your generation might think it archaic for there to be an order in which a queen ought to give herself to her dragons."

Hearing her speak of my generation reminded me of our age difference. Looking at the four of us seated together, you never could guess we hadn't been born within a few years of one another. Youthful, sun-kissed skin held their secrets, hid that they had centuries of wisdom locked inside them.

"Trust us. There are *many* traditions this island has upheld far too long," Lehua went on to say. "It's our prayer that, when the day comes for Kai to assume the role of chief, our change will finally come."

There was a sense of heaviness I hadn't felt from them before. It was also the first time I heard them say anything even remotely negative of the island.

A surge of boldness struck, and it sparked a question in my thoughts. Although, it may have just been that I'd held it in far too long, and simply couldn't anymore.

"Is … the lottery one of those things you hope will change?"

Three sets of eyes found me, and I guessed they had just been made aware of my knowledge of their island's dark secret.

Nayeli's shoulders rose and fell when she drew a deep breath. "I see the guys told you."

"They didn't," I confessed. "I snuck to the Firelight Celebration, and the performance told me all I needed to know."

All turned away, except one—Lehua.

"The lottery is one of our beautiful island's ugly truths. And, yes, it's one of those things many of us would like to change."

"Then why hasn't anyone done that? Our guys are among the most powerful, most revered dragons in the world. Why haven't they done … *something*?"

I hadn't meant to sound so harsh, so judgmental, but I was certain that's exactly what the queens detected.

"Because it's not that simple, Noelle," Kalea chimed in. "Yes, it's an outdated tradition and, yes, it's tragic. However, you're leaving out one very important detail."

"What's that?" I sighed.

"That it's worked," she stated. "So, try being the one to tell a mass of terrified citizens that you're going to outlaw the one ritual that's kept them at least *remotely* safe. Not only would you have a mutiny on your hands, there would be hell to pay once The Darkness realizes we've taken it upon ourselves not to uphold our end of the bargain. What you've seen of it so far is what it's like when it's tame, sated. Trust us, you don't want to see what it's like when it's angry." She paused and shook her head. "So, you're asking the wrong questions."

My eyes darted toward her. "Then what's the right question?"

She peered up, and there was grave conviction in her stare. "The right question is: What can we do to stop The Darkness? We need a new solution," she added. "Gone are the days of simply appeasing this great evil. It has to be destroyed. And until we figure out how that's to be done, we'll continue losing people. If not by way of the lottery, then it'll happen when The Darkness begins to spread again."

Tension creased my brow. "What do you *mean* again? It grows?"

Lehua nodded. "The territory it occupies has nearly doubled in the last decade, consuming some of our sacred burial ground, the ruins. Hence the rise of a new hive of Firekeepers."

"Four men from the Sigo bloodline, no less," Kalea cut in. "They're direct lineage from the first tribesman called by Spirit."

"Our men are doing all they can to keep it tamed," Nayeli said next, "and the Council's contribution to the effort has been to host the two annual sacrifices, by way of a random lottery.

But still, with all that's done to stop the dark entity, it's not enough." She peered up at me once more. "It's easy to judge what you don't understand, Noelle. It isn't a light decision to choose to sacrifice the few to ensure the survival of many. Our forefathers enacted the lottery, and no one's name is exempt, including those of us here today, our children," she added.

"The reason we haven't broken tradition isn't because it's been the easy thing to do," Kalea interjected. "We haven't broken it because—as ugly as it is—it works." She surprised me when she reached for my hand. "If you've been thinking your guys—or *ours*, for that matter—condone this practice, you're sadly mistaken. Their silence in the matter is only because they know it would only do more damage to revolt, than it would to ride this thing out until we find another viable solution."

"One that saves lives rather than ending them." Lehua's gaze was warm and understanding, probably knowing this was no easy pill to swallow. However, they achieved their goal.

They made me think deeper, made me look at this all from a different perspective.

"I hear you," I said quietly, turning toward the water again as I zoned out.

"You're troubled," Nayeli said with a sigh. "And for good reason, but talking about this won't change anything. Not *yet* anyway." She turned to face me. "May we take a look at your mark?"

Usually, I did my best to forget about mine being different whenever possible, but I knew this was her way of changing the subject, which I appreciated. There didn't seem to be a point in discussing the lottery further anyway.

"Sure," I agreed, lifting my hair to reveal the odd symbol.

A finger traced the outline of the anomaly.

"Does it scare you?" Nayeli asked.

I shrugged. "Some days more than others."

A flashback of Blythe and I in the basement came to mind, but I didn't share the memory out loud.

"Don't be frightened," she said sweetly, lowering my hair back to my shoulder. "There's always a challenge when you first accept your calling. This peculiar ordeal is simply your test, Spirit's way of strengthening you for life's journey."

"As Spirit is my witness," Lehua cut in, "I believe you'll come through this with a stronger sense of who you really are, and confirmation of what your *true* calling in life will be."

"And we know you have friends, but don't forget Spirit has given you three sisters, too," Kalea reminded me, making sure I knew that she and the other queens had my back.

"I appreciate that," I said with a smile, knowing she truly meant every word. Their love and patience was more than I expected, but exactly what I needed.

CHAPTER TWENTY-FOUR
NOELLE

The party livened up even more once the food was served and the sun had set. Torches kept the property lit, and loud music had most on their feet dancing. Even my friends.

Toni had gotten cozy with Caleb—a son of the Eros hive. He, like myself, was a newly shifted dragon, and from where I stood at the foot of the dock, he was super into her, too. The song changed to something slow, and while they weren't quite grinding on each other, it was close enough and I was two seconds from throwing a condom at them just for laughs.

"Dance with me."

I peered up to find Ori towering over me, and his eyes shifted to my lips just as a slow breath passed between them. I hadn't heard him approaching, but it didn't matter because I was done running from him, the others.

Speaking with the queens had planted a seed, one that grew throughout the day. They opened my eyes to the bigger picture, all that the Omegas had riding on their shoulders, and even that *they* were just as likely to be selected in the lottery as anyone else. This further drove my desire to find a way to bring change to Sanluuk.

I stood in place as Ori's large hand snaked its way around my waist, pressing flat against my stomach as he inched closer to my back. Warm air moved across my ear and down the side of my neck when he breathed against it. In response, my lashes fluttered over my eyes, threatening to close.

"Dance with me," he repeated.

The statement was neither a question nor a command, but something in between, making it impossible to find words to deny him. It was as if he *knew* he owned me—mind, body, soul—knew I had the hardest time resisting.

Before an answer could leave my mouth, he turned me slowly to face him and I didn't fight. As if I hadn't spent weeks putting space between us, I slipped both arms up over his shoulders, and then locked my fingers around his neck.

I didn't find it hard to look him in his eyes tonight, which was the opposite of how it had been lately. Although I'd been in my mates' presence, it still felt like we'd been apart for weeks. Which I can admit was all on me. However, based on the way he looked at me now—like I could do no wrong—I knew he didn't hold a grudge.

"I'm … sorry." The words tumbled from my mouth, and they'd barely reached his ears when a kiss landed on my lips.

If I hadn't already been over my misguided frustration, this would have done the trick.

He pulled away, and my mouth formed a smile. "You didn't even let me tell you what I did that warranted an apology."

Broad shoulders shrugged and I moved my hands down to them. "Because it doesn't matter."

"But I've been a huge dick to you guys for weeks. And I—"

"Doesn't matter," he repeated, cutting in. "Having you here, in my arms, that's all I care about."

He'd become so sweet—gentle toward me, and yet maintaining his image as a stone-cold warrior when he faced the world. The idea of me—the girl he wanted to strangle when we first met—now being his soft spot, it made me kind of crazy for him.

"Today's been good," he shared, bringing me closer as our bodies swayed in sync with the slow melody.

I let my cheek press to his chest before nodding against the soft cotton of his shirt. "It has. Then again, any day that ends with us together is a good day."

I'd missed this—the closeness, being vulnerable with my guys. Hardening my heart toward them was something I found easy to do in the past, but since our world had shifted on its axis, they were a part of me.

Still reveling in the feel of Ori's large arms engulfing my waist, my eyes opened slightly. For a second, I thought I heard something near the tree line, but from what I could see, there was nothing.

Then, I heard it again—the sound of twigs and underbrush being trampled as someone, or *several* someones, trudged through the rainforest.

Headed straight for us.

"Someone's coming," I whispered. "Do you hear it?"

Ori followed my gaze to the trees, and his body stiffened against mine. "No, but your hearing is keener than mine."

It was, apparently, my wolf that detected the quiet commotion, but I knew I wasn't mistaken.

"Have you spoken with Rayen tonight?"

The strange timing of Ori's question made my eyes dart up toward his. "No. And why is that relevant right now?"

Ori's chest swelled when he breathed deeply, passing a sympathetic gaze toward me. "Hurry and find him," he instructed. "I'll buy you two as much time as I can."

Confused, I didn't even know what questions to ask. His arms freed me suddenly, and he nodded toward the house as he took steps in the opposite direction.

Toward what sounded like an entire army making their way toward the bungalow.

I was nearly frantic when I burst through the front door, shifting my gaze in every direction until I caught Rayen's scent. My wolf led me straight to him.

I didn't bother knocking on the door when I found him in his bedroom, seated on the edge of his bed, deep in thought.

He peered up when I burst in, beyond curious why he'd be hidden in here while everyone else celebrated outside.

"Someone's coming and Ori said I should come find you," I panted, full of worry. "What's wrong?"

It only alarmed me more that he didn't seem surprised by what I shared. Now, all I could think about was how he'd tried more than once to tell me something today. Something important.

"What's going on?" I pressed when he hadn't answered my first question.

He stood and came close, reaching for both my hands. He was way too relaxed about all this. Meanwhile, I was lightweight freaking out.

"I met with the Council last week," he began. "In order to atone for breaking protocol, I was required to give a public, formal apology to Ori. Well, I did that," he added with a sigh.

My brow tensed, my heart raced. "And? That's still not telling me anything."

"I made atonement with Spirit, but my apology didn't renew my good-standing within the tribe. So, they're detaining me until further notice."

"Until further notice? Rayen, that's ... that's *insane!*" I was pacing and trying to keep my thoughts straight, but it grew harder by the second. "We did nothing wrong."

"I couldn't agree with you more, but there are rules."

"That may be, but you're not going anywhere."

He seemed surprised I'd make such a sure statement.

"Noelle, there's nothing we—"

"You're not … going *anywhere*."

Our stares were locked on one another, and Rayen's grew more sympathetic by the second. As if he knew I would be sorely disappointed in a moment, when he was hauled away to wherever it was he was headed. The thought of it made my eyes well with tears of frustration. My fist swiped one from my cheek when it fell.

"This doesn't make any sense," I choked out. When I blinked, more tears slid down my face.

Seeing me break down over this, Rayen pulled me closer and my forehead pressed into his curls, both arms tightening around him.

"It's temporary," he promised. "If I know Chief, he just wants to prove a point, show me he isn't afraid to assert his authority, then he'll release me."

My eyes fell shut, imagining him in some dark, dank cell. "I'm not letting them take you," I reiterated, meaning every single word.

They were on the dock now, their heavy steps trudging this way. With each foot that landed on the wood slats, rage multiplied within me. So intensely my skin burned as heat blazed just beneath the surface.

It wasn't until Rayen said my name that I reopened my eyes and saw the gleam of turquoise radiating off his white shirt. It came from me, from the symbols glowing all over.

Each breath that entered and left my lungs came quicker than the last. I was nearly beside myself with fury, practically blinded by it.

Concern spread in Rayen's expression like wildfire. I made myself back away because I'd seen more than once what I was capable of in this state, and I wouldn't have him caught in the crossfire.

"Stay back," I warned, hearing the crackle of fire as my hands lit with blue flames without me willing them to.

"Noelle, you have to relax."

I heard the false sense of calmness in Rayen's tone, and it did nothing to settle me. Authoritative steps stormed down the hallway, and my gaze darted there, bringing my wolf front and center with a deep, warning growl. Somehow, all three of my supernatural identities had come forth at once to protect my mate. Before now, I hadn't even known that was possible, but the proof was staring right back at me.

I'd caught sight of myself in the mirror — skin alight with sigils as my eyes turned dark, my dragon's fire surging from both hands like torches, the outline of my wolf fading in, defined by blue flames.

There was a loaded moment of silence that caused my breaths to come and go quickly. Then, as if they predicted I'd be waiting for them, fully prepared to unleash all hell if it came to that, Rayen's door burst open.

Chief Makana hung back, instead of leading the charge. A trio of witches rushed in — two with hands outstretched toward me, one aiming her palms toward Rayen. The sound of his pained groan forced a growl to rip from my throat.

"Don't touch him!" I yelled.

Chief responded with a brazen command to the witches. "Subdue her!"

A surge of magic swirled around me when they obeyed, but didn't render me completely paralyzed, like I'm sure they believed. But I played it off, letting them think they succeeded.

"Let him go," I screamed. My voice was my own, but … not. There was another laced with it, one deep and terrifying. Hearing the odd tone that left my mouth, Chief's eyes gleamed with intrigue, while Rayen's told of his growing concern.

Keeping both hands locked behind his back, Chief finally took a step into Rayen's bedroom.

"I see your instructors' reports haven't been exaggerated," he said, causing anger to spike within me. "You're at *least* as unstable as they've expressed." His tongue clicked several times, patronizing me from a distance. "Such a shame. All that strength, all that potential gone to waste."

His steps carried him toward me then, and I tensed, unsure what he intended to do once he reached me.

"Chief, I swear, if you—"

"Shut him up," Chief Makana ordered, and again, the witches did his bidding.

Another groan flew from Rayen's mouth as his knees buckled beneath him. Even when he cried out in agony, his brothers didn't rush in, which didn't seem possible. Not to mention, none from the other hives had come either. It was only Rayen and I, alone with Chief Makana and the witches.

The two who *thought* their powers held me in place were focused, their lips moving with whatever incantation they uttered.

Chief Makana came even closer, settling his stern glare right on me. Unlike most, he was unafraid of what he saw before him, unmoved by the freak of nature who was all three beings at once. Not even the deep grumble from within my chest made him back off. Which meant he had full trust in these witches.

"What did you have planned for me when I walked through that door?" he asked, letting his gaze wander over the detailed symbols glowing on my skin.

"That depends," I answered.

"On?" His eyes flicked upward and returned to mine.

"Whether you still think you're taking Rayen," I assured him.

He seemed to enjoy my answer. I guessed as much because the huge grin he wore widened with the statement.

"I see." Slow steps carried him in a circle around me. "And do you have any idea what the punishment is for anyone who even *considers* assassinating a chief?"

I shrugged. "Don't know. Don't care. But one thing I'm certain of, is that Rayen isn't going anywhere with you people."

Chief nodded, seeming to consider my words. "Well, what would you say if I told you I had a feeling you would have one of your … episodes, so I created a bit of a diversion ahead of time." He leaned in so close the flames rolling off my body danced over his shoulder, when he added the words, "Just in case."

My gaze was set on Rayen, noting how his nostrils flared with Chief being in my personal space. "What did you do?" He beat me to the question.

"Nothing yet," Chief countered sarcastically. "But that could all change if you two decide not to cooperate."

I faced him again when he cleared his throat.

"You see, these three standing before you are only a *few* of the friends I brought with me today. The others are outside waiting for my cue." Another slick smile touched his lips.

"Why are there even witches *on* the island?" Rayen seethed. "You have something planned. I can feel it."

To my surprise, Chief Makana didn't just completely ignore the question. Instead, he seemed more than happy to answer.

"They were invited," he revealed. "They've come to help us rid this island of the only enemy its ever known, once and for all."

"How?"

Chief smiled at Rayen. "Just leave that part to me," he said dismissively before turning to meet my gaze again.

"What have you done?" Rayen seethed.

Chief only spoke over his shoulder this time. "Again, the answer to your question is '*nothing yet*'. I'm simply prepared for the worst, should that prove necessary."

White-hot rage flooded my veins, flowing through my body at lightning speed, watching when Chief pointed toward the open window.

"Just beyond the bungalow, I've had the other witches gather each of the Firekeepers, their queens and children, using a spell to keep them entranced, and safe," he added. "Because, despite what you may think, the safety of my people, and the greater good of this island, is always my main concern."

Could have fooled me.

"Safe from what?" I asked, somehow holding back when the urge to curse at him came over me.

"From the fate your friends will meet should you not cooperate."

My heart skipped a beat.

"They're in the lagoon," he continued. My brow quirked, remembering that I'd seen each of them dancing near the speakers when I rushed past Ori to find Rayen.

"I have a witch posted just off the edge of the shoreline, and she's holding a vial," he explained. "And in this vial, there's a potion she concocted that will turn whatever water it touches into a boiling vat of acid up to a one-mile radius, for an entire hour." A satisfied grin parted his lips, and it pained me to see Kai's features reflected in his face. "Which, I'm sure you can guess, would not end well for your friends. They would likely heal, but only time will tell what the long-term effects of the spell will actually be."

"If you hurt them, I'll—"

"You'll what?" He asked, glaring. "This isn't a fight you'll win, Noelle."

Hot air passed over my lips as I panted, hating that I knew I had the ability to overpower Chief, his witches, but also knowing he'd make good on his promise to hurt my friends.

But I couldn't just let him do this, let him take Rayen when I believed I could stop him.

"Noelle, don't."

My head whipped left at the sound of Rayen's strained voice.

"You can't put your friends in danger because of me. He'll let me go soon," he promised, but I didn't just take that at face value.

"You don't know that," I shot back, feeling new emotions creep in, cuddling up right beside rage and frustration.

It was sadness and longing.

He hadn't even gone yet, and I missed him, regretted that I'd been so stubborn these past few weeks. Who was I to judge what he and the others ought to be doing about the lottery? Me, the imperfect girl who could barely keep from killing the people she loved. I should have known there was more to it than the black and white version I concocted on my own.

And now, I'd run out of time to make things right without even realizing the clock had been winding down.

"It's fine," Rayen said again, this time sounding as though the magic was starting to let up, but I was almost positive he only *pretended* it had, so I'd cooperate.

My eyes didn't leave my mate when I addressed Chief. "How long are you keeping him?"

"As long as it takes."

Still fuming, I shot him a look. "Why?"

"So those on this island who all but worship them, are reminded that the Firekeepers are not gods. They are mere men who must abide by the law like every *other* member of this tribe."

"Except you," I said flatly.

My shoulders heaved and I couldn't hold it much longer. The witches would soon be very much aware of my strength if I wasn't careful.

"Collect him and we'll be on our way."

Under Chief's instruction, the witch who'd harmed Rayen lowered her hand and he gasped with relief.

"On your feet," she commanded, prompting him to stand.

All this because we'd followed our hearts that night.

A warm glance passed over Rayen's shoulder and I caught it just before he disappeared around the corner into the hall, leaving me for however long the Council had in mind. Chief gestured with his head for one of the witches assigned to *me* to follow the other back out to the lagoon, giving her permission to release the captives.

I guessed that meant my friends.

Three of us stood in Rayen's room, so much tension swirling in the midst. I listened to the witch's footsteps, and then heard water slosh when Toni, Blythe, Manny, and Marcela were allowed to go ashore.

"Thank you for your cooperation," Chief said, feigning appreciation.

"Go to hell," I hissed.

That brought a smile to his face, and he looked me over. "Well, it appears one of us is already halfway there. And, call it a hunch, but I think it would only take one little push to get you there."

My wolf stepped deeper into the light and I felt my bones shift when she threatened to show herself fully. Her sharp hearing made me aware of retreating footsteps leaving the property. That meant my friends were in the clear ... and Chief Makana was fair game.

A guttural roar ripped from my throat and strength gathered in my arm, vibrating through the entire limb, until my fist balled tight. The blue flames engulfing my arm burned brighter and, without weighing my actions, I cocked back and swung straight for his face. With no time to react when I took him by surprise, I landed the hit cleanly on the broad side of his jaw.

Blue embers burst where I made contact, and his skin began to melt with a sickening sizzle as he cried out in pain.

He hadn't likely heard of what happened when a mainland dragon from my bloodline burned blue, but I guessed he understood now. It was the *only* fire to which other dragons were susceptible, meaning that hit hurt like hell.

Shocked, and a little fearful, his witch cowered to his side, bracing Chief's shoulders as the two backed toward the hallway. I'd both injured *and* angered the man, and that felt almost as good as killing him.

… Almost.

From that day forward, whenever he looked at the scar that would undoubtedly remain, he'd think of me and know the mistake he made crossing us, the Omegas.

"You'll regret this long before I will," he warned, letting his gaze settle on mine.

And then, he was gone.

I slumped to the floor, only now feeling the effects of all three beings having come forward at once. My head swam and it felt like every ounce of energy had been drained from me.

Several minutes passed and my intentions were to head outside to check on the others, but I couldn't seem to lift myself.

"She's in here!" Blythe yelled, and seconds later, the others came running.

First, three foreboding bodies came in to surround me, and then several others whose identities I couldn't place.

"We couldn't get to you." The anguish in Ori's tone made me feel for him. "I swear we tried."

I mustered enough energy to place my hand on top of his. "I'm fine," I assured him as I felt myself slipping under. "If you think *I'm* in bad shape, you should see the other guy."

I gave a weak smile as my eyes drifted closed, envisioning the look on Chief Makana's face when I landed that punch.

My guys laughed, as did most of the others surrounding me.

"Yeah, we saw," Kai chimed in next, amusement lacing his tone. "And trust me, Chief won't be forgetting anytime soon either."

"What happened to her?" I heard Paulo ask.

"I don't know. When I got to her, she was all lit up, and her hands were on fire, and I saw traces of her wolf," Blythe explained.

"All three?" Kai asked, unable to hide the concern in his voice. "At once?"

I saw Blythe's dark hair move over her shoulder when she nodded.

"I need to get her into bed," Ori spoke up. "She's stronger than any one of us in this room, so I'm sure she'll be fine, but she needs to rest."

There was no more conversation about it, just a powerful set of arms slipping beneath me, and then I was airborne, resting against a broad chest as I breathed in the scent of my alpha. He was more than gentle when he carried me from the room, placing me in his *own* bed instead of the one nearby.

I heard the rustling of a blanket as he pulled it from the foot of the bed where he kept one folded. It covered my shoulder and I relaxed there, knowing he'd keep me safe. A soft kiss went to the side of my hair and the whispered words spoken into my ear sent me off to sleep with a smile on my face.

"Rest," he said first, "and then we'll talk about that nasty right hook of yours when you wake up."

CHAPTER TWENTY-FIVE
ORI

We had a problem on our hands. Judging by the silence from the seven of us waiting in the living room for Noelle to awaken—her friends, my two remaining brothers—I guessed they'd all reached the same conclusion.

"All three manifested at once," Paulo stated gravely, pointing out one of many alarming factors that had come into play tonight.

Not only had all three of Noelle's supernatural sides shown themselves simultaneously, there was also the nasty burn she left on Chief's face. Between the two occurrences, I hadn't decided which was most dangerous.

"I didn't realize things had gotten this bad," Kai chimed in. "Or maybe I just didn't want to believe it." He stopped pacing and kept his stare trained out the window.

"I think that's been the case with all of us," I reasoned. "We care for her; therefore, we've been blind to how she's changing."

There was something I hadn't shared with the others. Continuing to hold it in was somewhat of a moot point.

"The day we visited Maureen, when she called me back inside alone, she revealed an interesting theory," I told them.

"What *sort* of theory?" Kai crossed both arms across his chest after asking.

There was a lump in my throat when I swallowed. "It had to do with what she said when first meeting Noelle. The part about her being an old soul."

"I heard that, but what about it?" Paulo inquired.

"Do you remember what Noelle shared with us right after she first shifted? It was during our conversation on the way to get her things from the dorm."

Paulo was thoughtful for a moment. "About her mother being killed, and then returning?"

I nodded. "Yes. She mentioned that a beast had been responsible for that. The same beast that later came for her mother *again,* while she was with child."

My brothers' expressions deepened with concern.

"Maureen seems to think there's a connection," I continued. "Like, that beast and The Darkness are two sides of the same coin."

"I don't follow," Manny spoke up, his brow knitting together with confusion.

There had to be a simpler way to explain this. "Maureen believes that all good comes from one source, and likewise, all evil comes from one source. So, if her theory is right, it would explain why The Darkness seems to know Noelle so well."

"Because it's been after her since she was conceived," Paulo said gravely.

"*Both* times she was conceived," I added. "So, this battle started way before she arrived on this island."

Silence ensued, and it became clear my brothers now felt the same sense of dread I'd carried on my own for weeks. Wondering just how long this battle had gone on, wondering how much bigger it was than any of us sitting in that room, it made hope a difficult concept to grasp.

"She warned that we should brace ourselves, because she believes it's entirely possible Noelle is already a lost cause," I added, revealing the last of Maureen's grim prognosis. "While I heard every word loud and clear, and I know things aren't looking good right now … I'm not willing to give up that easily."

I peered up after speaking, unsure of how the others would take the news.

"Neither am I. She just needs help." It was Toni who'd spoken up this time, huddled in a towel like the others from having been tossed into the lagoon by the witches.

"I agree, and I've tried," Blythe revealed, "but this has proven to be a *much* bigger task than I imagined."

All our gazes locked on her after she spoke. She peered up, blinking as unshed tears glistened in her eyes.

"What do you mean?" Paulo asked, staring fixedly at Blythe.

He was far more intense tonight than usual, which made him give off a menacing vibe that wasn't often seen. But he carried *two* burdens tonight—the uncertainty of knowing where Rayen was being held, and the instability of our queen.

"Noelle has worked very, *very* hard in secret," Blythe began. "She's tired of feeling like she's capable of hurting the ones she loves, so we've been meeting a few times a week, working on elevating her control, overpowering The Darkness."

"I take it there hasn't been much progress so far," Kai commented.

Blythe shrugged thoughtfully. "Well … *you* saw what happened today," she sighed. "Every win is followed by a huge loss, so Noelle feels like she's going backwards."

"And what makes *you* qualified to help her?" There was no missing the distrust in Toni's voice when she asked.

Blythe's hands shot up in surrender. "Listen, I'm guessing Noelle told you about our past, but trust me, I'm not the enemy here."

I wasn't sure what past she spoke of, but I agreed our biggest threat was not in this room, despite the scent of dark magic coming from Blythe.

"We're all on Noelle's side," I interjected. "And she'll need us *all* to be around to get her through this. Which means we need to keep an open line of communication between us. No secrets when it comes to her, especially if it's something that can help or hurt her."

"Agreed," Paulo grumbled.

"Facts," Marcela answered.

The others offered some variation of the same response to signify that we were all on one accord.

"So, what do we do from here?" Manny peered up to ask.

When everyone turned to me, I assumed that meant they thought I had the solution. Naturally, I didn't.

I considered our options, knowing our allies were limited to those of us here in this room, the other Firekeepers and their families, Maureen.

"For now, I say we do what's in our power to keep her safe, stable. We're not at full capacity without Rayen, and Chief's had his witches block our tether. That means we have no idea where he is, how long he'll be detained, nor can we communicate. In the meantime, our best bet is to try and enlist as much outside help as we can get." I turned to Toni. "Any idea how to get in touch with Noelle's family? Her people are powerful and well connected. If we can get them here to the island, it could only help."

She didn't look hopeful. "Easier said than done. Communication to the mainland only gets spottier by the day."

I nodded. "I'm starting to think that's not a coincidence." When no one disagreed, I guessed I wasn't the first to have this thought.

"So, basically, we're screwed," Manny sighed, standing to walk off his frustration.

For a few seconds, we were plunged into silence.

"I … might be able to help with that."

We glanced toward Blythe, waiting for her to explain.

"There's a spell I can try, but it'll take me a while to gather ingredients, and then I'll need to practice," she added.

"If there's anything we can get or do to speed things along, let us know."

Blythe nodded when Kai offered.

"The sooner you can do the spell, the better," I interjected, "because I think it's painfully clear that our Chief, and our Council, have been severely compromised."

"You could say *that* again," Manny scoffed.

"Then that's our plan." Marcela rose from the floor, standing beside her brother. "We stick by Noelle, and work together."

I sighed, wishing we had more options, more allies.

"That's basically the long and the short of it. We'll keep eyes on her, report anything strange, and keep our objective in mind."

"And what's our objective?"

I met Toni's gaze to answer. "We have to get Noelle off this island … by any means necessary."

CHAPTER TWENTY-SIX
NOELLE

The Overseers hadn't exaggerated when they said exams would be tough this term. Not only had we taken finals all week, we also faced intense evaluations to test our physical abilities, as well as our psychological fortitude.

Now, it was all coming to a head for me right here in the gym.

As if it wasn't insulting enough that I'd been forced to do my final evaluation on the opposite side of the room, my instructors—Sira and Claire—had put up a magical barrier between me and the other students as well.

Just in case.

My nerves were frayed, and my head had been all over the place since Rayen was taken. It'd been two weeks with no word, no update as to where he was being held or how long he'd be there.

The guys had been to Chief's office daily, pleading for information, only to be turned away. I promised Ori I'd give it a little more time, but if he didn't tell us something soon, I would be paying their island's leader a visit myself.

Apparently, I, too, was at risk of being arrested – thanks to that little love tap I'd given the man—but I wasn't afraid of him. Not even with his gaggle of nasty witches hanging around.

All of this made for a very crowded mind, and it definitely reflected in my final grades. Straight C's so far. Now, lucky me got to bomb this last test in front of the instructors, my peers, and of course the three scouts from The Guard who watched from the far corner of the gym.

Fun.

I mean, only my entire future hung in the balance. No big deal, right?

"Again!" Sira yelled, prompting us all to resume our stance.

Others around me, including Blythe and Toni, created brightly colored forcefields that moved from their bodies slowly, inching toward the opposite side of the room as they doubled in size, and all I'd done was make a few pink sparks fly from my hands.

Frustrated, I peered up at the scouts as they watched me, whispering.

"Is that her?" one asked.

"It is," the other answered with a nod. "Such a waste. All that power and no talent to back it up."

"The worst part is the lack of self-control. Apparently, she's injured others during her time here. One girl has even lost her magic after partnering with her."

Heat flashed across my face after my wolf stepped forward to eavesdrop. They had no idea I could hear their quiet conversation, but I could.

Loud and clear.

I shook with anger and tried channeling it when I took my stance again, letting my feet press into the mat. I focused on my hands as a surge of energy filled them. Next, I imagined myself getting this right. A shield would form right before me, and then spread outward as it moved away. Just like everyone else had done.

Don't screw this up.

A deep breath left my lungs and I pushed, waiting for some display of magic to manifest. It was all I could do to redeem myself in front of the scouts, although I feared my reputation here preceded me. Meaning, it was already too late. My thoughts snagged on that idea, and I lost focus. Instead of a pink shield shooting from my hands, there was a huge fireball that filled the room with heat.

Screams and gasps echoed off the vaulted ceiling, making the scene *way* more dramatic than necessary.

Of course, all eyes were on me, and I was certain I'd just sealed my own fate. The looks of exasperation on the scouts faces told me as much.

I felt both Toni's and Blythe's gazes locked on me, but I didn't turn their way. The last thing I needed to see was the look of horror I was positive each wore. I knew how badly this had gone without their expressions confirming it.

I'd done it, ruined everything.

"Well, I … think that's enough," Sira said, putting me out of my misery. "Hit the showers, everyone. Your final grades will be posted right outside the gym at nine a.m., one week from today."

The sound of feet shuffling from the room and quiet conversation were the soundtrack of my failed attempt at impressing those who held my future in their hands. I turned, heading toward the door slower than everyone else, defeated and angry with myself.

"Noelle, it's not—"

"Don't. Please," I said sharply to cut Toni off.

I knew what she was going to say. She'd tell me it wasn't that bad, and that this wasn't the end of the world, but I couldn't let her spin such a huge lie. It *was* that bad.

Blythe caught up and stood on my other side. Only, I wanted nothing more than to be left alone.

"Listen," I sighed. "Why don't you two just go ahead without me. I'll catch up with you this evening."

Neither spoke after I made the request, but they shared a concerned glance.

"I'll be okay," I assured them. "I just need to clear my head."

Eventually, Toni released a deep breath, and then nodded for Blythe to follow her, granting me the space I desperately sought.

The exit opened and the two flooded out with the sea of bodies that moved out into the hallway. Meanwhile, I trailed far behind on purpose.

"The crazy part is, her dad's a living legend. Didn't he teach her anything?"

I paused, hearing the scouts speaking about me again.

"Apparently not. Maybe he expected her status as a princess to carry her through life," the other laughed.

"From the looks of things, she should have stuck with that plan."

My chest felt tight and I recognized the rage right away, but their careless words not only awakened my dragon. The deep growl humming in my chest meant my wolf hadn't taken the comment well either.

I breathed out slowly, hoping to dispel some of the anger. However, it didn't dissipate, and I knew I'd have to let it out somewhere if I didn't want to lose my cool. As I neared the door, my eyes flitted to the cinderblock wall, and without thinking, I slammed my fist into it, leaving a basketball-sized crater behind.

The red stain on the cracked white paint meant I'd busted my knuckles, and the sickening crunch that accompanied it meant I'd broken at least a few bones as well. Still, somehow, I felt relief sweep over me.

I didn't turn back to see the shocked looks on the scouts faces. They officially didn't matter anymore. The sooner I put them out of my head the better. My dreams of joining The Guard were over before they really even started.

It just took me falling flat on my face in front of them to realize it.

I pushed the door open and stepped out into the hall long after it had emptied. The rest of my classmates were already in the locker room, so the two sets of footsteps hurrying toward me belonged to Ori and Paulo.

"What the heck happened?"

"Is it broken?"

I kept walking when both called out. "I'm fine. It's already healing," I said quickly, never looking back as I made a beeline for the doors straight ahead.

I didn't want to talk about any of this. I just wanted it to be behind me, and I wanted Rayen back, and I wanted to be normal—all things I had no control over.

I left them on the other side of the threshold, hearing the entire locker room go quiet when I stepped in and my classmates laid eyes on me, which meant I'd been the topic of conversation.

Nice.

As I passed each one, they lowered their gazes to the floor, and I could practically smell their fear just from being in my presence. Taking shampoo and a few other items from my locker, I headed toward the shower without a word, turning on the water to block them all out.

The clothes I'd worn to gym were in a heap on the floor, and I stood beneath the stream. The wound on my hand stung a bit, but the bones had already shifted back into place, leaving only the broken skin to mend now.

My eyes closed. Everything was falling apart, slipping right between my fingers, and there was nothing I could do about it. I felt lost, broken, like a piece of me was missing without Rayen. Our unit had five members, and with any *one* of them missing, we wouldn't feel whole.

Minutes passed, maybe fifteen when I lifted my head at the sound of a gasp hitting the air.

"What are they doing?"

"Are they allowed in here?"

The questions had come from the few girls who still hung around, and the sound of heavy steps crossing the tile told me exactly who they spoke of.

I whipped my head just in time to find Ori and Paulo approaching, as I stood naked, in all my glory beneath the water.

"Seriously? I'm not the only girl in here," I reminded them, passing a look toward them from over my shoulder. "You can't just barge in like that."

"Tell us what happened to your hand," Ori demanded, ignoring my comment. Apparently, I'd taken too long to come out for their liking.

"It's nothing," I said dismissively. Honestly, now that I'd settled down a bit, I felt embarrassed to tell them it was self-inflicted.

"I'm gonna need a better answer than that," he grumbled.

A deep sigh left my mouth and I lowered my head beneath the water, letting it run down my body. This day had been one humiliating event after another, culminating with these two not letting me shower in peace.

"I punched a wall," I admitted on the tail end of a sharp breath.

"Why?"

I pictured Ori's confused expression, but didn't turn to witness it.

"Because today sucks. Because I'm losing myself. Because Rayen's gone and I miss him. Because … everything's a mess," I unloaded, adding, "Especially me."

It was no relief sharing my burden with him. Mostly, because I knew no one could fix it all. This was simply the state of my life, and I'd just have to deal with it.

"What happened in there?" he asked, taking a few steps closer.

His question went unanswered, because I couldn't even find the words to say that I'd singlehandedly sent my future up in flames. Literally, considering the fireball I'd just made a little bit ago. To put it plainly, nothing was going the way I imagined.

There was a long span of silence and I didn't move, just let water hit my shoulders.

A deep sigh left Ori's mouth. "Clear the room and wait for me outside. Don't let anyone back in," was the vague command he barked at Paulo.

There were no questions asked, and a few seconds later, I heard the remaining girls being rounded up and asked to leave. There were shuffling footsteps, the sound of a door closing, and then just the water.

My shoulders heaved when I breathed deeply, feeling like they held the weight of the world. Ori was somewhere behind me, but I didn't open my eyes. He stepped closer, his feet moving across the wet tile, until the next thing I felt against my back was his skin.

At some point, while making his way over to me, he'd come out of his shirt. A breath of relief passed from my lips and my head reared back, landing gently on his shoulder. His hands splayed across my stomach, slicking over the moisture that gathered on my skin. It was on the tip of my tongue to tell him he couldn't stay, that we could get caught even with Paulo standing guard, but I didn't bother fighting the fact that I wanted him here.

Needed him here, because the guys were my one, continuous source of comfort.

Without giving permission, I was turned to face him seconds before his mouth crashed down on mine. The heat that rushed to my lips radiated through my entire body. He moved lower, letting his tongue trace slow swirls down my neck to my collarbone, then then to the valley at the center of my chest.

I leaned into the tiled wall behind me, panting as feather-light kisses trailed down my stomach, until he lowered to his knees.

When his lips found me again, air wouldn't leave my lungs. I held it in, feeling dizzy with pleasure as my thigh was lifted to his shoulder.

It felt like, lately, my life had been in ruins, but my guys had been there at every turn. Their undying devotion had given me back something I thought I left behind when I came to the island.

Not only family, but … love.

My fingers wove their way through his soaked strands as I began to pant, feeling that weight I carried lighten just a little, lifting more and more as I gave in to him. Gave into the feeling of letting go.

When I squirmed, he only held me tighter, forcing me to endure the relentless swells of pleasure that came in like a flood, making me lose my breath as I gripped his shoulder. My voice carried into the air when it all got to be too much, only for the sudden high to come crashing down again, plunging us in silence after the release of one final cry.

Every limb felt weak as I struggled to keep standing. My foot was lowered to the ground, and my gaze followed Ori's tall frame as he rose to tower over me again. He stared with a sated expression that somehow made him even sexier than before. Leaning closer, soft words touched my ear.

Words that made every concern seem just a little less damning.

"You're not alone," he reminded me. "Ever. In any situation. We're all in this together, right beside you, no matter what happens."

The room went dark when my eyes fell closed, when my arms went around his neck ... when I chose to believe him—my alpha—with my whole heart.

Chapter Twenty-Seven
Noelle

I stared at the cloudless sky while I lie there, flat on my back on our claimed, stone bench in the courtyard.

"It is what it is?"

My friends seemed shocked by my response to Toni's question: "Are you ok with not being invited to join The Guard?"

"It is what it is?" Marcela asked, as if she thought she misheard.

I simply nodded and focused on the flock of birds that flew overhead. "Yup."

At first, it stung a bit seeing others celebrating after receiving their prospect letters when break first began, but I had a week to cope with my new reality.

"Never know," Manny chimed in, mumbling as he bit into a sandwich from where he sat on the grass beside me. "Not being invited to join doesn't mean you won't be accepted. Just means they need you to prove yourself a bit more."

I heard him, but knew that wasn't the case for me. He hadn't heard the things the scouts said, hadn't heard how they had clearly judged me before that first encounter. There was no amount of showing and proving I could do, that would convince them to let me in. However, I wasn't as broken up about it *now* as I'd been the day of our final evaluation.

No cinderblock walls were in danger this time.

Part of the reason for my level-headed reaction was that my priorities had shifted. Not seeing or hearing from one of my mates for just over three weeks would do that for a girl. Every time I laid my head on the pillow, I wondered if he was comfortable, if he was safe, being taken care of.

Daily, I had to remind myself that Chief Makana thought the Omegas needed to be taken down a peg. Taking Rayen was mostly about showing them who's boss. It made me worry a little less about his wellbeing, but there was nothing I could do about missing him.

"I think I might be meant to do something else with my life, ya know?" I reached to steal a grape from Toni's baggie. She playfully slapped my hand before deciding to share.

"But being a part of The Guard has been your dream since you were a kid," Blythe added. "Sure that's not frustration talking?"

I shook my head. "Nope. I've had a solid week to think it all over, and I've come to the conclusion that being a soldier isn't the only way I can help people. That was always my real objective," I shared. "The title and division had little to do with it."

Manny shrugged when I guessed my reasoning made sense to him.

"Besides," I continued, "my little sister, Lea, intended to follow in my footsteps and join once she's of age. Who knows? Maybe she'll get to be the one to carry the torch for our family."

"So, what's the new plan?"

I didn't have a clear answer to Blythe's question, so I didn't pretend to. "I'm honestly just taking it one day at a time."

What I kept to myself was that I'd honestly considered withdrawing from my final term at the academy, although I'd been forbidden to leave. There just seemed to be less of a point in putting myself through all the studying, training, and then exams if I wasn't even certain having a certificate from the academy would make a difference in my future. For now, I'd keep my thoughts, and my uncertainty to myself. Once I knew for sure, I'd let them in on my plans, too.

"Well, whatever you decide, we've got your back," Manny concluded.

"Definitely," Toni concurred.

I didn't doubt that for even a second, because they hadn't left my side much since Rayen was detained. If I wasn't surrounded by my friends, I'd been looked after by the Omegas. When Ori said I wasn't alone, he meant it.

"Well, I'm due for my midday nap. That's my routine from now until classes start again, and I'm not breaking it for *anybody*," Manny declared, groaning as he stood from the grass. "I'll be awake for dinner and dessert," he promised. "I heard someone mention they've got cupcakes in the dining hall."

Kid loved his food.

"Sleep well," Blythe said with a laugh, and I didn't miss how her gaze followed after him as he trudged toward his dorm.

Deciding not to call her out, I simply smiled to myself, wondering how long it would take for the two to hook up.

"I think I'm gonna catch up with you guys later, too," Marcela announced. "Mr. Montrose agreed to work with me a little during break. I didn't do so hot on my math final. Your girl needs all the help she can get."

"He charging you anything?" Toni asked, cocking her head to the side.

"If he was, I wouldn't be going," Marcela laughed.

Toni was on her feet the next second. "Then count me in. I barely passed that sucker myself."

I laughed watching her scramble to gather her trash from lunch, and then hustle behind Marcela.

"See you guys in a few," she said with a wave. I didn't miss the look she and Blythe exchanged before leaving the two of us alone. It wasn't the first time I'd seen it, and I was pretty sure I figured out what it meant.

It was their way of wordlessly checking in, asking if the other was cool sticking with me until someone else could cover the shift.

I appreciated their concern, and kept it to myself that I saw right through them.

"Looks like it's just us for a while," Blythe sighed. "What should we get into?"

I smiled, not having to give it very much thought. "Manny mentioned cupcakes, so…"

"You had me at cupcakes. Let's go," Blythe replied, standing quickly now that she had frosting on the brain.

I was on her heels, hightailing it across the courtyard, when a strange sensation in the pit of my gut stopped me cold in my tracks.

Blythe noticed my steps had halted and turned to me.

"What is it?" Concern riddled her expression as she came closer.

"I don't know." It was so hard to explain, but I was certain of one thing. "Something's wrong."

"Do you feel sick? Should I get Paulo?" When she said his name, her gaze flicked to where he stood leaning against a tree across the courtyard. It seemed as though he noticed my expression and was now coming toward us.

"It's not me," I told her, starting to breathe heavier as panic set in. "It's … one of the guys."

Paulo reached us just as the words left my mouth. "What do you mean?"

Confused, I shook my head while trying to explain. "It's like I can feel him, whoever it is. I can feel he's in danger, or … hurt maybe?"

I hated not knowing what it meant.

The entire left side of my body began to tingle, and I couldn't shake it. Without thinking, I took a step that way, which made it grow even stronger.

One step turned into two, and then many, and I was gaining speed. Paulo and Blythe were sticking close, although I still had no idea where I was going or why.

'Guys, you there?'

I was vaguely aware of Paulo's inner conversation as he checked in on the others, dialing in on some sort of magnetism that pulled me toward it.

'Yep, what's up?' Kai sounded off.

'Here,' Ori said next. *'Everything good?'*

They were safe. I breathed deeply, hearing their voices inside my head, but then that sense of relief left just as quickly as it came. Because if it wasn't them …

"Rayen."

His name rolled off my tongue as we neared the border wall. I hadn't been great in flight, but it seemed my body had forgotten about that as fire consumed my skin, and within seconds, my pace quickened to an unfathomable speed until I was airborne.

"Noelle, where are you going?"

I didn't glance back when Paulo called out to me, but I wasn't surprised that he was still sticking close. Just like Blythe. She, too, had taken to the air, but not with wings and fire.

With magic.

"I have to go to him," I tried to explain, speaking loudly to be heard over the wind as it passed beneath me, as my wings sliced through with ease.

"We don't even know where they're keeping him."

I couldn't make him understand that it suddenly didn't matter that we hadn't been given an address, or coordinates. At that very moment, my dragon and Rayen's were in sync, and I only knew one thing.

He needed me.

And he needed me right away.

CHAPTER TWENTY-EIGHT
PAULO

'She's headed toward Jacob's Ridge. Meet us in the air in two minutes.'

'On it," Ori answered.

I was on Noelle's trail as she tore through the sky, fast and precise, like she'd been doing this for years. Something primal drove her in Rayen's direction. There was nothing more powerful than a tether, and I was positive that was what pulled her in his direction.

Which left me to wonder, what had been so dire that she'd taken off so urgently?

Two bolts of fire joined us in the air, and I made out the outline of broad wings aimed straight back as my brothers rose to our height, startling Blythe at first. She hadn't even hesitated to take off after Noelle, despite having no idea where she was leading us. I wasn't sure what kind of rocky history Toni hinted at several times, but it seemed that was behind them.

The only ones who follow you blindly are true friends.

A dense expanse of trees lie up ahead and Noelle began to lower toward it. Those of us trailing her did the same. Within seconds we were on the ground and our dragons had only retreated enough not to be visible, but mine was certainly on high alert.

She'd taken us to a stretch of land dangerously close to the northern border, near the forbidden land where The Darkness roamed uninhibited.

"What's she doing?" Blythe whispered.

I shrugged and kept my eyes on Noelle. "I believe she's looking for Rayen. She seemed to sense that he needs help."

Confused, Blythe frowned. "But I thought you all couldn't feel him, couldn't communicate with him because of something the chief's witches had done?"

"That's true, but … Noelle's different," I reminded her. "It's not so hard to imagine that her connection to him, to all of us, reaches beyond whatever the witches have done to sever the Omegas tie to Rayen. We can't reach him, but that doesn't mean Noelle can't feel him. If his situation is dire enough …" I trailed off then, not wanting to think the worst, but it couldn't be helped.

We'd worried about him for weeks, doing what we could to reason with Chief Makana, going out and looking for Rayen ourselves when we got tired of being dicked around. Every effort left us emptyhanded and frustrated. Ori did his part to keep us levelheaded, reminded us that once Rayen served whatever time Chief deemed necessary, he'd return home, and everything would return to normal.

Only, this trek deep into the rainforest, with Noelle searching frantically for our brother, made me wonder if his prediction had been wrong.

"Do you still sense him?" I had to ask, unable to keep quiet.

Noelle's gaze darted back and forth as her feet carried her straight ahead. "I do, but … it's starting to get faint."

"Are we headed in the wrong direction then?" Kai chimed in.

She shook her head and I didn't miss the strain of emotion in her tone when she spoke again. "No, that's not it."

Which meant her sense of him was fading.

Which meant … maybe he was fading.

"Let's speed up," Ori urged.

Our fast-paced walk turned into a full-on sprint. Noelle paused a moment, before veering slightly to the right as her intuition pulled her in a new direction.

We ran for miles, staying right with our queen, moving closer and closer to the border. So close smoke from the ever-burning blaze we Firekeepers kept lit was now visible. I glanced toward Ori as a question passed from my thoughts to his.

'Do you think they sent him there? Into the northern hemisphere?'

I hated that this idea even seemed possible. However, with Chief's behavior lately, I honestly couldn't put anything past him. Even the idea of him endangering one of us—a warrior sent by Spirit to protect this island. An island he claimed to love and regard higher than his own life.

'Wherever he is, we're going in after him.'

I couldn't have agreed with Ori more. Even if it meant we would all be endangering our lives to save his.

My hands braced against Noelle's shoulders when I nearly ran into her. She stopped cold and pointed. I followed her gaze to a dark mound up ahead.

"He's over there," she panted, out of breath from how we raced to get here.

None of us questioned her, just picked up the pace again and ran full-steam ahead, this time with a clearer sense of where we were headed. We came to a stop at the base of the oddly placed hill, circling around it until we reached the other side and discovered a wrought-iron gate sealing some sort of entrance.

The five of us stood there, staring at the darkness beyond it.

'We can't let her go in there,' Ori said, taking the words right out of my mouth.

'Then what's the plan to keep her out?" I asked. 'Because we all know simply stating that it's not safe won't stop her.'

'You and Ori can go in after Rayen,' Kai reasoned, "and I'll keep her here. If I thought I could convince her to trail me back to the bungalow, I would try, but I don't think it'll work. She's stubborn.'

'Think her friend could use a spell to maybe sedate her?' I knew it was a longshot, but had to ask. We didn't have very many options.

Ori sighed, thinking harder. 'Kai might just have to take her by surprise, subdue her and carry her to safety.'

"Try it," Noelle seethed.

All three of our eyes snapped toward her when she seemed to have responded out loud to our thoughts. With a threat no less.

"What are you talking about?"

At first, it seemed Kai's question would go unanswered as Noelle continued to stare at the gate that stood between us and Rayen. Then, when she was ready to talk, she pivoted on her heels to face us all.

"I can hear you," she said with a sigh. "Your thoughts. All of them. Since the day I shifted."

My brow tensed with confusion, and my brothers wore similar expressions.

"At first, I didn't say anything because it was kind of cool knowing what you guys were thinking, and then eventually, I didn't say anything because I was kind of embarrassed I hadn't told you sooner."

This new info had me running through the ultra-long list of crass things that flowed between my brothers and I on a daily basis. If I hadn't been so focused on Rayen, I would have probably felt like an idiot, but I was certain there would be plenty of time for that later.

"So, no," Noelle said flatly. "I will not stand out here while you guys go in after him. And, no, I will not leave."

With that, she didn't waste another second debating, instead turning back toward the gate to see if she could pry it open. It shuttered when she tugged it hard, but didn't budge.

"We might be able to kick it in, but I'm not sure we should make our presence known. There are others inside," she informed us. "I can smell them. Dragons."

Blythe stepped forward and placed her hand on the bars. "Here, let me try."

Our gazes were locked on her as several pulses of purple energy vibrated from her hands to the metal, and then the hinges creaked quietly.

Noelle passed her friend a quick smile, thanking her as we moved inside.

Darkness surrounded us completely. One sharp turn left as the ground began to slope downward cut us off from even the light at the entrance. We were descending quickly, headed into what could have very well been a trap.

The smell of damp earth greeted us when we went deeper. So far, there was only one direction we could travel, which made things only marginally easier. Still, something didn't feel right.

My steps halted when Noelle gripped my wrist from where she walked beside me.

"Someone's close," she barely whispered.

No one moved, listening harder.

"I need to go first," she insisted, warranting an abrupt protest.

"Absolutely not," I said flatly, putting my foot down. "We have no idea what's ahead of us."

"I can protect myself," she reminded me. Not that I needed reminding. Having seen her in action, I knew what she was capable of. Still, that didn't change the fact that she was our responsibility. Didn't make me forget that she was important to our hive, or that any one of us would choose death for ourselves before we'd let harm come to her.

"Paulo, I need you to trust me."

I couldn't see a thing down there, not even my own hand in front of my face, but I felt her. I knew she stared at me with that unwavering conviction in her eyes.

My only response was a deep sigh, and she took it for what it was. Me letting her have her way.

Her soft steps were right ahead of me now as the passageway narrowed, and I didn't let her move more than an arm's length away.

Another turn—this time to the right—and faint light could be seen up ahead. Orange light outlined Noelle's dark hair and features as she crept forward, until the glow surrounding her brightened into a golden aura.

"Guards," she said, having a better view around the bend than the rest of us. "I'm gonna go talk to them."

"What?" The whispered question flew from my mouth as I managed to grab only the hem of her shirt, which wasn't enough to pull her back.

She stepped forward, and before either of the guards could get the wrong idea, thinking they'd simply overpower her, Ori, Kai and I fell in step with Noelle, creating a wall behind her.

Our girl was insane, and brave to a fault, but only when it came to stepping up for one of us. She made it clear on more than one occasion that she'd put it all on the line if she had to, solidifying her place within our hive.

"Take us to the prisoner," she said with confidence, not bothering to ask if there was even anyone being held down there. She knew beyond the shadow of a doubt this was the place.

One stepped up, wearing a look of concern as his gaze shifted behind Noelle, to the three of us. "On ... whose authority?" he stammered.

"Mine." Noelle didn't back down. In fact, her shoulders squared a bit when she answered. "The dragon you're holding doesn't belong here, because he hasn't committed any crime, so we've come to see to it that his sentence ends today."

The guard turned to look at his partner, still smirking. "Abe and I can't let you do that," he answered, sounding bolder now. "We've been given strict orders by Chief not to let anyone down here without proper clearance. So, unless you have the same credentials as the last visitor, we're going to have to ask that you leave."

His partner, Abe, stood to his feet as well, as if the two expected trouble out of us.

"Wait. What visitor?" Noelle asked, confusion apparent in her tone.

The two stared blankly, defiant.

"Answer her question," Ori commanded, his voice thundering inside the small space. The guards may not have known yet who Noelle was, but they certainly knew of the Omegas.

Abe's gaze rose to meet Ori's. "The truth is, we're not sure."

Tension spread across my brow. "What do you mean you're not sure?"

"The person was cloaked and they didn't speak. We were simply handed the proper paperwork and then opened the gate. We're not here to ask questions or dig into why Chief grants certain ones access. All we're here to do is make sure that those who aren't authorized don't make it beyond this point."

My fists clenched when I sensed a challenge in that statement.

"Or what?"

I peered down at Noelle when she asked. Faint, just beneath her skin, I noticed the glow of blue light beginning to show through, angular symbols that always seemed to show up before she did something wickedly insane.

Or violent.

"If someone were to try and force their way through … we'd have no choice but to take action against them," Abe said with confidence.

He had no idea what hell he would face if he tried. From us, from our queen.

Noelle's shoulders heaved as she began to breathe deeper. In the tight space, I thought I heard the deep rumble of her wolf, but wasn't sure.

"I'm going to ask one more time," she seethed, speaking through clenched teeth. "Please … take us to the prisoner."

The guard who first greeted us faltered a little, seeing how the markings on Noelle's skin brightened to almost full strength. I imagined he'd never seen anything like it, because we hadn't either before her.

His gaze flitted from Noelle's to mine.

"I already told you," he started. "If you don't have proper paperwork, I—"

A sound similar to a rock being smashed exploded into the hollow space where we stood bargaining, and all of a sudden, the guard's words cut off. His entire body crumpled to the ground in a broken heap when Noelle's hand jutted out, and then closed into a tight fist. It was as if she'd smashed the man's large frame like a soda can, with nothing more than a gesture.

Dead silence.

My gaze panned to Ori as he watched Noelle with disbelief and concern overshadowing all else.

Abe, shivering and sweating, slowly shifted his eyes to what was left of his friend.

Noelle took steps forward, lessening the distance between herself and the one remaining guard. He was terrified, which became evident as he backed closer to the wall that stood only a foot or so behind him. He had nowhere to run, nowhere to hide.

"Your friend gave me the wrong answer," she said calmly—too calmly to have just killed a man, simply because he stood between her and Rayen. "So, I'm giving you a chance to get it right."

Abe took zero seconds giving Noelle's offer any thought. Instead, he began fumbling with a large ring with keys clanking around it before she even finished her thought. The gate behind him was quickly unlocked, granting us access to the next section of the cave.

CHAPTER TWENTY-NINE
PAULO

Every so often, as he led the way, Abe's eyes wandered over his shoulder, carefully scanning Noelle. I guessed for signs she'd see to it that he met a fate similar to his friend's.

A five-minute trek took us deeper into the narrow cave. When Abe finally stopped, it was as we turned abruptly and approached the mouth of another passage. One void of the mounted, intermittent torches that had provided a sparse source of light to this point.

Abe gestured in the direction of the dark walkway. "He's down there."

All our gazes shifted toward the stone corridor that appeared to have no end.

"You'll take us," Noelle insisted.

The guard hadn't even had a chance to agree or disagree when his collar was gathered into her fist, and he was forced to take steps ahead of us. Of course, he made no attempt to argue, and I didn't blame him.

Blythe had been completely silent the entire time, and it was hard to read her. The only thing I knew for sure was that she, like the rest of us, grew more concerned for her friend as time wore on. Noelle slipped into these states where she acted without thinking, and it was during those moments that none of us were ever really sure what to expect from her other than violence. It was as though, as a witch, she had access to The Darkness' power, and could tap into it at will.

Or ... *against* her will.

"What is that?" We'd gone down this new path for what felt like a quarter of a mile when Noelle stopped to ask.

She peered through the darkness and we did the same. It took a moment longer for any of us to see what her sharp eyesight had revealed to her a moment before, but there it was.

A strange, green glow coming from what I guessed to be the end of the hallway.

"Rayen." Noelle called out to him with desperation woven into the syllables. I hung on the silence a moment, unsure of why he hadn't answered.

When only *her* voice echoed against the stone, my heart raced.

Abe released a startled grunt when Noelle took off running into the darkness with him in tow. We managed to keep up, but barely. Even with our heightened speed, she was hard to catch.

Eventually, her steps slowed, and I could now make out the dark silhouette of bars. The odd light we'd seen from a distance glowed behind them. It was magic, energy moving in waves from the ends of three sticks jutting upward from the ground.

Dirt and loose gravel crunched beneath our feet as we moved closer.

As the outline of a body lying on the ground caused my heart to stop cold.

As the objects that glowed became clear.

Arrows—three right to the center of Rayen's chest.

Noelle dropped to her knees and finally released Abe from her grasp.

"What did you do?" she screamed as the sigils burned brighter, lighting up the darkness we'd barely been able to see through before then. "What did you do to him?"

She scrambled quickly toward the cell that held our brother. Reaching between the bars, she found Rayen's hand to take hold of it. Tears race down her cheeks and the heart-wrenching sob that left her mouth broke my soul.

My stomach turned as the finality of it all hit me like a ton of bricks, seeing the one I'd come to love like my own flesh and blood lie there on the stone floor of a cave.

Lifeless … where he'd died alone.

Kai's back fell against the wall, and he stood speechlessly, shocked into silence by what all our eyes were having a hard time believing.

My chest burned with rage, but sadness kept the intense anger in check. I couldn't seem to grasp the concept of him simply … not existing anymore.

"Who did this?" Noelle turned from where she knelt, her now pitch-black eyes contrasting her glowing skin. And those eyes were locked on Abe.

When he shrugged, Ori seemed to come from nowhere, rushing the guard into a wall. Loose stones fell to their feet and the entire cave echoed with the sound.

"Who … did … this?" our alpha asked, repeating the question.

"I—I don't know. The visitor was completely covered. I told you, they had a signed statement from Chief Sigo to enter, and we let them in. That's all I know."

"It was a witch," Blythe spoke up. "Only a cursed weapon could mortally wound a supernatural. Otherwise, he would've healed and been fine. Not …"

Her voice trailed off and I was grateful for it. Hearing someone say the words out loud would have been more than I could take.

Noelle's head whipped back toward Rayen and her desperation was so strong, it could be felt by those of us connected to her.

"I have to fix this," she said quietly, seemingly to herself. "Open the cell."

I glanced toward Ori, finding that he already had his gaze locked on Noelle.

Abe, panting, turned toward her, and it only took him half a second to remember why it would be unwise to keep her waiting. The keys dangling in his hand rose to the lock when he made it there.

"Noelle, what are you doing?" It was Blythe who asked the question we were all thinking.

"I'm doing what has to be done," she reasoned. "It can't end like this. Not when I can do something about it."

"But you *can't* do anything about it," Blythe reasoned, stepping closer. "If you're thinking about bringing him back, necromancy requires a *ton* of dark energy, and you can't go there."

The warning resonated with us all, and I stepped forward. When I reached Noelle's back, just as the gate swung open, I placed both hands on her shoulders. Beside me, Blythe stood, breathing deeply. When her eyes flitted toward me, and I caught a glimpse of the terror in them, my heart sank. It let me know the extent of the damage this could do to Noelle, possibly pushing her to the point of no return.

"This isn't what he'd want," I told her, getting the words out as calmly as I could. "If you do this, we might not be able to pull you back. There's a chance this will be the thing that pushes you beyond our reach."

I breathed deep, praying she listened.

"No," she breathed, making my eyes fall closed when she stood and slipped from my grasp. "I can't leave him like this."

"*None* of us wants that, Noelle, but you can't—"

"I'm sorry." She turned to me when the words left her mouth, and those ink-colored eyes that seemed to make her behave like a completely different person locked on me. Then, with the wave of her hand, my body flew to the cave wall, as well as my brothers, Blythe, and Abe.

We were pinned there, paralyzed by her magic as she moved into the cell, where she lowered beside Rayen.

"Blythe, can you break us out of this? Can you counter her spell?"

I turned to her after Kai asked, spotting a lone tear as it streamed down her face. "She's stronger than me," Blythe admitted. "I can feel it dampening my powers as we speak."

Hearing those words, I attempted to move my shoulders, a finger, *something*, but it was no use. The only thing I *could* do was speak, which meant my only defense, the only way I could possibly convince our queen to turn back while there was still time was to reason with her.

"Noelle," I called out, hearing her name echoing off the stone surfaces. "This is wrong, and you can feel it. We all want to undo what's been done, but … not like this."

"Then how?" Her question was harsh, resolute. As if her mind had already been made up. "You want me to just leave him like this?"

"What's done is done," I answered, feeling as though sadness might strangle me to death. The longer the seconds wore on, the more reality hit—my brother was gone.

She stared down on him, shaking her head in disbelief.

"The only thing we can do from here is find out who did this, and bring them to justice."

She laughed a humorless laugh from where she stood over Rayen, clearly disagreeing with me.

"And you think that's enough? Bringing them to justice?" She shook her head once again. "No, I'm bringing him back. And even then, I'll find whoever did this and make them *beg* … for death."

My eyes slammed shut, feeling like I'd lose this battle when she declared this promise.

"And what if this is it?" I asked. "What if it's like Maureen said. It's up to you which side you choose, and what may seem right and necessary, might not be so black and white," I reminded her. "She seemed to think you'd reach a tipping point, one final decision that pushes you from straddling the line … to crossing it."

Noelle didn't answer right away, which gave me an inkling of hope to cling to. I saw her shoulders heaving as she thought, weighing my words, weighing her options. When her eyes found mine, I held my breath and prayed I'd said enough to sway her.

But then, that morsel of hope was dashed by two words.

"I'm sorry."

Her gaze slowly returned to Rayen as she mourned him in silence. The caves began to whistle in the distance, and then seconds later, the wicked gust of wind that caused it finally reached us. Noelle's long, dark hair swept across her face and up into the air as she placed both hands over Rayen's chest, where she'd just removed the three arrows. Despite the chaos ensuing around us, she appeared calm when her eyes fell closed.

The bluish-green markings that covered her skin were beginning to change, slowly fading to a striking purple that made my heart race with uncertainty. I stared as Noelle's lips moved, and somehow, the whispered words could be heard loud and clear, as if the wind carried them throughout the cave, filling the atmosphere with their power.

The purple aura rose from her skin like a halo surrounding her, and then engulfed Rayen as well. Meanwhile the rest of us were powerless, forced to be onlookers.

Then, right before my eyes, I saw his hand twitch. I hated the relief that one, tiny movement brought with it, because I had no idea what the cost would be.

To us.

To Noelle.

Our hive as a whole.

Her lips moved faster, faster than humanly possible, and the aura brightened into a blinding white flash that forced my eyes closed. Through my lids, I was aware of the moment the space suddenly went dark.

Pitch black.

The wind faded to a howl before it died completely, leaving us with nothing more than the sound of Noelle's labored breathing from somewhere in the distance.

And then … a loud gasp that didn't belong to her made my heart stall. Noelle's breaths quickened with excitement, then there was frantic shuffling inside the cell.

"You're okay," she panted. "You're okay."

Harsh coughing from the same direction reverberated off the cave walls, and I struggled in vain to free myself.

"It worked!" The triumphant tone of Noelle's voice felt displaced, because those of us who'd tried to stop her had a very different outlook on what she'd just done.

A bright, orange glow illuminated the cell when she ignited her fingertip and found a torch to light on the wall. Now, we were able to see for ourselves. Our brother who once lie fatally wounded on the ground, was sitting up, trying to catch his breath.

In the center of his shirt, three blood-stained holes marked the spot where the cursed arrows had entered his heart. In that moment, the consequences seemed secondary, because … he was with us again.

Noelle's spell still held us in place, unable to move.

"You can free us now."

Ori's voice was stern when he addressed Noelle, and I glanced over to find that his expression matched. He seemed leery of her now, or perhaps just angered that she'd gone against him.

She pressed her hand gently to Rayen's cheek, staring at him through a tearful gaze as she ignored yet another command. Leaning in, her forehead rested against his, and it was clear she was still racked with the emotion of having nearly lost him forever. The two shared a single, unhurried kiss as Rayen finally started to get his bearings, and then Noelle stood to her feet.

She took steps in our direction, but stopped in front of Abe. The wicked smile that curved her lips upward caused beads of sweat to bud across his forehead.

"Tell me everything you know about the witch who did this," Noelle demanded calmly. "And I don't need to tell you the lengths I'm willing to go to get the truth."

He could hardly catch his breath as fear filled him to the brim. "I-I-I already told you what I know," he stammered. "The person came in wearing a big, dark cloak, handed me the paperwork from Chief, and we let them in."

"When this person left, which way did they go?"

"I have no idea," he said, almost apologetically. "We didn't escort them out, so they could have gone anywhere."

Noelle's jaw clenched when the answer filled her with frustration.

"So, what you're saying is, not only did you cause this, but you're also useless to me now." When the last word left her mouth, dark liquid began coloring her irises and the whites of her eyes.

"No," Abe said in a panic. "I wish I had more to tell you, but that's all I know."

Noelle stared wordlessly, and I don't think any of us knew her intentions, which terrified me.

"Well," she sighed, "have it your way."

"No, please!" Abe's plea ricocheted off the stones, and then went silent when his head abruptly jutted to the side with the closing of Noelle's fist.

We all heard his neck snap.

We all saw the look of satisfaction that filled Noelle at the sound of it.

She backed away casually, slipping a necklace off over her head. I watched as she made her way to Ori and placed it around his neck.

"What are you doing?" His hard tone hadn't changed as he glared at her.

She met his gaze and seemed unphased by his disappointment in her actions. My guess was she felt perfectly justified because it worked—she saved Rayen, and would have done the same for any one of us.

"Just hang on to this for me for a bit," she answered, touching the stone that now hung at the center of Ori's chest. "I'd never forgive myself if I lost something so important to you."

"Where are you going?" It wasn't until asking this question that Ori's concern finally reared its head. He was angry with Noelle, yes, but he still cared deeply. That was more than apparent as he searched her expression for an explanation.

She blinked, and despite the fury swimming in her eyes, there was softness toward our alpha. "I can't just let this go," she reasoned.

"Noelle. Please." The desperation he'd fought hard to hide was beginning to bleed through, and Noelle lowered her gaze at the sound of it.

Still, his words didn't draw a response, I guessed because her heart was already set on exacting revenge for Rayen, and there was nothing any of us could do to stop her.

"So, that's it," Ori said with a blank stare. "You're giving me the necklace because you don't want to harm what's important to me. Yet, you're putting the most valuable thing of all right in harm's way."

Not quite understanding at first, Noelle's gaze narrowed as she questioned Ori with her eyes. And then it hit home.

He was referring to her.

She lowered her head again, and I wondered if I begged, would she change her mind and stay put? But then I remembered who I was dealing with—the most treacherous princess-turned-queen the mainland, *and* our island, had ever known.

"I should be back at the bungalow before nightfall. Look after Rayen until I get there." The softly spoken words left her mouth as she placed a hand on Ori's chest, seconds before taking off at lightning speed.

I imagined she'd gotten a good enough distance away to avoid being tracked when the spell finally lifted. Within me, there was a conflict between chasing her down, and going to Rayen. However, knowing Noelle had done everything in her power to cover her tracks, I moved to the cell.

"What's going on?" Rayen asked, his voice sounding strained.

"What's the last thing you remember?"

He closed his eyes to think about my question. "I was sitting here, and then someone rushed me, and —"

His gaze shifted toward his chest and he grabbed at the wounds in a panic. Well, they *would* have been wounds, if it wasn't for Noelle.

"She brought you back," I explained. "How do you feel?"

Still confused, Rayen shook his head. "Like me, just a little out of it."

"I can imagine." I couldn't help but to smile at him, feeling relieved beyond words. As much as I regretted what Noelle had done, I was grateful to her.

"Take him back to the bungalow and make sure he's okay," Ori commanded, prompting me to nod. He turned toward Kai next. "You, come with me. We have to try hunting her down. Who knows what she'll find out there?"

He was right, although I was starting to believe it was the *world* who needed to fear *Noelle*. Not the other way around.

I got Rayen to his feet, and we shuffled out of the cell. Blythe was several steps ahead, in a rush to leave.

"Where you headed?"

She slowed down when Ori asked, seemingly even more unnerved than *we* were. I found myself wondering if, as a witch, with knowledge of these things, she wasn't panicking for good reason.

"Back to my room," she answered. "I'm not really any use to you all here, so I'm going to do the one thing I can."

My brow pulled together. "And what's that?"

She met my gaze and took a deep breath. "I'm gonna try to get us some help."

EPILOGUE

BLYTHE

"Out, *NOW!*" I yelled, moving quickly around my room.

"Everything cool?"

Pausing from dumping the contents of three purses onto my bed, I glanced toward Kip, certain impatience had darkened my stare. It was confirmed when she hopped up from her seat and scrambled into her shoes.

I returned to spilling the items from my bag onto my comforter as the door slammed behind her.

Finally, the lighter I'd been searching for tumbled out.

Rushing to grab the metal trash can from the corner, I emptied it on the rug, next moving to my dresser. There, sealed in a bag inside the top drawer, were the ingredients I'd worked my butt off to gather. I was still missing a few items from the list, but time had run out, which meant I'd have to improvise.

One by one, I took inventory as I dropped each item inside the trashcan, and then stood to rush toward the door. Remembering I'd need a couple things, I doubled back to grab an earring and a loose bottlecap from Kip's nightstand.

Bursting out into the hallway on a mission, I went straight for the door next to mine. My fist slammed into it with three swift knocks, and the one inside opened up in a panic.

"What the—"

"Here, use this to prick yourself," I said, handing over the earring without explanation, "and catch a few drops of your blood in this."

The kid stared at the bottlecap when I handed that to him next.

"Why on earth would I do a thing like that?" he practically laughed. "Because I need the blood of a virgin, and that ship sailed for me a *long* time ago, and … because I'll show you my boobs if you cooperate."

He scoffed at the offer. "What makes you think I'm a virgin?"

My brow shot up and the incredulous expression he wore melted away. "Fine," he conceded, "but boobs first."

Rolling my eyes with a sigh, I reached for the hem of my shirt and flashed him the goods.

"Blood. Now," I urged.

Taking a moment to gather himself after likely seeing a half-naked woman in the flesh for the first time, the kid did as I asked, wincing when the needle broke skin.

"There," he said, cautiously handing the bottlecap to me. "I don't know what this was about, but if you need more, you know where to find me, and you know how to get it."

"In your dreams, nerd," I sighed, already halfway back to my room.

Locking myself inside again, I added the blood to my concoction, and then exhaled deeply as I clutched my lighter.

"Please, *please* let this work."

With one final breath, I ignited the corner of a sheet of paper, and then let it fall into the can.

The items lit with a loud *whoosh* that made me fall back on the heels of my palms, staring as an array of colors illuminated my room. My eyes glanced toward the sprinklers above, praying they didn't turn on and ruin everything.

There was a sign I waited for, one that would let me know this had all worked, and at the sight of the flames turning black, I was grinning from ear to ear.

This was it.

If I hadn't been relieved to the point of tears, I might have celebrated having been so sweet with my magic. Because, I totally was.

However ... priorities.

Rushing to grab an ink pen from the floor beneath my desk, I scribbled a message on a piece of paper, along with a name, and then crumbled it into a ball before tossing it into the fire.

If this worked, then Noelle's Aunt Hilda—a witch who'd been hard on us both, but loved us even harder—would soon receive this smoke signal of sorts. Assuming the phone lines weren't the only form of communication on lockdown. It may have been a longshot, but it was the only hope we had.

And we really, *really* needed this to work, because things had gotten so far out of hand. It was this revelation that prompted me to take this step. Prompted me to take even *more* extreme measures.

For instance, that sheet of paper didn't only request that Noelle's Aunt Hilda come to her rescue. I'd asked her to bring *everyone*.

Swallowing the lump in my throat, I accepted that Noelle would probably hate me for what I'd just done, because she'd never want to put those she loves in harm's way. I couldn't afford to worry about losing her friendship again, so soon after the fence between us had begun to mend. What was important at this point, was her survival.

Hopefully, with any luck, the entire royal family would be stepping foot on Sanluuk in the near future, prepared to fight alongside us.

Sooner rather than later.

For Noelle's sake ...

***

BONUS CONTENT

DFA 3 releases January 2020; however, if you want more of Noelle and the Omegas NOW, visit www.theomegahive.com where you'll find these exclusive bonuses:

- *A huge, HUGE secret I was supposed to keep under wraps for a bit (hint: It may or may not involve Noelle's family ... shhhh)*
- *Omega Hive Character Profiles*
- *The DFA Soundtrack (new songs added with each installment)*
- *A Special Invitation*
- *My Inspiration Board*
- *A teaser gallery*
- *A link to Noelle's Origin Story*

THE LOST ROYALS SAGA

Experience Noelle's legacy from the very beginning.

Hotheaded dragons, ferocious wolves, powerful witches ... this series has it all!

Grab THE LOST ROYALS SAGA today!

Always FREE with Kindle Unlimited.

Thank you for your purchase!

Come hang out in "THE SHIFTER LOUNGE" on Facebook! We chat, recommend YA Paranormal Romances, and engage in other random acts of nerdiness. We also have tons of giveaways, exclusive ARC offers from me, and guest appearances by some of your favorite YA authors!

For all feedback or inquiries: author.racheljonas@gmail.com

Made in the USA
Columbia, SC
03 December 2020